D0482373

GOOD NEIGHBORS

GOOD NEIGHBORS

A NOVEL

JOANNE SERLING

TWELVE

NEW YORK   BOSTON

Copyright © 2018 by Joanne Serling

Cover design by Jarrod Taylor

Jacket photograph by Getty Images

Cover copyright © 2018 by Hachette Book Group, Inc.

Twelve
Hachette Book Group
1290 Avenue of the Americas, New York, NY 10104
twelvebooks.com
twitter.com/twelvebooks

First Hardcover Edition: February 2018

Twelve is an imprint of Grand Central Publishing. The Twelve name and logo are trademarks of Hachette Book Group, Inc.

The publisher is not responsible for websites (or their content) that are not owned by the publisher.

The Hachette Speakers Bureau provides a wide range of authors for speaking events. To find out more, go to www.hachettespeakersbureau.com or call (866) 376-6591.

Library of Congress Cataloging-in-Publication Data
Names: Serling, Joanne, 1966- author.
Title: Good neighbors : a novel / Joanne Serling.
Description: First hardcover edition. | New York : Twelve, 2018.
Identifiers: LCCN 2017034571| ISBN 9781455541911 (hardcover) |
ISBN 9781478941415 (audio downloadable) | ISBN 9781455541898 (open ebook)
Subjects: LCSH: Married people—Fiction. | Neighbors—Fiction. | Families—Fiction. |
Domestic fiction. | BISAC: FICTION / Literary. | FICTION / Family Life.
Classification: LCC PS3619.E75 G66 2018 | DDC 813/.6—dc23
LC record available at https://lccn.loc.gov/2017034571

ISBNs: 978-1-4555-4191-1 (hardcover), 978-1-4555-4189-8 (ebook), 978-1-4789-4141-5
(audiobook, downloadable)

Printed in the United States of America

LSC-H

10   9   8   7   6   5   4   3   2   1

To my family

PROLOGUE

What We Thought We Knew

WE KNEW WE LIVED on the nicest street in the nicest neighborhood in Fair Lawn. A neighborhood with views of a golf course. Grand houses. Wide-open sidewalks.

We knew we were never going to be the kind of parents our parents had been: hopelessly authoritarian, yet clueless and also uninterested in parenting. We knew that no matter what kind of parents we were, our children would most likely suffer from our mistakes and good intentions. Or disappoint us. That they would never be as smart or as swift or as popular as we imagined we had been. That they would very likely never grow up to live in a neighborhood quite as nice as this one. Our good fortune as much of a blessing as it was a mystery to us: born of hard work and birth order and a kind of easygoing luck that we were the first to acknowledge having benefited from. Our luck carrying us to this street at the same time at the same stage in our lives, when our children were two and one and some of them infants.

We knew that we would never have been friends if we didn't live on the same street at the same time with kids the same age. But we were happy to have found each other. To have discovered each other's good-natured camaraderie. Eager to watch our kids play freeze tag. Eager to share cocktails on a Saturday night. To throw pool parties in heat waves and make chili during snowstorms.

We knew that we knew almost nothing about each other that we didn't want known. But the things we knew drew us closer. We hated strivers. Abhorred social climbers. Were impartial to religion, yet felt obligated to carry on the traditions we'd been brought up with. Some of us Jewish. The rest of us Catholic.

We were modest. We were moneyed. We were all of us self-made and the most successful siblings of our respective families. A fact we laughed about as soon as we knew each other well enough to admit it. That our extended families weren't as smart or as kind or as socially mobile as we were. More serious issues didn't get mentioned, but nonetheless trailed us. Perverted uncles. Troubled sisters. Brothers who were white-collar criminals. The weight of the secrets pressing us deeper and closer together. We were eager for each other's friendship and reassurance. Convinced that our friends could do for us what our spouses were supposedly doing but simply couldn't: alleviating the boredom and the isolation of middle age, helping us to navigate this strange furlough called parenthood.

FEATHERS

PAIGE INSISTED ON BUYING Indian headdresses. Faux leather bands. Intricate beading. Dyed and colored feathers. They were hideous. Impractical. Quite possibly racist. Still, I defended her.

"It's cultural," I told Lorraine when she called to complain about them.

"How are presents at Thanksgiving cultural?"

"I don't know. Maybe it's a Christian thing. Like a stocking stuffer?"

Silence from Lorraine, who was Jewish and didn't know from stocking stuffers. Aware that I didn't, either.

"Who cares?" I asked, gesturing toward Lorraine on the phone, even though I knew she couldn't see me. Lorraine no doubt pacing her office, her team of admins pretending not to hear her through the glass-walled partition. Not that it mattered. Lorraine, a trim, athletic blonde with the kind of freckled face and easy demeanor that made everyone like her, no matter how much she gossiped.

"It's rude, for starters," Lorraine said. "Now we all have to chip in forty bucks for a stupid gift that our kids don't want and don't need. It's a neighborhood leftovers party in a cabin in a park. The whole idea was *not* to spend money!"

"They could put on a skit while we're eating," I offered, walking toward my front hall mirror to examine myself, my dirty blond ringlets mashed against the side of my face, my green eyes staring back at me skeptically.

"It's just so Paige! Who buys a group gift without asking first?"

"Let's just forget it and next year we'll make sure she doesn't do anything without permission," I suggested, idly fluffing my hair with my fingers before walking away from the mirror and heading up to my second-floor office.

"That's what you said last year!" Lorraine reminded me. "And Paige brought the 'washable' window paint. Remember the lost security deposit?"

It was true. I had said that. She had done that. But what did it matter, really? Paige Edwards was unpredictable. Lorraine Weinberger was bossy. And Nela! Nela Guzman-Veniero could barely acknowledge us, claiming to be too exhausted from her job as a corporate lawyer in Boston, happy to leave the socializing to her husband, Drew, who owned a baseball card store on Main Street. He was more one of us than she was. Sort of. Not really. But we didn't care. We cared but we'd made a trade-off—to accept everyone as they were in exchange for the comfort of the group's camaraderie. That's what we were now. A group. A thing. A neighborhood clique. The kind of friends who made up holidays to celebrate together, like this one, Leftovers Day, a senseless ritual that made us feel like we belonged to one another. Lorraine needed to drop the headdress complaint, not because Paige was right, but because being right was beside the point.

"Just be overly solicitous when she presents the gift, then dump it in the trash as soon as you get home!" I said, turning on my computer. The whir making me feel productive even though I'd quit my corporate job four years earlier; my desk cluttered with bills and paperwork instead of writing assignments.

Lorraine laughed. Lorraine said, "I just don't understand her!"

I agreed. I commiserated. I said, "I know what you mean!" Even though I didn't. Not really. Paige wasn't a mystery to me. I understood Paige in my own peculiar and hard-to-explain way: her dramatic flair and self-deprecating humor, her silk scarves and handsomely furnished Tudor. Hers was a life that functioned perfectly, as long as people didn't know her well. Or didn't question her. I didn't question her. I didn't look too closely. Her fights with other people were ceaseless and comical. The rookie cop who pulled her over for speeding. The naive mother who accidentally cut Paige off in the car wash driveway. Paige always eager to tell us about these incidents. Always eager to explain how *awful* the other party had been. And in the telling I'd shake my head. I'd murmur support. I'd pretend to understand her side of the story. But I always knew the other side, too. Could always feel the crevasse where the rest of the information lay.

In my ear, Lorraine was saying, "We didn't even tell her to buy a group gift this year. Did you tell Paige to buy a group gift?"

"Well, I didn't say she *couldn't* buy a group gift," I offered, hoping this would perhaps make Paige's transgression all right, forgivable, at least to Lorraine. It was already forgivable to me in the way that all acts that weren't deadly—and even some that were—could be made forgivable by me.

A sigh from Lorraine, not content yet. Lorraine telling me again about Paige's rudeness. Her presumption!

I stood up from my desk and peered out my office window toward Paige's herringboned Tudor, enchanted, as always, by the home's grandeur: its handsome brickwork and stylish gardens. The house in the middle of our cul-de-sac circle; its kidney-shaped pool a frequent scene of our impromptu get-togethers. All of us eager to enjoy the soothing rush of the waterfall, the luxury of the whirl-pool. Even though I imagined the gardens were barren now, the pool covered and puddled with water.

Lorraine was still talking. Phones ringing in the background. Lorraine a corporate recruiter who spent her entire day on the telephone. In another moment, she was saying she had to go, but not before telling me how excited she was for our leftovers party.

"It'll be great!" I agreed, even though I knew the actual event would be loud, the cabin uncomfortable, the kids no doubt tripping over tree roots and other hidden obstacles. The women shouting at the kids to *slow down, be careful,* to not punch or kick one another, while the guys stood in the corner drinking from the makeshift bar, their halfhearted attempts to organize kickball or Duck, Duck, Goose never materializing into anything other than reminiscences about their own days as children. How much freer they'd been. And also more self-sufficient. All of it a salad of half-truths and carefully massaged memories, the ages of their independence no doubt older than they remembered, their parents more neglectful than they cared to admit to themselves. Not that it mattered. None of it mattered. Their memories weren't the point. The party wasn't even the point. The point was the group. Our neighborhood. The romantic and somewhat unlikely notion that we'd all wandered into this storybook setting and created something magical for ourselves. Something fulfilling and fun and full of future promise. Which never failed to surprise me. How I'd become the kind of grown-up I could never have imagined as a child. Someone happy.

LEFTOVERS

When the appointed day came and the women were appropriately attired to chase the kids and still look like they belonged at a party—expensive boots, quilted jackets, soft fuzzy sweaters over T-shirts and leggings; when the wine had been uncorked and too many appetizers consumed; when the kids had been fed and were busy with a hired babysitter playing charades, we finally sat down for dinner: sticky cranberry relish, leftover corn casserole, dark turkey meat that had been sliced and made ready for sandwiches. The dinner half consumed when Paige announced her big news by tapping on a plastic wineglass with a knife, blushing, then fidgeting, then bursting out, "We're adopting."

What had been a din of talking over talking suddenly collapsed into a moment of silence, of paying attention. Paige had our attention. She was adopting. Her husband, Gene, looked on solemnly, if a man that handsome could ever look solemn. His sandy hair, his hazel eyes, even his square jaw all conspired to make him look more like a playboy than like somebody's middle-aged husband and father.

"Well, you know we've been waiting, right?" Paige asked sweetly. Innocently. As if the adoption weren't a loaded topic.

Some of us knew. I knew. I'd known Paige the longest, except for Lorraine, who'd met Gene at some sort of fundraising dinner.

I glanced at Nela. Nela and Drew lived in a sprawling ranch house right next door to the Edwardses. She had to know. But Nela's face betrayed nothing, her emotional scale somewhere between bemused and uninterested at all times, the result of our failure to be either brown-skinned or her cousins. ("In Puerto Rico you don't get involved with your neighbors!" she was always quick to point out, looking at Drew, her suburban-born husband, as if it were *his* fault she'd fallen into this mess.)

In a moment, Lorraine lifted a plastic wineglass to toast the Edwardses, causing a commotion of cheering and clapping.

At the far end of the table, my husband, Jay, caught my eye, his slim, narrow body pitched forward, his face wary. Was he or wasn't he supposed to know about the adoption? Gene had never once mentioned it to him directly.

I shrugged. It didn't matter. It wasn't a secret. Paige had been saying it for years. How much she wanted a second child. How she was dying for a ton of kids! Which I doubted. How much Paige truly loved children. Paige wore her motherhood like some sort of old-fashioned coat, belted and done up, proper and attractive from a certain distance. Her son, Cameron, always dressed in new clothes, told to behave, sit up straight, use his manners. Paige always smiling frantically, a thin veneer that rarely hid her irritation. Her desire to control the situation always shimmering just below the surface.

"I know, world's oldest mother, right?" Paige was saying at the other end of the table when the toasts had died down, her sleek silver hair curled delicately around her earlobes; Paige prematurely gray, which did nothing to detract from her considerable beauty. Or how chic she was.

Lorraine said, "Give me a break, you're barely forty."

Lorraine was the oldest living mother! She'd had her second child three years ago at forty-three. A surprise she hadn't necessarily wanted, which she made no bones about admitting. Lorraine more interested in tennis and socializing than in the day-to-day business of parenting. Especially now that she was divorced. Evan gone with barely a ripple.

"I had honestly given up," Paige was saying at the other end of the table, her mood suddenly shifting as she dabbed her eyes with an orange paper napkin. "When the agency called over the summer, I thought it was to take us off the list because we've been waiting so long."

We nodded expectantly. I wondered, was there an expiration date?

"But then they offered us a preschooler," Paige added shyly. "She's just turned four. We met her in August."

She had?

"So this could be better than a baby with unknown issues," Paige said, looking around the long lodge table for agreement that no one was able to give her. Not until we knew which way she had chosen.

"I mean, Cameron's already seven. He'd rather have a sister he can play with. And she has no issues besides a lazy eye. So we said yes. Yes!"

The women nodding more vigorously, our voices rising over one another to reassure Paige of the wisdom of her decision. We were all at least forty. Of course a preschooler was better! The men silent, swirling their wineglasses or chugging from beer bottles, embarrassed, perhaps, to be acknowledging Paige's reproductive failures. Or maybe they were merely weighing the pros and cons of an adoption, whether they could go through with it themselves. I could go through with it. I had wanted to do it instead of having my own children. A fact which had shocked Jay and was never something he could take seriously. The risk of bad genetics. Of taking on an unknown story. Which was, of course, the whole point of it to me. To create a different kind of family than the one I'd grown up with.

Next to me, Gene was loudly proclaiming, "We're flying to Moscow in January. Two thousand bucks per ticket!" Gene shaking his oversize head, running his hands through his thick sandy hair. "Not even for first!" he complained.

Now, here was a topic the men could warm to: the cost of things. The recession three years behind us, but still casting its sickly gray pall on us.

"Inflation!" Jay asserted, suddenly coming to life at the other end of the table. Economic doom among Jay's favorite topics.

"When I was a kid, my dad took three kids to Europe on a salesman's salary!" Gene boomed, shaking his head like he couldn't imagine how his dad had managed it, even though we all knew that *salesman* was a euphemism; hadn't Gene's dad run a biotech company?

"That's when the stewardesses were still stewardesses!" Drew said, raising his eyebrows suggestively while the other men all nodded appreciatively, Nela calling them animals. In another moment, Lorraine rose from behind her long bench seat to hug Paige and Nela came around from the other side of the table to join them. I was shocked. Paige was, too. You could tell by the way she opened her mouth in an O when Nela reached out to her, then closed it quickly and leaned forward to clasp Nela's back. Paige's face not just happy but thankful, too, as if by hugging her, Nela was granting Paige something she'd never dreamed of getting: Nela's blessing.

I watched Nela as she asked for particulars about dates and medical exams, about whether Cameron would go with them, how they would manage it all. Something had shifted in Nela's delicate face, some sort of acknowledgment or acceptance, as if Paige was not who Nela had suspected she was but, instead, someone better. Someone to be hugged and even celebrated. Or maybe this was just what I was thinking, relieved that someone else was thinking it, too, that maybe this would make it true.

I rose and gave Paige a hug, her back bony beneath her white cotton blouse, ideas about the adoption flitting through my head like images in a silent movie. The girl adorable in a fur-trimmed snowsuit, even though I doubted a Russian orphan wore anything with real fur. The girl rosy-cheeked and fair, waiting at the orphanage. I wondered if she fully understood what was about to happen. I wondered if she was excited. I wondered if she had any way of imagining the perfect idyll to which she was being transported. The Edwardses' giant Tudor with its coffered ceilings and stained glass windows. The long hallways filled with silver picture frames and fine Oriental carpets. All of it elegant and lovely and no doubt beyond the imaginings of a child who had grown up with rough blankets, industrial beds, metal cribs. I could barely wait for Paige and Gene to go to Russia and return again, to be part of their daring and wonderful rescue.

OFFERINGS

Suitcases were packed. A passport acquired for Cameron. Timers attached to light fixtures. All of this relayed to us in a long group e-mail from Paige, who wanted us to keep an eye on the house while she was gone. This despite Yazmin's daily dispatch there for dusting and checking up on things. Which was so Paige: overly privileged and overly waited on. Who needed daily dusting while they were away in Russia? Why couldn't her nanny enjoy a vacation? But still. I dreamed of her voyage. Longed for her return. Tried to imagine the moment when she would become the girl's mother.

For three long weeks the house sat silent, vacant, like an expectant pause in a soon-to-begin drama. And then, all at once, it was Thursday. The day of the Edwardses' return. The plane descending into Logan within a few hours. The light already fading into a purplish dusk at five o'clock as Lorraine and I converged at Paige's house with our plates of homemade food and our group gift. We'd agreed on two Burberry scarves, one for each child. Lorraine had suggested it, and I'd eagerly gone to the mall for them. Certain that Burberry was exactly what Paige would want, if she'd been able to ask us for it.

Nela totally disagreed. She was actually miffed by our suggestion. Didn't we know that Burberry was overpriced and not that attractive? Didn't we know that Burberry was the ultimate in phony tradition? Of course I knew this. I wore flea market necklaces. Bangles from Mexico. But phony was what Paige went for. Couldn't Nela see that? She couldn't. She declined to go in on it with us.

Now Lorraine and I were at the Edwardses' front door, leaving our separate driveways to converge in our overcoats and winter boots, standing on the Edwardses' slate stoop in the February cold, ringing the bell, waiting as we were greeted by Yazmin, the nanny Lorraine had found for Paige when her own search had turned up two qualified candidates. Even though I'd counseled Lorraine against getting involved in Paige's business, nervous about how Paige treated the women who worked for her. Which I suspected was poorly. Several quitting suddenly, complaining to my housekeeper about Paige's condescending behavior. But Yazmin had stayed. She'd been there a year now, maybe two. Which just went to show you. How maybe Paige wasn't so bad. I greeted Yazmin, handed her my coat, which she insisted on hanging up for me. Yazmin overly solicitous, calling us Miss Nicole and Miss Lorraine, neither of us bothering to insist on just our first names as Yazmin offered us coffee and freshly made cake.

We declined the cake even as Yazmin brewed us the coffee. We eagerly accepted it in Paige's good coffee cups, the ones with mint-green leaves curling around the thin porcelain lip, the cups nothing like my own coffee mugs, with funny sayings or bank promotions. Paige's house always filling me with a warm and satisfied feeling. The marble more gleaming than my own. The inlaid cabinets more ornate, the daily china of better quality. A feeling of luxury and entitlement sweeping over me completely when I was there, happy to let Yazmin wait on me and bring me coffee in a way I would never allow Idallia to do in my own house.

When we'd finished our coffee and our pleasantries, we arranged our Burberry boxes in the center of the island, one for Cameron, one for Winifred. The new daughter apparently named after Gene's grandmother. Which was ridiculous. Naming a Russian girl anything like Winifred. Naming any girl Winifred! Which I suspected we both thought but neither of us said. Happy to hear from Yazmin that the Edwardses planned on calling her Winnie. Both of us eager to hear what else Yazmin knew about the Edwardses' trip and imminent arrival. Lorraine peppering Yazmin with questions as was her customary manner: Had she heard from them today? What time exactly would their plane land? Had they said everything was going smoothly? Was the girl healthy and happy? Was Cameron? And to everything Yazmin smiled vaguely and said, "I'm not sure" or "I don't know" in her heavily accented English, as if by knowing something about the Edwardses she would risk revealing how she really felt about them, too. Or maybe it was only I who sensed this: a shrinking into herself whenever the idea of Paige and Gene entered the room, a sudden pretending to not understand what we were asking.

In the hallway we heard the stomping of feet, a voice calling, coming closer. It was Nela. We'd left the door ajar, invited her to join us. Nela's short, sleek hair plastered with snowflakes, an armful of white lilies in her arms, their scent dense and sweet, the bouquet gorgeous and exactly the right thing for the occasion. Which suddenly made me ashamed of my Burberry gift and plate of cold chicken.

"From a family event," Nela said as I complimented her on the arrangement, not wanting to suggest, I supposed, that she went out and bought them. Not wanting to suggest that she was in any way like us. Which she was quick to show us as she turned to greet Yazmin in Spanish. Shedding her fleece to reveal a tight Harvard T-shirt, black leggings; Nela no more than five feet, but her figure curvy and perfect.

Yazmin smiling toward Nela, speaking rapidly in Spanish, reaching up to a high cupboard to get down a vase from the spot where Paige kept them. Nela helping her arrange the lilies, fussing with the stems while Lorraine and I sat blankly at the island, afraid to break into English and seem like we were speaking over them. Lorraine checking her gold watch, then getting up to open the fridge again, to wonder if the dinner would be visible as soon as the Edwardses opened it and whether we should tape instructions to the refrigerator door. Shrugging my shoulders, not wanting to interrupt Yazmin to ask for the tape or the pen. Nela finally joining us at the island, allowing us to drop the petty concern about the note. Nela announcing that she had wanted to throw a shower for Paige.

She had?

"But she said no, she would be too tired," Nela added, looking from one to the other of us for some sort of response we couldn't give her. Nela had never once had us to her house for a party or even dinner. Why was she suddenly being so solicitous of Paige?

"I just thought it was the right thing to do. To honor her decision to take this on," Nela continued, softly, as if she was already disappointed and sad about it.

"That was really nice," I said, trying to be encouraging. Not sure exactly what Paige was taking on that the rest of us hadn't already taken on—namely, having children and raising them.

"Do you think she's embarrassed?" Nela pressed, resting her chin on her thumb and forefinger and staring at me as if I had some sort of special insight. Which was flattering, even if I wasn't going to give it to her.

"What's Paige got to be embarrassed about?" I asked instead, curious to know what it was that Nela was thinking, her reasoning opaque and confusing to me in the best of circumstances.

"To have a daughter who isn't hers. Who doesn't even *look* like an Edwards," Nela said, glancing from one to the other of us for some sort of response we weren't prepared to give her. "Some Russians look Asian," Nela added.

"She's probably just nervous about who she would invite. I wouldn't read too much into it," Lorraine cautioned. Not reading into things was Lorraine's specialty.

"I'm sure she addressed all her feelings at her group," I offered. Eager to move off the race issue. Eager for there not to be a race issue!

"What group?" Lorraine practically shouted, causing Nela and me to look toward the sink to see if Yazmin had heard her. Yazmin's back toward us, the water running over the coffeepot noisily.

"My friend saw Paige at her group a few times," I said, lowering my voice. "She wasn't supposed to tell me, but when I told her Paige was in Russia, she let it slip," I offered, fiddling with my bangles, nervous that I'd betrayed a confidence.

"What group?" Lorraine pressed again, her mouth open in disbelief, her entire body poised on the verge of laughing. My breach of privacy of absolutely no concern to her. Lorraine wanted to know only one thing: had Paige been to some sort of group therapy? Paige Edwards the last person in the world any of us could imagine doing anything that required self-evaluation.

"It's a group for couples to explore different paths," I explained, looking from Lorraine to Nela to see if they were getting it. If my faux pas had been worth it. Lorraine's mouth still open, revealing her perfectly square white teeth. Nela's face blank, her pursed lips and high cheekbones giving her an air of superiority.

"Like whether you want to do an open adoption, or how you feel about adopting a foster child. It's really tricky. My friend has all this shame around using a surrogate. It's much more complex than I ever realized," I said.

"So you're telling me Paige Edwards went to group therapy?" Lorraine repeated, glossing over any family confusion, laughing lightly, causing Nela and me to laugh a little bit, too, even as we pointed to Yazmin's back and put our fingers to our lips.

"So anyway, not having a shower. I don't think it has anything to do with shame," I continued. "I mean, she's got to know women who adopted black babies and brown babies, even crack babies. And half those parents are in jail!"

Nela silently running her tongue under her top lip, no doubt steaming that I'd just associated brown babies and black babies with jail and with drug abuse.

"I'm just saying that adoption is pretty commonplace these days," I said, looking directly at Nela, trying to cover up my insensitive comment. Which wasn't all that insensitive in my book to begin with. Couldn't we ever just be honest?

"Can we have a party at your house anyway?" Lorraine joked, not eager to linger over anything unpleasant.

Nela smiling reluctantly. Nela seemingly relieved that the shower wasn't a reflection of how Paige felt about her new daughter's ethnicity or appearance. Willing to forgive my insensitivity. Or at least to accept it in the spirit in which it was intended. Yazmin done with her coffeepot, turning to us, asking if we needed anything else. Not kicking us out but nervous, perhaps, that we might tell Paige if she didn't do everything exactly right. All of us saying, "No thanks!" and "The coffee was delicious," aware that it was time to leave. That we couldn't have a party and gossip in Paige's kitchen without her. Even though we'd been doing exactly that for the past half hour.

We said our good-byes and slipped out the front door, Nela rushing next door in some sort of hurry to get home while Lorraine and I stopped for a minute to acknowledge the moment and hug each other lightly. The moon casting its glow across the blackened trees and snowy lawns of our neighborhood.

NOTES ON HOW TO BEHAVE

THERE WERE SNOWBANKS STACKED against bushes, wind gusts sweeping the neighborhood. Paige hadn't called. Hadn't sent a thank-you for our presents, even though she'd been back for nearly a week, a fact that amused Drew, who called me to joke about it, but irritated Lorraine, who couldn't see the humor in it. "Why wouldn't you call?" Lorraine asked me. It was our fourth call of the day. Lorraine prone to constant calling once you'd answered and seemed willing to talk, which I was. The kids home for February break, Lorraine a welcome distraction.

"Maybe she's jet-lagged," I offered, certain this wasn't the reason but aware that Lorraine needed one.

"So what, you're jet-lagged. You pick up the phone and say, 'Hey, we're back. We missed you. And by the way, the rice pilaf with Craisins was really good!'"

I laughed lightly. Lorraine so clueless about how the real world worked. Lorraine living her whole life in Fair Lawn within ten miles of her extended family. Everybody getting together for holidays and birthdays. Everyone arriving on time, speaking civilly to one another, agreeing to play by the same rule book. Difficult topics weren't mentioned. Like the fact that Lorraine's aunt was a compulsive shopper or that Lorraine had a new boyfriend before her divorce was even final. Everything papered over with money and good manners and plans for next time. It would have been laughable and pathetic if I weren't so jealous.

I said I had to go. I said the kids needed me, suddenly eager to retrieve the mail, which I'd heard drop through the slot. I found a thick, wet envelope, half covered with snow, my name in pen on the outside of it. Inside, a note from Paige explaining what to say to our children about "the event." About the fact that Paige and Gene and Cameron had traveled halfway around the globe one January morning and come back three weeks later with a new daughter for themselves, a sister for Cameron.

"Don't say 'real parents' when referring to her Russian family," the sheet intoned. "*We* are the real parents. Say 'biological parents.' Winnie had biological parents in Russia who could not keep her."

This was good, I told myself. Instructive. Not the tone, which was bossy and supercilious. But I liked the content. The content was obviously well researched, if not by Paige, then by some adoption professional she was trying to mimic. There were other rules, too. About not saying that Winnie was "given away." About not mentioning the orphanage. Or her lazy eye. But none of these were as interesting to me as the stuff about the real parents. I liked it. It fulfilled my own idea about what was possible: how a person could be saved with love and will and a little bit of money.

In the kitchen I heard laughter and the sounds of marbles pinging against each other. I walked with Paige's envelope toward the boys' voices, eager to share something important with them.

"Did you know Cameron Edwards has a new sister?" I began, standing over the kitchen table, fumbling with my silver bracelets. Murmurs. Heads bowed. Fingers collecting marbles from a series of hollows in a long wooden plank.

"She's adopted from Russia. Do you know what *adopted* means?" I asked sweetly, wondering if Lucas was aware of the adopted Ethiopian boy in his second-grade class.

Lucas ignored me. His long, narrow torso resting on top of the kitchen table; his thick, curly head of hair nearly on top of the game board. Lucas constitutionally unable to stay in his seat. Josh sitting quietly across from him, his lips pursed in concentration before saying, "In China they wrap the girls in blankets and leave them near the river," not looking up from the game. Then adding cheerily, "They don't like baby girls!"

This was all wrong. But this was so true! How cruel some cultures were. I wanted to correct him. To praise him. To find out where he was getting this outside information from, this dark and carnal truth about the world. He was only in kindergarten! His cheeks still chubby, his sweetness not tempered yet. But before I could refer to Paige's sheet, gather my thoughts and my own brand of protective, tender truth, there was Winnie in the stroller outside my kitchen window. Paige and Gene pushing through the heavy veil of falling snow while Cameron walked slowly alongside them. I ran outside in my bare feet, eager to catch them before they passed, eager to be the first one to see them. To greet Winnie.

"Welcome back!" I shouted when I reached the street, kissing Paige and Gene, hugging Cameron before taking in Winnie's lazy eye, the snot dripping from her nose, the pale and crumpled face that peeked out beneath the pink, fur-trimmed parka hood. She looked like a disfigured doll, not at all like I'd pictured her. Not at all like I wanted her to be. A shining star of girlhood. The lucky one who'd gotten away.

"Can I hug her?" I asked Paige, no longer wanting to but feeling like I should.

"She doesn't really like hugging strangers," Paige said, cocking her head to the side so that the weak sun hit her pale and aging face, the tiny cracks and places where her cheeks fell in.

I was surprised and disappointed. I thought it strange that Paige would say something so definitive after knowing the girl so briefly. But I didn't really feel like hugging Winnie anyhow; she seemed dirty and unreal to me, more like an old man in a wheelchair than a child in a stroller, which was embarrassing for me to think about.

Beside the stroller rail, Cameron stood mutely, wisps of blond hair escaping from his plaid cap, the flaps lowered over his ears. Already he resembled Paige, with his high cheekbones and delicate chin. His neck long and elegant.

"Are you happy to have a sister?" I asked, suddenly aware that I should be making a fuss over him, too, not just his new sister.

Cameron nodded silently. A smirk on his face. Cameron always quick to create conflict whenever there were more than two kids in a room. But maybe that was only-child syndrome?

I smiled again at Cameron, worried he could tell I disliked him. Worried I hadn't said enough to let Paige know how wonderful I thought he was. But already the wind was growing colder, making it difficult to think and to speak, much less to soundlessly communicate anything meaningful.

"We should keep going," Gene said, his face red and soggy in the cold.

I agreed. It was freezing. My toes were wooden! And yet I didn't want to let them go, either. I wanted to know more about Winnie. To bask in the possibilities of her new life. But already Gene was turning the stroller away from me, the back wheel cutting through the snow, revealing a thick black smudge where once there had been white.

A FOREIGN PLACE

THANK GOD WE'D FINISHED eating. Gooey boeuf Bourguignon, which was typical of Paige's French cooking, served on good china with Baccarat stemware. It was our official Winnie dinner—a month since the Edwardses' trip. All of us in the dining room waiting for coffee, the kids relegated to the basement. Winnie nowhere in sight, sent to bed after the quickest of greetings because six thirty was the absolute latest she could stay up. "She has sleep issues," Paige had explained, not elaborating.

Now Paige was telling the story of the trip itself, which I'd been dying to hear about, hoping they'd enjoyed it. Or at least gotten something meaningful out of it. But already I was cringing.

"Wait till you hear what happened in Gorky Park!" Paige was saying. Her face flushed with laughter and wine. Her silvery-white hair making her look queen-like at the head of her mahogany table. "On our way there, Winnie's resting on Gene's shoulder, and she suddenly starts shouting to this crowd of people in Russian, which we ignored, because, you know…"

"Because you don't speak Russian," I offered, embarrassed that Paige thought it was okay to make fun of her daughter's distress, as if the fact that Winnie was speaking in Russian made it count less. Paige held her palms up in halfhearted agreement, then continued.

"So anyway, Winnie's yelling in Russian, which sounds like gibberish to us, but the crowd behind Gene is getting sort of loud and coming closer, and after a few minutes, people are tapping Gene on the shoulder and pulling at Winnie!"

Yazmin came through the swinging door to the dining room, clearing plates, head bowed, some of us greeting her, Paige ignoring her.

"So now we're getting scared," Paige continued. "And Gene and I are like, 'Where is the adoption agency guide?'"

Everyone around the long dining room table nodded, eager, I knew, that Paige not get derailed by a complaint about the adoption agency guide.

"She's nowhere," Paige continued, answering her own question. "And the crowd is getting loud and unruly, so we start jogging. And the crowd starts jogging with us! And Winnie's still screaming toward them in Russian! Finally, after five terrifying minutes, the adoption agency guide sees the crowd and tells them something that makes them stop following us. Then she tells us the deal. Get this: Winnie was telling them we gave away her brother!"

A brief, pregnant pause. Was there a brother?

"She doesn't have a brother!" Paige said, shaking her head, giggling a little. "I think she was thinking of someone from the orphanage."

"Jesus!" said Lorraine.

"Doesn't the adoption agency explain anything to these kids?" Nela asked, her face dubious, her attitude of disdain lowering its mantle upon us, the white folk who didn't understand hardship. I always wanted to bang something down on Nela's sleek, seal-like head at these moments, she who had been poor but otherwise fortunate. She who had gone to Harvard on scholarship and had a mother and father who were sane and loved her.

"Well, and here's another weird thing," Paige said, ignoring Nela's question as if it hadn't been asked. "Winnie starts saying that she has to go to the bathroom, and we've just gotten to the park and there's not a Western bathroom in sight. I have nowhere to take her! But the guide tells me, are you ready for this, to, 'just put Winnie down and let her go to the bathroom like she's used to going'!"

We nodded. We waited for her to elaborate. I knew what the others didn't. I'd traveled to Russia for a month in college as part of my foreign policy minor. I'd used the holes in the ground, shitting while squatting and wishing desperately for toilet paper. I imagined the scenario couldn't be dissimilar to what Paige was hinting at, even though it was twenty years later. Even though they supposedly had capitalism now.

"Holes?" I finally ventured.

"Cesspools, Nicole," Paige said, turning toward me. "Shit-covered cesspools with little tread marks for your feet. And no walls between them! I set Winnie down and she does her business and starts to pull up her pants without wiping herself. Like an animal!"

We were startled. We were amazed. Had Paige just invoked feces at her dining room table? Just compared her new daughter to an animal? The men covered their eyes with their hands, rocked their heads back and forth in disbelief or possibly disgust while Lorraine laughed loudly. Nela merely raised her thick eyebrows in my direction, which I met, but only momentarily. I didn't want to get drawn into Nela's disapproval. I wanted to hear the rest of the story, to hear the parts that made Paige's behavior laudable, or at least not embarrassing. At the head of the table, Paige looked flushed, happy, eager to be the teller of strange and funny tales, which were not, it seemed, about Winnie exactly but about the barbarism of the Russian people.

"It's hard," Paige said when the room had quieted down, her smile fading, causing her deep lines and wrinkles to come into sharper relief. "The things you don't know."

Some of us leaned forward in our chairs, curious to hear this bit of honesty. I was eager. I was hungry for it, certain it was possible for Paige to be sincere with us now that she'd been in a support group.

Paige took a breath. Then, as if steeling herself for something necessary but difficult, she said, "Winnie doesn't really sleep. I mean, she needs to sleep, but she's exhausted from all the stimulation of our lives."

We nodded and waited for her to go on. This was the Paige I believed we all liked best. The honest Paige, the vulnerable and occasionally introspective Paige, right here, side by side with the Paige who told insensitive stories about people she deemed less civilized.

"Well," Paige continued, taking note of all the eyes around the table on her, "in the middle of the night, Winnie wakes up screaming. Really screaming. I used to go to her to try to calm her down, but that just makes it worse."

"It does," Gene chimed in quickly, defending Paige against some unspoken accusation.

"We've had to make some hard choices," Paige said, and we all nodded, all knew exactly what she meant. Lucas had slept on our floor for eight months during one particularly bad spell when he was six. Eight months with a blanket and a pillow and a red plastic mat! I'd hated him for it. But what could I do? I'd tried to lock him in his room once, holding the handle so he couldn't get out, and the screams were still too horrible to fully conjure and admit to. Had I really been that mother? I had. Which meant I was in no position to judge Paige.

"We've installed baby gates in her room," Paige was saying at the other end of her table. "We're trying to help her learn boundaries. She needs to stay in her room. Not come to our bed."

Everyone nodding as if the gates explained everything. I nodded, too, even though the gates merely raised more questions for me. Couldn't Winnie climb over the gates? Of course she could climb over them. Which meant they were just a symbol, and Winnie could go to Paige and Gene for comfort when she needed them? Or maybe they weren't gates as we thought of them? The story didn't make sense, but then again, Paige's stories seldom did. They often started in the middle and lacked cohesion and relevant facts.

Meanwhile, all around me, people were murmuring their support for Paige. Lorraine laughing, shaking the ice in her empty highball glass as she reminded us that her two-year-old, Jesse, had slept in a bouncy seat for the first four months of his life.

"Remember, you were outraged!" Lorraine said, laughing, turning to me.

"Not outraged," I corrected, smiling at the memory of the incident. "I was just surprised. You said Jesse slept through the night after four months. You never mentioned the bouncy seat. Then I go into his nursery and the crib's not even put together!"

Lorraine laughing, her mouth open, her perfectly square, white teeth making me wonder whether they were real. Everyone talking at once about their children's strange sleep habits. Drew reminding Nela that they'd had to run the garbage disposal to get the twins to calm down. Lorraine admitting that she had hired a sleep consultant to teach Gabe how to transition to a "big boy" bed. Which was insane. What parent hired a sleep consultant? But I was glad, too. That I didn't have to hear more about Winnie and what she did or didn't get from Paige. Didn't have to wonder about the strange gate situation. Certain that it was probably something I could live with. Winnie, too. Soon Winnie's fears would die down and she wouldn't need to scream in the night or try to leave her room. I believed in this. That things worked out. That the things you ignored couldn't harm you.

And then, as if on cue, Winnie appeared at the arched entrance to the dining room in pink footie pajamas, a teddy bear at her chest. She looked nothing like the girl in the stroller, haggard and a little bit ugly. Nothing like the girl presented to us in the red-and-green plaid dress at the beginning of the evening, nervous and more than a little uncertain. Now she was playful. Charming. A little bit devilish. Her lazy eye covered by a lock of silky black hair that she twirled in front of her face. Her other hand waving at us.

Gene was smiling right back at her, waving wholeheartedly like he already adored her. Which was lovely and charming and made Gene so much better than just another preppy golfer from that club of theirs that didn't admit Jews.

"Come," Gene said, reaching his arms out toward Winnie as she skipped into the dining room and climbed into Gene's lap, snuggling close but still peering out at us, smiling. She had, despite her Slavic features, a kind of American smile, confident and flirtatious.

Paige said, "Winnie's a daddy's girl, aren't you, Winnie?"

Winnie said something unintelligible, which for some reason spurred a round of questions that had no doubt been bottled up all night. Did Winnie speak any words of English? How did Paige and Gene communicate with her, and what did she say back to them?

Gene started to speak, half answers about speech delays and vision tests. The preschool they planned to send her to for children with special needs. Gene leaning over slightly, his lap suddenly smaller, causing Winnie to uncurl herself and begin walking around the table, peering at people, saying, "Hi" in a strange, high-pitched voice, the effort apparent, as if she were pushing the word through a wind tunnel in her throat.

When she got to me, I placed my thick cloth napkin over my eyes and said, "Peekaboo." Quickly. Before I lost her attention. Winnie laughed, motioned for me to do it again. Which I did. Five, then six times. The same laugh every time. And then she took the napkin and put it over her own head.

"Winifred Leigh Edwards, don't put someone's napkin on your hair!" Paige called down the long table. Her voice ugly and shrill.

"She doesn't realize," Paige continued in my direction, as if I was expecting something more of her new daughter. Clearly she was. Which was ludicrous but not unusual for Paige. She thought all the kids should conform to some idea of childhood behavior she'd gotten from a Christmas catalog. Smiling in their best finery. Daintily nibbling on canapés. I didn't begrudge Paige her fantasy—it was why her house looked so good whenever she had us over—but I wasn't going to spend my energy getting Winnie to conform to her dream. It was just too much trouble and not possible, anyway.

I waved Paige off with a smile and turned to Winnie, who had started to speak and was trying to tell me something. The consonants tumbling out on top of one another in a way that was familiar to me. It was the sound Lucas had made when he was learning to talk. He'd been delayed. His tongue not always cooperating.

But I'd always been able to understand him. I leaned in closer to Winnie, sorry I didn't know her particular squeaks and rattles well enough to interpret for her.

"Hug?" I said instead, opening my arms wide to show her what I meant, hoping the offer would cover up the fact that I couldn't help her. That she couldn't make herself understood.

I expected a hesitation. A pause as she considered it. But Winnie flung herself toward me, forcing me to reach forward and clasp her tight lest she topple the both of us.

"She'll hug anyone," Paige called from the other end of the room. "It's part of the orphanage thing."

This seemed odd. And mean. Even if it was true. But then, hadn't Paige told me that Winnie didn't like to hug strangers? Out on that snowy walk? All of this quickly flitting through my mind as I felt Winnie's warm arms clasped around my back. Who cared if she loved too much or too little or without forethought? She had that inimitable thing that couldn't be taught and that everyone wanted. Charm. I hugged her back, a thick, syrupy feeling creeping up from my chest and into my throat. There it was. I loved her already.

DARKNESS

THE SNOW FELL OUTSIDE our windows like white rain, seemingly delicate but relentless in its toll. Nearly a foot piling up in the back-yard, until it was too dark to even see it. I gathered the boys in the kitchen to play a game, eager to pry them off of the TV set. Josh running to the basement to get checkers just before the wrought-iron chandelier started to flicker, the candle-shaped bulbs dimming to a faint glow before going out completely; the house was pitched into darkness.

Josh started to scream. A high-pitched wail from the basement. "Get me! Get me!"

"I'm coming!" I shouted, disturbed by how upset he was. Josh normally so calm and easygoing, The darkness obviously frighten-ing him. Trying to reassure him that I was on my way, even though I needed a flashlight, or a candle. Fumbling with the childproof lock on the drawer where we kept them. Hating the damn lock. Josh screaming louder.

Lucas saying, "I know a thing or two about electricity," then standing up on a kitchen chair to tighten a lightbulb in the wrought-iron fixture. The bulb cracking. Lucas crying.

"Everyone stop it!" I screamed. Hating my nasty tone but unable to stop myself. Determined to control the situation. To make the children listen. Jay clomping down the stairs with flashlights, asking, "Why is everyone screaming?" As if it weren't already obvious! His judgment of my parenting apparent and undeserved. Which made me furious!

"Go get Josh!" I snapped at him. Jay making a face at me. Jay silently descending the basement steps while I took a flashlight and helped Lucas with his hand, which thankfully wasn't cut too badly. Taking a deep breath and giving him a hug, even as he began to squirm away from me. Lucas hopping toward the basement steps, then banging into Jay. Josh screaming, "You left me!" over and over again even as I rubbed his back and tried to soothe him. Jay sulking, refusing to look at me. The entire scene a misery. How did we get here, and so quickly?

And then, my cell phone ringing.

I lunged for it, happy for the distraction. Hopeful it was Drew or Lorraine or even Paige telling us that they, too, had lost electricity. Hopeful the evening could turn from a washout into some sort of party.

"Hey," I said, even though I didn't recognize the number. Which was risky and something I normally avoided. I heard deep breathing. Then my name, slurred and barely audible.

"Hello!" I said, hoping the volume and forced cheer of my voice would make the caller go away. Pretty certain I knew who it was even though I wanted to believe it was a telemarketer.

"Nicole?" The voice louder this time, but still slurry, followed by more heavy breathing.

"Yes?" I said. Still aloof. Still pretending I didn't know it was my older sister, Penelope, a name we both detested for its pretentious aspirations.

"This is so fucked up!" Penny slurred.

I held up my finger to Jay and the boys, mouthed, "One minute," and took a flashlight with me to the paneled study, away from where the boys could hear me.

More heavy breathing from Penny as I walked the darkened hallways.

"Where are you?" I asked, trying to flip on the lights in the study and then, remembering about the power failure, flopping down on the sofa and staring out into the darkness, a dull throb beginning behind my eyes and nasal cavity.

"Bob broke up with me!" Penny wailed, burping, then hiccupping.

"Where are you?" I asked, pinching the bridge of my nose, hoping Penny was home, even though home was a dilapidated house in Ohio thirty minutes from where we'd grown up together. Every inch of the small rented kitchen covered with coffee mugs and used glasses. The mess supposedly a reflection of her and Bob's shared creativity. Penny a former pianist and sometimes piano teacher. Bob an artist, or was it an illustrator? Bob always distracted the few times I'd met him, his mood slightly hostile.

"It's thirty-five hundred dollars."

"What is?"

More sobbing. Then, "Forget it. It's not worth it."

"What's not worth it?" I asked, jumping up to turn on the lights and then remembering about the blackout again and feeling like an idiot.

"I'm done," Penny slurred between sobs.

"Please!" I commanded.

On the other end of the phone, the line went dead.

I felt my breath catch and my heart begin to pound. Guilty and worried that I'd caused Penny to hang up on me. Praying we'd been disconnected.

I quickly dialed Penny's cell phone, even though clearly that wasn't the number she'd called me from. Alarmed when I heard the busy signal. How did cell phones ring busy? I called again. Busy. I called repetitively, ten, twelve, twenty times, finally reaching the voice mail only to hear it was full. I wondered if I should call a suicide hotline, if Penny really meant to do herself in. I stood up, pacing, thinking, worrying, wishing there were some damn electricity! Knowing somewhere in my mind that Penny wasn't going to do herself in. Probably. She'd been this upset before, when Bob had left her or she'd lost a job. And in those times, she had managed to pull herself up to normal, or at least her version of it. My mother paying for one disastrous stint in rehab in which Penny went directly from her program to the supermarket to load up on wine coolers.

I dialed Penny again.

The phone ringing through to voice mail. No room for messages. I told myself that could mean anything, not necessarily a long bender. I called Penny's house phone and learned it was disconnected. My heart beating wildly, I wondered if I should call my mother. Aware that wasn't an answer either one of us wanted. I held my face in my hands, counting the seconds until someone might need me, unable to decide which was worse—being alone with my sorrow and hopelessness or trying to act normal with the rest of the family.

In the distance I heard the doorbell ding-donging in a slow succession through the foyer, which seemed like an answer. I pushed myself up from the couch and followed the narrow beam of my flashlight through the front hall and around the corner to the kitchen. Drew and Jay standing near the granite island discussing how much gasoline to buy for our generator or whether to wait a few hours to see if the lights would come back on. Drew fingering his beard with his thumb and his forefinger. Nela and the kids still in their coats and boots. Nela calling out to me as soon as she saw me, saying she was so sorry to barge in like this!

"Don't be ridiculous," I said, waving her off. "Let me make you hot chocolate," I offered, hugging Sebastian and Matias, laughing at their long hair, wild with static electricity. Squeezing Sophia's hand, pretending this was a fun moment for an impromptu party. Terrified my sister was wandering around, about to be hit by a car or somehow taken advantage of. Penny a petite brunette who could be easily over-powered. Penny once showing up at Thanksgiving with tiny hatch marks all over her face, marks she claimed she'd gotten from falling into some branches. As if a mulberry bush could do something like that! Suddenly wondering what Nela would think if she knew about Penny's drinking or everything we went through as children. Wondering if she would cut me a break for being white and seemingly spoiled. But my urge to tell her was no match for my urge to cover it up, to pretend that everything was normal, to prove that I was.

I busied myself with the instant hot chocolate while Jay mouthed, "Who was on the phone?" his back to the Guzman-Venieros.

"Penny," I mouthed, waiting for his reaction.

Jay shrugging his narrow shoulders. Jay mouthing, "Sorry," which made me want to kill him. For his pat remark. For never understanding how responsible I felt! Even though I knew how much he loved me. Jay reaching out to rub my hair, to call me "Poodle" before returning to his machinery discussion.

In another moment, Jay asked, "What do you think, fire up the generator or wait a couple of hours?"

"You can wait," I said, not eager to have him leave.

"What about the food that will spoil?" he asked, antsy, I knew, to show off his preparedness plan. He'd strung two generators together with a custom cord that doubled their capacity. The whole rig stored on a cart with holes for rain and a tarp to protect it from wind gusts. Jay an engineer before he became a financial analyst.

"Don't worry about the fridge," I answered, eager for fewer problems to worry about, not more.

"What about all the food in the freezer?" Jay insisted. "You have a ridiculous amount of steak and chicken in there!"

I shrugged. I didn't answer. Hadn't he insisted we have lots of extra food in the house in case of catastrophe? I heard the doorbell ring again.

It was Lorraine with a bottle of Grey Goose in her hand, the boys trailing behind her. Gabe looking more and more like his mother, with his easy smile and straight dirty-blond hair, Jesse dark and thin like his father. Both of the boys pushing past their mother and clomping their way to my basement in their wet boots while Lorraine handed Jay the vodka.

"Should we start drinking?" Lorraine asked, looking around, I could see, for a glass. Her pageboy tousled and newly colored, a strand of pearls at the neck of her cashmere sweater. Didn't she ever just throw on sweatpants?

"I'll take mine straight up with lots of ice," Drew said, smiling and nudging me slightly.

I pushed Drew playfully with my shoulder as Jay went for the ice, my mood buoyed by the possibility of alcohol and camaraderie. Telling myself there was nothing I could do about my sister with a house full of people and no electricity. Aware that I'd surrounded myself with a lifetime of people for exactly this purpose.

Next to me, Lorraine started to pour vodka on the rocks as she regaled us with a story about passing Paige and Gene in the street.

"They booked a room at the Mandarin Oriental. A suite!" Lorraine said.

"Of course they did," Drew said, shaking his ice cubes, trying his first sip of vodka. In front of me, Nela raised her eyebrows, causing a flow of ripples across her high forehead, the implication being, of course, that the Mandarin was the worst possible indulgence you could engage in at a time like this.

"Paige loves the Mandarin," I said, ignoring Nela's judgment and pointing out what everyone surely knew, namely that Paige was a fan of the Mandarin even when there wasn't a blackout. Especially when there wasn't a blackout! Going there regularly to enjoy the spa and the pool and the hushed atmosphere of money. No doubt enjoying the way the hotel staff called her "Mrs. Edwards" and kissed her ass for the generous tips she always left. Which I understood wholeheartedly. The desire for luxury nearly the same as the desire for privacy, both of them protecting you, making you feel invincible. Suddenly wishing I was at a hotel, too. Glad that Winnie was there and wondering what she would make of such opulence.

Slowly we abandoned the kitchen and settled into my gray velvet couches. Tea lights scattered on my glass coffee table; all of us sipping our healthy shots of vodka as Drew leaned forward and announced that he had a solution, not just to the present blackout but to the constant lack of services we experienced. The recycling trucks frequently passing us by. The plows ignoring our cul-de-sac.

We leaned forward, anxious to hear what he had to say.

"Doesn't what's-her-face have a brother in the councilman's

office?" Drew asked, pointing to the house next to mine. The house dark except for the kitchen, where a congregation of people could be seen huddled around a table, a lantern lighting up their faces and the gleaming refrigerator behind them.

"The Williamses?" I asked.

"Her brother is, like, big in Boston politics!" Drew said. "How could you not know that?"

Everyone nodding like this fact explained something. Which maybe it did. Drew's ideas half-cocked but sometimes working. Drew once bribing a security guard to get us backstage at Blue Hills Bank Pavilion.

"So we call Debbie Williams and we see if she can work the back channels; I mean, those city guys are totally plugged in at the state level. Her complaint could go straight to the governor."

"We live in the suburbs, not Boston," I pointed out, amused and grateful for the distraction from my sister's well-being. Aware that as soon as I thought this, it wasn't working anymore. My guilt and my worry flooding back to me. Why hadn't I been a better sister to Penny? I barely called her. I always tried to get off the phone with her. I was overwhelmed by all the problems she was experiencing— with her unemployment benefits or why she could no longer teach piano. Things she'd hinted at that I couldn't follow. Things that didn't fully make sense—about carpal tunnel syndrome and a law-yer who overcharged her. But look at me—wasn't I just a tiny bit shallow, scheming and joking with my friends about how to get the governor to help us while Penny wandered the streets, drunk and no doubt depressed that Bob had left her? I hated myself and I loved my life, and the two things seemed irreconcilable in my living room.

Abruptly the subject switched to Stephanie Peterson and her

new natural gas generator. Everyone getting up and walking into my dining room to try to make out the outline of the Petersons' generator in the darkness.

"It's too fucking loud," Nela complained.

"I'm sure they rip you off on the maintenance," Jay added.

"I'm calling Olsen's tomorrow. They do it fast and they service it," Lorraine said, always quick to spend her sizable divorce settlement to avoid the first hint of a struggle.

"You and the rest of the neighborhood," I joked as we returned to my living room. Eager to be part of the good-humored complaining. Knowing I would have to leave everyone soon. Would have to try to track down Penny. Guilty I wasn't looking for her now. Certain a better person would have jumped on an airplane and gone searching for her. Certain that Lorraine would do it, probably even Drew and Nela. Even though I doubted they'd ever had to deal with something like this. Which made me feel ashamed and alone and completely helpless.

"Let's make a big batch of something," Drew said, done with his back-channel scheming and ready to start cooking.

"Definitely," Lorraine agreed. She'd had at least two drinks but didn't seem drunk. If anything, Lorraine merely got more energetic when she drank, more up for anything, including making an elaborate dinner in this case. "We have all this defrosted turkey meat in the fridge. Let me go get it," she offered now, looking toward Drew to see if he would get it for her.

"I have the world's best hot sauce," Drew said, not budging. "Here, take my key and I'll explain where it is. It's easy."

The room spontaneously bursting into laughter. Nela and Drew's kitchen was decked out with state-of-the-art appliances, yet famous for its state of disarray, their refrigerator packed haphazardly with Styrofoam takeout containers and half-eaten casseroles.

My cell phone suddenly buzzing, the strange number from earlier flashing. I lunged for the phone and hustled out of the room with a flashlight before anyone could ask me anything. Running up our spiral staircase, whispering, "Penny, I'm here. Don't go, okay?"

Quietly shutting my bedroom door, I walked farther into my suite, happy to be surrounded by the chocolate-brown walls and thick cream carpeting. None of it visible in the darkness but all of it a comfort to me nonetheless as I positioned myself on the tufted chaise we kept there, hugging my knees in my arms as I waited for Penny to say something.

"Phyllis won't help me!" she slurred, referring to our mother by her first name, the way she always did.

"How do you know? Did you call her?" I asked, dreading the thought of my mother now calling me, too. Our mother furious that Penny hadn't joined AA and gotten on with her life the way all the celebrities seemed to do. My mother always pointing out the rehab stories in *People* magazine to me, then talking about what great looks Penny had. As if the two were somehow linked: good looks and an ability to conquer your problems.

"They say I could die!" Penny said, not bothering to answer my question.

"Who says you could die?" I asked, confused and also desperate for some authority. For someone who wasn't Penny to be telling me these things.

On the other end of the phone, Penny started to sob again, deep, heaving sobs that I pictured racking her frail and beleaguered body. The last time I'd seen her, she'd been thinner than she was in childhood, which made me think she didn't eat properly.

"Ask Phyllis to bring my stuff to the hospital," she said between tears. "You know how my skin is."

"Okay," I said, casting around wildly for another solution, aware that without Bob there was none. My sister suffering from lifelong eczema. Claiming that only three hundred thread count could soothe her ravaged skin. My mother outraged that I had gifted the sheets to Penny on more than one occasion. Insisting that I spoiled her. On the other end of the line, I heard loud voices: someone shouting, then the phone dropping loudly in my ear, Penny in the background shouting, "Here, come here!"

"Who are you talking to?" I shouted.

I could hear muffled voices arguing, then a woman's voice, annoyed and businesslike, saying into the receiver, "Hello? Is this a family member?"

I was suddenly embarrassed. To be the person associated with Penny.

"Yes," I said, trying to sound authoritative.

"Do you wish to pay for this person's detox?" the voice asked.

"Oh," I said, surprised, although why was I? What had I thought the thirty-five hundred was for? Penny never direct with what she was asking, which always left us plenty of wiggle room to pretend we weren't talking about the things that we were.

The woman took my credit card number, then said, "Your sister came in earlier but she doesn't have insurance. We gave her some pills to take the edge off, but she came back. She thinks she's dying. Which is normal."

So Penny thought she could die, not the hospital staff. Which was a relief. Even if it was infuriating. The way everything always got so twisted up with my sister. The truth always buried under layers of detritus.

* * *

I hung up the phone and dialed my mother. Quickly. Before I could change my mind or get nervous. My mother exploding when I told her where Penny was. My mother saying, "She probably cracked up the car getting there!" Which was so shocking. I hadn't even thought of this. Why was she introducing this?

"Do you know she's driving with a suspended license?" my mother continued, barely pausing. "She told me that you told her it was okay."

As always, my mother was going too fast for me.

"I think I told her she should go to a driver's ed class to get it back," I said, trying to remember if the license was suspended or merely expired. Trying to figure out why my mother was focused on this!

"You think it's funny if she goes to jail for a DWI? Who do you think is going to bail her out? Are you going to fly here from Massachusetts and take care of things? Of course not."

"Mom, she's not in jail! She's in detox. Or a psych ward. Or some combination of both. I'm not sure how these things work."

"Of course you don't know. Because you don't bother to educate yourself!" my mother roared.

"I've been to Al-Anon!" I shouted, immediately embarrassed by my sudden outburst, afraid someone downstairs might hear me.

"Oh yeah? When? How many times? You drank with her the last time she was here. You bought wine coolers and drank with her!" my mother screamed at me.

"That was five years ago!" I shouted, unable to contain myself and furious that we were still talking about this incident.

"You think you know everything. That's why Penny's in this situation!"

"How did I cause this? How?" I hissed at her, reaching up to grab the roots of my thick, curly hair, tugging in fury and frustration.

"You told her it was my fault she dropped out of college!"

"That was fifteen years ago!" I screamed, unable to restrain myself.

"It's a pattern!" my mother shouted at me. "If you didn't enable her, she wouldn't be in this mess."

"I think Penny could use some bedding," I said, lowering my voice and letting go of my hair. "You know how itchy she gets."

My mother guffawed.

"Bob broke up with her," I added, hoping this might trigger some sympathy from my mother, even though my mother had been single twenty-plus years and never even dated, a state she implied made her both stronger and smarter than her friends, many of whom had remarried and divorced again.

"I can't do it. I'm too old!" my mother shouted, ignoring the issue of Bob altogether. "I have diabetes. Do you realize that?"

I did realize that. Sort of. Even though I tried to forget about it, too. My mother's enormous weight gain and her ill health. Loath to point out to her that her compulsive overeating wasn't so different from Penny's drinking. Furious she couldn't see it for herself!

"Can't you ask a friend to pick up the sheets from Penny's apartment?" I asked, a tone of frustration and subtle judgment creeping into my voice. A tone I immediately regretted. Hugging my knees and closing my eyes as I waited for the bomb blast of retaliation.

"You disgust me!" my mother began to shout. "I raised two

daughters alone on a secretary's salary, and you sit in that big house with your husband and your money and dare to judge me!"

"I'm not judging you," I insisted, my eyes clenched shut, trying to breathe my way through the tunnel she was now taking me through.

"How would you like it if Lucas or Josh were in the hospital? Huh?"

I grabbed my wrist and sank my nails into my pale white flesh.

"God forbid you should understand one day."

I dug my nails deeper. Refusing to answer her. Refusing to let her know how upset she had gotten me. After a pause, my mother blew her nose loudly and asked, "Are you still there, or did you conveniently hang up on me?"

"Just forget the whole situation. I'll buy the sheets and have them shipped," I offered, releasing my nails from my skin, breathing deeply so that my mother wouldn't hear the tears that were now bunched up at the back of my throat.

"Fine. You handle it!" my mother shouted, starting to cry again.

I knew I should say something kind to my mother now. Something supportive that reassured her that she'd been a good mother in a tough situation. That Penny was responsible for herself. But I just wasn't capable of putting on that particular record. It felt scratchy and ruined and the words simply couldn't find their way to the surface.

"We're in the middle of a blackout," I said, aware that this was a way out of the conversation. My mother started crying more loudly, her words no longer intelligible. I told her to get some rest. I told her she was overwhelmed. I hung up the phone and immediately felt sorry for her. Trying to imagine what I would do if I had a child who was an alcoholic and struggling, the thought chilling in the bleak gray air of the dressing room. Not willing to picture Lucas or Josh in my sister's situation. My empathy for my mother growing like an ink stain, blotting out my fury. Embarrassed about digging my nails into my skin. Wondering how I would hide the marks, from my friends, and from Jay, who hated the habit and thought I should have long ago learned to handle my mother.

In another moment I got up and went into the bathroom, my pale skin splotchy, my blond ringlets wild and frizzy. Smoothing the flyaway pieces and staring at my face in the mirror, looking for something I wanted to understand about myself. My green eyes staring back at me in the weak light from the moon. I took a deep breath, then pulled my sweater lower on my wrists, carefully hiding the ugly red marks before I made my way out of my bedroom and through the blackened house, the merriment of the living room rushing up to greet me.

SELECTIVE HEARING

THE SNOW MELTED AND the skies darkened. Long, rainy torrents soaked our yards and pounded our thinly mulched gardens. The sky finally clear and the ground just starting to harden when Paige and Gene invited us to their country club for a spring scavenger hunt. Pink and green goody bags, hand-printed maps, the promise of fresh air and sunshine, wholesome good fun. I waved at Paige as I approached from the parking lot, Jay, Josh, and Lucas trailing behind me.

"I'm so excited!" I called to Paige as we got closer, thrilled for the warm April weather, thrilled to not be on the phone with my sister, who was possibly sober but still not fully functional. My own life slipping away from me as I listened to her long litany of problems: a leaking roof, insomnia, eczema that refused to retreat. Bob's absence like a canker sore Penny touched over and over again while I tried to reassure her it was for the best. That she was beautiful and had an enviable figure. That she was a talented pianist and a very good music teacher. Even as I worried over her loneliness. Her lack of a steady job. Uncertain whether she was even attending AA. The truth confusing and hard to unwrap. The truth swirling around me like a mist whenever I tried to grab hold of it. Confused and depressed myself by the time I got off the phone with her. •

But now here I was, heading toward Paige and Gene's stately brick clubhouse, eager to indulge my fantasy of a perfect country club Sunday. The dining room no doubt decorated with pretty porcelain pots and tall, elegant flowers. The patio dotted with couches and club chairs for lounging. All of it filling me with envy and desire before I'd even seen it. Pretending to not know what had probably transpired before we arrived. Paige in charge of the decorating committee. Paige short-tempered and easily frazzled. Paige no doubt yelling at the help all morning as they prepared.

From the corner of my eye, I saw Lorraine and her boyfriend, Jeffrey, appear on the walkway in matching golf shirts and freshly pressed khakis. Jesse holding Jeffrey's hand while Gabe ran wildly between parked cars, Lorraine oblivious. Lorraine already waving and saying something I couldn't hear to Nela and Drew, who had come up behind me. Turning to see Nela in her fleece jacket with something on her feet that looked like slippers. Drew in ripped jeans, a flannel shirt, some sort of faded gray motorcycle jacket. For a country club brunch! The Edwardses kind enough to not say anything as we entered the club's main dining room, all of us exclaiming over the lovely food spread, the deviled eggs and mini quiches, the asparagus tarts and chocolate-covered strawberries.

We fed the kids. We fed ourselves. We tried to clean our kids' fingers lest they threaten the club's French country furniture with smeary deviled egg remnants. The scavenger hunt imminent. The kids clamoring for it as they raced around their tables, barely listening to Paige as she sternly explained the rules from her microphone in the corner. About no pushing. About no trampling the bushes or going on the golf course. About lining up at the French doors from shortest to tallest. Cameron interjecting in a loud stage whisper to point out what his friends already knew. That it was his club! That he already knew where all the treasures were hidden! The rest of us starting to roll our eyes at each other. Drew murmuring, "Get the gong," when after five minutes, Paige was still talking about the rules, completely oblivious to the commotion her son was causing.

"One more second," Paige said to the assembled crowd. "Then you can get the hook in the closet," she teased. "Finally, most importantly, kids five and under get a head start!" she announced. Winnie spontaneously taking the twins' hands in hers, which caused Nela to beam with pleasure as the three of them skipped toward the club's French doors. Winnie so lovely in a lavender dress. Sebastian and Matias in purple bow ties as if they'd planned it. Drew reaching for his video camera as I snapped my own photo. And then, the doors opening into the sunshine and fresh air, the spring smell washing over us, filling the room with a certain expectation and happiness.

After a few moments, the rest of the kids released and already squealing, I took my mimosa outside, ready to be part of this magical day—the children laughing and running as they knelt to scoop up their treasures. I'd done something similar with my father and his girlfriend Tracy once. Even though it wasn't similar, not really. All of us huddled around Tracy's small kitchen table making Easter eggs for a hunt in her parking lot, the curtains drawn against too much sun. Against any sun. My father's girlfriend loved it that way. Dark. At twelve I found it mysterious. And slightly glamorous. And then I found it ugly. And slightly tawdry. The memory shifting back and forth over time as I grew older. As I tried to come to terms with the truth about Tracy. Things I realized later, or that were eventually told to me. Her drinking and her sketchy employment. The way she never had any food in the house. And yet, even now, my heart still clung to what it knew then. That Tracy was beautiful and fun to be with. The past impossible to write off, even when you knew that you should.

I shook my head slightly, dismissing the memories, walking across the patio and out toward the hunting grounds, trying to find Lucas. To make sure he was discovering some treasures, not getting frustrated. Aware that Lucas was a terrible looker. A worse sport. Someone who insisted on getting his own way and was impossible when he didn't. Which I hated about him. His temper. His inability to be flexible. Which I worried about constantly, despite everyone telling me it would get better with age and good parenting. Which seemed so exhausting. Waiting for it to go away. Knowing I was responsible for fixing it. Afraid that if I wasn't vigilant, he'd become some sort of addict. Which was ludicrous and farfetched but always present, just beneath the surface.

I found Lucas near the side of the clubhouse, a half dozen toys in his polka-dotted goody bag, his mood seemingly fine or at least oblivious to my presence. Leaving me free to watch Winnie nearby, silently darting between the tennis courts and the low row of holly bushes alongside them, her hands quickly ferreting out the colorful plastic toys and dropping them in her bag.

I was surprised by it. Pleased by it. Embarrassed to not have imagined it! That a Russian orphan could be so graceful. So athletic. I watched her skip toward the flower beds and gently scoop up two foil-wrapped chocolates from alongside the peonies.

"You have so many prizes," I said to her, pointing at her nearly full bag, smiling even though I doubted she could fully understand me. Winnie stopped her hunting and turned toward me, her lazy eye making it hard for me to know where to train my gaze. Making me all the more astounded by her skills. Could she see fully?

"You are so good!" I told her, pointing at the bag but really meaning her.

Winnie nodded once, a hesitant smile on her face, clearly unsure what the words meant. I gave her a squeeze around her narrow shoulders, then said, "Go, go!" pointing toward the other kids and smiling encouragingly.

Winnie quickly turned and raced away toward the farthest corner of the green, where none of the children were looking for hidden treasure. Gene suddenly beside me, watching Winnie as she skipped off.

"She's so good at this," I told him. "Did you see how many items she's found?" Wondering if Gene was as proud of her as I was.

"It's on account of the orphanage," Gene offered, shrugging. "She's used to battling it out to get her fair share."

I thought this was terrible. I thought this was probably true! But I wished he hadn't said it. Hadn't given her this label that set her apart from the other kids.

"But she's so smart!" I insisted, eager for him to see that she was special, unique, not a misfit they'd picked up from the unwanted clothing bin.

"Definitely," Gene said, starting to back away from me. Obviously not interested in my assessment of Winnie. Or in my assessment of him. Which was so annoying. My annoyance immediately replaced by embarrassment. That he wanted to get away from me so quickly. That he clearly didn't like me all that much.

* * *

When the masses of brightly colored toys and foil-wrapped candies were collected, heaped in bags, and spilling out clumsily from pockets, the children gathered in the shade of an oak tree to compare their findings while the rest of us lounged on the country club terrace. The air too cool for sunbathing but luxurious in our newly purchased spring clothing. Lorraine teasing Gene about his monogrammed socks while Drew described a cache of old baseball cards he'd found at some yard sale. Out of the corner of my eye, I caught a glimpse of Lucas, laughing. Thick, smeary chocolate remnants visible in his teeth as he reached into Winnie's bag to take a handful of candy. I desperately wanted to say something. To stop him from embarrassing me. Was tempted to shout at him, but knew it would backfire. In another moment Gabe reached in to steal some of Winnie's toys, then so did Sebastian and Matias. Sophia starting to slap at her brothers' hands, the boys shouting that she was hurting them. Nela finally noticing and saying to all of them, "Stop taking Winnie's things!"

"Winnie says we can have them. She doesn't mind!" Lucas shouted back at Nela, the chocolate on his teeth so noticeable. So embarrassing!

"It's true!" Gabe added, reaching into Winnie's bag to boldly grab a bouncy ball.

"She did not," Lorraine said. "Winnie doesn't even speak English!"

I cringed. Why did she say that? Why did she have to call attention to Winnie's differentness? And so loudly.

"She actually understands everything," Gene said, sitting on one of the terrace's stone walls to face us. "She's just never seen so much candy in her whole life. She doesn't care if they take it."

Next to me on her chaise, Paige sighed. Loudly. As if she were already tired of the subject or simply didn't want to get into it. Lorraine, who never caught a cue or simply didn't believe they applied to her, refused to let the subject drop. She sat up in her own chaise and leaned toward Paige, asking, "So Winnie understands English now?" Her muscled forearms on her knees like she was getting ready to negotiate something.

Paige combed her fingers through her fine silvery hair before saying softly, "Winnie understands, but she pretends not to."

Jay laughed at the table next to me.

"Selective hearing!" Drew added.

Lorraine said, "I honestly thought Gabe was deaf. I had his hearing checked when he was four."

All of us cracking up except for Paige and Gene. Gene looking at Paige seriously before coming to stand behind her lounge chair. "It's different when you adopt a child. Right, Pip?" Using her pet name in case we missed the fact that he had her back, in case there was any doubt whose side he was on.

We waited. We wanted an explanation. Paige reaching down to hug her knees under her dress, turning toward us with a face more tired than we had realized earlier. Which made me immediately feel sorry for her. And worried.

"Her speech is a lot more delayed than we thought. Which is something the agency didn't really reveal to us," Paige said, sighing. "They basically lied to us."

"Lucas couldn't speak till he was five!" I jumped in. Hoping to make Paige feel better. Lucas far away enough that I doubted he could hear me.

"He could, too!" Jay protested.

"Not intelligibly!" I argued. "We got him tons of speech therapy," I went on, insistent that Paige understand this fact, even if Jay couldn't. Even if Jay still believed Lucas would have talked normally regardless of what we'd done to help him. Which seemed like an odd and risky way to live your life. To believe that things either worked out with your kids or they didn't. That there was very little you could do to influence them. Even though I secretly suspected Jay was right, their basic temperament was out of your control, which frightened me.

"The eye surgery will help," Gene said smoothly. His salmon-colored golf shirt like an expensive flag. A colorful promise.

"It will?" I asked, excited and confused. What did her eye have to do with her language skills?

"Not directly. Not immediately. But she'll have better vision afterwards. She'll be more likely to read. She can progress," Gene said, sounding for all the world as if he were quoting a social worker. Which was strange coming out of his mouth, but not unwelcome. I was pleased he and Paige were getting help. Taking advice.

"When are you having her eye fixed?" Lorraine wanted to know, eager to put a cap on this conversation, to no doubt start planning the group gift we would get for Winnie post-surgery. Mylar balloons with a "Get Well" teddy bear. Flowers. Something sent to the hospital during her recovery

"As soon as she doesn't have a cold," Paige said. Obviously peeved. "Have you noticed she's always sick?" Paige asked no one in particular.

How would we have noticed? Winnie had just gotten here. We hadn't seen her since the welcome dinner. Or at least I hadn't. And everyone had a cold in the winter, didn't they?

"Assuming Winnie doesn't get sick again, we have something on the calendar for next month. Early May," Paige said. Still sounding aggrieved. Still sounding for all the world like Winnie was a burden she'd inadvertently been stuck with. I told myself I wasn't hearing this. Nobody else seemed disturbed by her tone, which I told myself was proof that I was reading too much into things.

We offered congratulations. We offered to help with anything Paige needed. To babysit Cameron. To drive carpools.

Paige declined. Paige thanked us. Paige hugged her knees tighter and told us we meant the world to her! But no, she had everything covered. An old school friend was taking Cameron. They would only be in Boston for a couple of days. Maybe fewer.

I felt disappointed. I felt left out. I wished Paige would let me do *something*, if only so that I could be part of this transformative process. The surgery the thing that would assure Paige that she had nothing to worry about. The surgery was the thing that would allow Winnie to catch up to the other kids. Especially if Winnie really understood English like Gene said she did! Even though it gnawed at me. That this was what Paige seemed to require in order to love her new daughter.

A MISUNDERSTANDING

It was early afternoon. Sunny. Not hot. I was leaving Paige's front door, crossing under her cherry blossom tree, the May sun pleasantly thick on my neck, when I heard it. Someone begging. Then an adult voice. Mean. Low. Insistent. A door slammed followed by miserable crying from somewhere deep in the throat. It was Winnie. Somewhere behind the boxwood hedge. Of course it was Winnie. But I couldn't look. I couldn't peer between the bushes that guarded Paige's backyard, my face pressed against the greenery. What would Paige think if she saw me? I shouldn't have come over unannounced. Shouldn't have rung the doorbell in search of some baking soda. I started to walk faster, at an angle, heading for the sidewalk, off her property, away from the commotion and noise, the sadness and fear. But before I could fully escape, I heard her voice. Paige's. Calling after me. Desperate. Insistent.

"Nicole? Nicole?"

I turned and tried my best to look friendly. Normal. Not alarmed. Paige emerging from her front door, walking fiercely toward me in a boldly patterned wrap dress. Her face narrow and pinched.

"I'm so glad I saw you there," Paige insisted, her upset shimmering just below the surface.

"I ran out of baking soda," I said, desperate that she know I wasn't trespassing. Not spying.

"Winnie's had her eye fixed," Paige said, ignoring my statement or else simply not hearing me.

I nodded. I said, "I'm so happy!" clasping my hands together for emphasis, to show her how supportive I was. Eager to go. To get away.

"She has to wear socks. Over her hands. So she won't scratch and pull off the patch," Paige said, looking at me like she was asking permission. Like she was asking to be excused. For what, I couldn't tell yet. I didn't want to know.

"I may have to tie her to a chair. So she won't scratch!" Paige said.

"I'm sorry you're going through this," I said, transferring my weight from one foot to the other, not looking at her. I didn't want to hear more. Already I was certain I had misheard her. It was important that I leave before she clarify. "Josh is home alone," I said more loudly and enthusiastically than it made sense to.

Paige opened her mouth as though she wanted to say something else, but I merely turned and started to sprint down the middle of our road, shouting again over my shoulder that Josh was home alone. As if his being alone in front of the TV were a desperate thing that needed attending to. Not something I had planned for and calculated so that I could borrow baking soda, knowing full well that five-year-olds shouldn't be left alone. Which meant I wasn't a perfect mother, either. Bursting into my kitchen out of breath, feeling guilty and remorseful about an accident that hadn't happened, hugging Josh close and telling him I loved him.

* * *

Gene came home early from work. I saw his silver Mercedes glide
into the Edwardses' short, curving driveway and disappear behind
the house. I checked my watch. Almost three o'clock. Was he playing golf? I knew I should look away. Clean a closet. Get a job! But
I stood at my desk, staring out my office window.

In a few minutes, Winnie and Cameron stepped onto the front
stoop holding giant lollipops, licking the edges round and round.
Winnie's hands covered in mitts, or maybe they were socks? From
around the corner, Gene came out of the garage with Wiffle balls.
A batting stand. White rubber bases were tossed around the yard
and Matias and Sebastian came to join them. Teams were formed,
Winnie the permanent cheering section. I knew I could go over,
too. Bring my boys. Subtly ask why Gene was home, whether anything was the matter. But I preferred to stay where I was. Content to watch the action from behind my windowpanes. The scene
charming and animated when observed from a certain distance.

* * *

Gene stayed home the rest of that week. The children outside with
him in the afternoons. Winnie usually on the stoop doing something with chalk while Gene and Cameron ran around the yard.
Cameron clumsy. Awkward. Tripping over branches or else throw-
ing a Wiffle ball badly. Gene in turns patient and frustrated. All of
this observed by me from my office window, if also ignored. Not
eager to find out what Gene was doing home. Not eager to find out
what was or wasn't happening with Winnie's surgery, her urge to

scratch. The days flipping slowly forward until it was the weekend again. Until Gene was supposed to be home.

On Sunday, Drew bought a croquet set from an estate sale: ten wooden mallets and matching striped balls. Lorraine suggesting a neighborhood tournament and Paige insisting on hosting us. Pastel-colored macarons set out on a doily-covered plate when we arrived just after lunchtime, miniature cocktail napkins fanned out next to sweating pitchers of lemonade.

But nearly as soon as we arrived, the croquet mallets chosen and the spikes spaced out accordingly, Paige wanted to escape. To get away from the tournament and the children and the sunshine.

"Come inside," she said to Nela and Lorraine and me. I tried to inch closer to where Josh was studying his striped green ball; eager to see if he could complete the complicated technique Jay was insisting on explaining to him. Josh's mouth a straight line in his slack and pudgy face. His focus far exceeding his years.

"Don't you think we should make sure a fight doesn't break out?" I asked, trying to delay the inevitable. Being cornered. Being monopolized. Being stuck in the house with Paige, far from our husbands and our children with no ready-made excuse to get away from her.

"I have to show you something," Paige insisted, laying her pale arm on my shoulder in a gesture of sisterhood and solidarity. I snuck a peek at Nela and Lorraine, who, I knew, were relieved it wasn't their arms she was touching. Nela in the same tight Harvard T-shirt she wore every weekend; her breasts straining against the faded burgundy fabric. Lorraine in tennis whites and a full face of makeup, obviously on her way somewhere else. Which was astounding. Wasn't it her idea to have this tournament?

Inside, on the marble island, there was a black velvet jewelry envelope, a name I didn't catch embossed on the cover. Paige already reaching for it by the time I'd settled onto one of her bar stools. Paige opening it up to reveal a ruby and diamond necklace, the diamonds brilliant, the rubies like liquid wine, beautiful and exotic.

"Birthday?" Lorraine practically shouted, nervous, I knew, that we'd somehow missed the occasion and would now look foolish with what could only be an inferior group present. Paige smiling a mercurial smile, bending her long, slender neck forward to clasp the choker behind her hairline, then lifting her chin and spreading her shoulders so that we could better admire the jewels that now lay perfectly along the prominent bones of her neckline. They were stunning. Magnificent. The contrast with her hair making her ethereal beauty even more dignified.

"Anniversary?" shouted Lorraine again, determined to guess the occasion that had motivated such an extravagant gesture.

"Gene brought it home earlier this week," Paige said. "I told him no baby gift, but he insisted. I think he's feeling a little bit jealous of Winnie," Paige continued, pressing her pale lips together, her cheek color rising.

I felt the fullness of her statement settle into my chest. "Earlier this week" just so happened to be when Paige might or might not have tied Winnie to a chair. Been out of control.

"So anyway, besides the necklace, Gene decided to stay home with me. He couldn't do it before. You know how much he travels..."

We nodded. We knew. He was an executive at some expensive tableware company, traveling to Italy at least once quarterly, not to mention his domestic travel.

"So anyway, if you see him around, that's why," Paige said, looking carefully at each of us in turn.

I suspected all of this to be false. Not the particulars: that Gene loved her. That Gene had bought a lavish baby gift for her. But the reason for it, surely. Convinced that Paige needed to be propped up. Reassured of something. That she now wanted to reassure us, too.

"Evan once tried to pawn off somebody else's jewels on me!" Lorraine said, apropos of nothing. Or maybe apropos of this. Eager to show Paige how much better off she was in the love department than she had been. All of us turning to look at Lorraine.

"We got engaged three months after we met—and he didn't have a ring because it was sort of spur of the moment, which I thought was romantic," Lorraine said, fingering her blond pageboy as if remembering the failed possibility.

"So, a week later, Evan comes to me and shows me this huge diamond that he says was in his family, and asks what kind of ring do I want made?" Lorraine continued. "So I say, 'Gee, Evan, that's a big diamond. Where'd you get that?' because I just could not picture Evan's mother or grandmother wearing something like that. I mean, it must have been four karats, a huge pear shape, but sort of ugly, with obvious inclusions. And Evan says, 'Well, I bought it for my ex, but I figured you wouldn't mind if we used it.'"

"That's fucked up!" Nela said, reaching for one of Paige's perfectly polished apples on the island and taking a loud bite out of it. All of us looking at her as if she'd just fired a gun. Nobody just reached for things in Paige's house. Paige once yelled at Lucas for helping himself to a Kleenex.

But Paige seemed not to notice, so intent was she on Lorraine's story. Fingering the necklace and shaking her head from side to side in polite agreement about Evan's gauche behavior.

"Evan didn't understand. We almost didn't get married. Can you believe how different my life would have been if we hadn't?"

I couldn't imagine it. It was strange to think about. Would there be another family in Lorraine's house if she hadn't married Evan to begin with? Would we all be belong to each other without Lorraine, who had brought us together and insisted we were like family?

"Drew and I bought silver bands from a flea market when we got married," Nela said, smiling and crunching into her apple again. "Our fingers turned green on the honeymoon, so we had to throw them out."

I looked at her and smiled. Aware that she didn't really give a shit about Paige's routine or about Lorraine's story. Nela intent on showing us how different she was from us, how we couldn't understand the first thing about her. Which I understood, even if I thought it was self-serving. To be so convinced that other people couldn't possibly understand you. To not bother to try to understand them, either.

But neither Paige nor Lorraine seemed to notice Nela's disinterest, or her derision. Paige leaning back against one of her mahogany cabinets, pleased, I could tell, with the attention she was receiving, and also with the success of her story. The fact that we all seemed to believe her cover-up. I sensed that's what it was—a cover-up—even though I had not one shred of proof to rely on.

* * *

After that first week, Gene stayed home for three days, still around, but not quite so present in the front yard with the kids and the games and the candy. Once I saw him cruise by in their Mercedes convertible with Paige in the front seat, both of them waving at me. Paige admitting later that they'd had a couples massage at the Mandarin spa, which I thought was nice for them, if a little weird. In the middle of an afternoon on a Tuesday.

The following week Gene was home for two days, and Lorraine made plans to play tennis with him on one of the afternoons. The other afternoon I ran into him at Home Depot with Winnie, his cart stacked with wicker storage baskets. Gene talking to Winnie in a high voice as I rounded the corner. Saying something I couldn't make out, his face close to hers as if he'd recently kissed her on the forehead. I felt my eyes tear up with gratitude that Winnie had a father who so clearly adored her, making a point to stop and say hello, even though Gene never seemed eager to engage with me. A fact that embarrassed me.

"A full-time nanny and Paige needs me to help organize the third-floor bonus room," Gene said, rolling his eyes as soon as I asked him what he was up to.

"How's the eye?" I asked, nodding toward Winnie, whose left eye was still red and swollen. Wanting to let him know I was supportive, hoping I didn't sound nosy.

"Perfect. Everything's on schedule. We're going back to Boston on Monday," he insisted with false friendliness. His normally handsome face appearing puffier than usual. His hands clutching the cart too tightly.

I nodded. The silence stretched out. I wished I could ask Gene something more about Winnie. But already he was moving his giant cart away from me, Winnie smiling and waving as Gene said, "We're off to get wooden hangers."

In the final week of Gene Edwards's supposedly romance-filled paternity leave, he was home just one day, a Friday, when he and Paige were spotted in town by Lorraine.

"They were definitely not holding hands!" Lorraine reported to me. "Paige was furious with him. I think he was letting the kids drink soda!"

RETREAT

GENE WAS BACK AT work and the weather was consistently warmer when Paige retreated into her house and wouldn't come out. She didn't stand on her stoop to supervise the kids on her lawn or invite us for drinks at her pool. She didn't return phone calls or even preside over her gardener as he labored around her yard. Paige, who had studied landscape design and always had an opinion. Paige, who had ripped up the Mediterranean-style beds the previous owner had installed and replaced them with an English floral design. Not that anyone could tell the difference.

But now there were no marathon planning sessions in the front yard. No scolding of neighbors to keep their dogs off her flowers. Cameron and Winnie were seen with the nanny, or with Gene, who took them to our houses on weekends. The other kids accepting Winnie's presence as if she'd always been one of them. Everyone happy to watch the children play kickball or freeze tag, to trade gossip and share cocktails, to pretend it was just another season in our ongoing idyll of childhood and parenting. The days wonderfully long and happy except for the static that hung over Paige's house. Where was she? Gene hinting at shopping trips and spa visits. Gene rolling his eyes at her need for yoga and calming respites.

His smile and jocular manner still on display, even if I sensed a hint of melancholia, a certain wariness just beneath the surface.

Nela not interested in Gene's mental state. Nela appalled by Paige's absence, criticizing Paige to anyone who would listen. Eager to point out that no one had the luxury to indulge oneself in the neighborhood that Nela had grown up in. Drew nodding his head vigorously like he agreed with Nela, even if he seemed more amused by Paige's absence. Lorraine endlessly speculating. Wondering what Paige *did* all day. She couldn't get massages and go to the mall endlessly! Lorraine's stories repetitive, unfounded, full of gaps and holes we couldn't fill in. Like whether Paige sometimes drove around late at night. (Drew claiming that her car pulled out frequently at eleven p.m.) Like whether she was seeing a doctor who told her to get more rest. Soon it was August. Paige's absence having gone on for nearly three months, and still Lorraine wanted to talk about it.

"She blew off Faye Crosby's fortieth birthday party!" Lorraine reported one cool evening, the sky milky, with hints of gray at the edges. Lorraine in her Range Rover, still in her work clothes, parked in front of my driveway to chat like she always did on her way home from the office. If I wasn't outside, she'd pull into my driveway, ring the bell, walk in before I answered. Not that I minded. Most of the time.

"And it was at Paige's own club," Lorraine added. As if this were the ultimate faux pas. Not showing your face at your club. I nodded. I didn't care. Or rather, I did care, but not in the way that Lorraine did. I didn't need to wonder and analyze and discuss. I already thought I knew what I thought. That Paige had had some sort of breakdown. Some sort of collapse in confidence. Which could be good, in a way, I told myself. Promising. People got better after such a thing, didn't they? If they got help. I imagined Paige resting as she gathered her wits about her, or even talking to some-one that Gene had found for her, and I felt better just knowing it. That in the darkness of her room, Paige was morphing from one person into another. Someone calmer. Someone better able to man-age the stress of parenting an adopted daughter.

"Well, maybe Paige is seeing a professional," I said vaguely, unsure where Lorraine stood on therapy. Lorraine shrugged. She wasn't really interested in the specifics of what was wrong with Paige. In how she could or couldn't get better. She was interested in reporting the news. In showing me how Paige was strange. Inde-finable. A mystery for us to solve.

Or maybe she didn't really care about the mystery at all. Maybe she merely wanted to string sentences together, to bind us closer with what she considered a shared but ultimately minor concern. Surely she thought Paige's absence was minor; otherwise why would she be talking about it in the same way she talked about everything else? The new bar at Charlie's Steakhouse or the no-texting rule at her country club pool? All of it reported with the same mix of frustration and amusement. All of it fodder for conversation, an excuse for daily discussion.

I waited for Lorraine to switch topics. I knew that she would. In the next breath, Lorraine wanted to know what I was doing Saturday night. Was I going to the Lipmanns' party, or was I still annoyed with Diana for what she'd done at the school book fair last fall?

I told her I was annoyed. I told her I hated Diana Lipmann! I told her we were going anyway because it was a party, wasn't it? And besides, I liked Roger Lipmann. He was funny and smart, even if he was bald and had lost too much weight. Which didn't make him look good. It made him look old. Lorraine agreed. Lorraine was the kind of woman who never had to lose weight.

"I'm having a fiftieth birthday party for Jeffrey this winter," Lorraine said, referring to her boyfriend apropos of nothing, suddenly turning off her engine.

"Fun," I said, surprised that Jeffrey was so much older than the rest of us.

"Do you think I should do passed hors d'oeuvres or a buffet?"

I sighed. I didn't care! Couldn't she decide later? But clearly Lorraine needed this diversion. This task she'd created for herself. To free herself from her own boredom or else from anxiety about her present and her future. Of course I understood this. Of course I could see the entertainment value in this. It was why I wanted to go back to work. Was even now weighing the pros and cons of asking my old boss for freelance work. So that I could have something concrete to focus on, something with hard edges and clear rewards. The opposite of kids, with their murky motives and strange behaviors. The opposite of neighbors who were unpredictable and made you worry.

I tried to get into the spirit of Lorraine's party planning. Together we considered the benefits of a rented dance floor. Of a red carpet rolled out from her stoop to the curb. The Sutherlands had done it. Which I thought was lovely and my decorator had claimed was tacky.

"Jason Fried would totally give me a deal on a charter if I wanted to make it a destination thing," Lorraine said, starting to explain how Jason, our neighbor who owned a small jet-for-hire business, had kissed her once in middle school. How hot he once was, before he developed a twitch.

I started to protest about the flying, but Lorraine's cell phone rang. Jeffrey's voice suddenly booming from the dashboard. Lorraine telling him about a client's funeral and then instructing him to make a dinner reservation for the weekend. Which was so annoying. Having to listen to their minutiae. So embarrassing! Not telling Jeffrey he was on speakerphone. I mouthed, "Go. Talk to Jeffrey!" and Lorraine nodded, waved distractedly, then kept talking as she turned on the engine and rolled down the street.

I went inside and stared out my kitchen window toward Paige's imposing brick Tudor. I imagined her resting in her pale yellow bedroom, the shades drawn, someone attending to her once, twice, maybe three times a day. Yazmin maybe. Or some temporary person she'd hired. Paige's shrill voice weakened with illness and fatigue. Her body listless. I imagined her drinking weak tea and contemplating her mistakes, or else not contemplating anything at all. Just miraculously changing into someone calmer and more loving, into her best and truest self. I believed this image with every fiber of my being; I believed this in a way that wasn't even belief but some hard kernel of knowledge that I carried inside me always, like faith. That if you waited long enough, the people you loved would become the people you wanted them to be.

I left the window and rummaged around in my refrigerator for dinner. Paige already replaced in my mind with images of Penelope; feeling guilty that I hadn't called my sister in months, hopeful that the money I was sending her was enough of a remedy. Aware Penny didn't want to talk to me, either. At least not consistently. The phone ringing. Nervous that it was Penny and pretty certain that it was. Caller ID confirming my hunch. Unable to ignore her now that I'd inadvertently conjured her. I picked up the receiver and answered with a cheery, "Hi, Penny!" Eager to appear happy. Welcoming. Hopeful we could start on good footing.

Penny began immediately without greeting me. "I know you're going to think I'm crazy, but I think Bob may have come back and stolen from me."

"Didn't you change the locks?"

"It's not like I have a spare hundred dollars lying around," Penny retorted.

"I'm just saying..."

"Listen, Nicole, that isn't the point. The point is that the land-lord may evict me!" Penny said, her voice suddenly rising.

"I'm sure the landlord isn't going to evict you because Bob came back and took your stuff!" I said, wishing desperately I hadn't picked up the phone.

"Would you please just let me finish!" she demanded. "There's more to this story!"

"Okay," I said, returning to the fridge, getting out the ingredients for dinner—trying to focus on the steps I needed to make pork chops: the eggs and the flour and the bread crumbs all in their separate dishes—while following Penny's long, complicated story about the neighbors' cousin who was a not-so-secret drug dealer and a recent bout of vandalism to her garage.

"Vandalism?" I asked, nervous and confused.

"It wasn't serious. But I did call 911," she continued, telling me another long, complicated story, this one about the guy the landlord used to do simple handiwork, whom she suspected was involved.

"I'm really sorry things have been hard," I interjected when I thought she was through with her story and the pork chops were lined up neatly on my white cutting board, ready for the grill even though I'd forgotten to turn it on.

"Don't be sorry," Penny said. "Please! I'm not calling to make you feel sorry for me! I'm calling to update you about my life. So that you know what's going on with me. And also because I have some good news."

"Great!" I said, my voice too high and too artificially happy but the best I could manage as I went outside to stand in front of my grill, listening carefully.

"Listen, I found out I can finish my bachelor's degree in five months online. Then I can start substituting, maybe even as a music teacher, while I do my teacher preparation program. In eighteen months I can be a full music teacher with benefits. No more freelance. No more bitchy moms!"

I cringed at her description. Didn't she know she was going to have another pool of difficult parents to contend with? Not to mention difficult colleagues? But I tried to push this thought out of my mind as I considered this piece of good news. Certain that a college degree would be the thing that would help Penny regain some self esteem. Hopeful that once she felt better about herself, she'd stop using the drinking as a crutch. Stop being so negative about other people.

"Tell me more," I said, opening the grill cover and turning on the burners, the flames bursting to life in a way that always pleased me in their efficiency but startled me in their exuberance. The whoosh of the fire loud and sounding for all the world like a mini explosion. Penny talking in my ear about the fact that she needed someone to pay half her tuition.

"Of course I'll help," I agreed, cringing as I said it. Knowing Jay would kill me for continuing to dole out money without talking to my sister about her drinking problem. My sister barely bothering to thank me. My sister telling me a story about her upstairs neighbors, then announcing that she was going to work the late shift as a waitress to pay for her other expenses. Something about an after-hours club.

"Maybe you shouldn't hang around that sort of element," I cautioned, realizing as I spoke that the pork chops would soon be ready but that I didn't have a plate for them. I turned and ran into the house and toward the kitchen, the distance not inconsequential. The distance reminding me for the hundredth time that we should have installed French doors and a deck off the kitchen to avoid this problem!

"Nicole, let me stop you right there!" Penny was saying as I finally reached the kitchen and grabbed the platter. "Please don't talk to me like I'm a child who needs advice. You have no idea what it's like to be inside my head!"

I nodded, afraid to imagine what it was like to be in her head, running back through the house to the backyard, trying to think what I could say to make Penny understand that I cared about her and hadn't meant to be condescending. But before I could open my mouth and begin to explain myself, Penny said, "You are basically a spoiled housewife who spends thousands of dollars on her hand-bags and looks down on me because I'm not more successful. I'm done with this conversation!"

"I'm sorry," I said, struggling to flip the pork chops. Because I *was* sorry. For anything I had done to inadvertently hurt her. Even though I was furious, too. Because I was the last person to spend a thousand dollars on a handbag! Even though I could afford to. Which somehow made her accusation true, or at least damning. For my having so much more than she did.

On the other end of the line the phone clicked dead, and I went back to the kitchen confused and guilty and furious. Lucas wait-ing for me by the granite island, wanting to know if he could go to Target.

"Maybe," I said distractedly.

"I want to get a LEGO set. With my own money," he said. His dark, curly hair nearly covering his forehead.

"Okay, maybe Saturday," I said, trying to scrape the burnt crust off the pork chops and wondering if with enough applesauce they would taste all right. Jay stuck eating cold food at eight p.m. anyway, which meant maybe it didn't matter?

"I want to go now!" Lucas whined. I looked at him and wanted to tell him to please shut it, but I refrained. Instead, I said, "I can't now," opening the cupboards, searching for the applesauce.

"Why? Give me one good reason," Lucas demanded, ready to negotiate a settlement with me.

"Because I'm cooking dinner," I said. Furious that Lucas didn't understand that no meant no. That Jay had taught him to never take no for an answer! Training Lucas for a career in business was how Jay had explained it.

"We can eat later with Daddy," Lucas persisted.

"No!" I said, raising my voice in an attempt to intimidate him.

"You never do anything for me!" he said, starting to shout.

"Lucas, you are not the most important person in the world. Do you fucking understand that?" I asked, furious that he wasn't being the docile child I wished him to be. Slamming the cutting board down on the counter to make my point, which only served to make Lucas scream louder, high-pitched keening followed by crying and garbled words about the fact that I didn't love him.

"Stop it right now!" I said, grabbing him hard by the shoulders and forcing him to look at me, which merely had the effect of causing him to scream in my face. I wanted to hit him. I wanted him to understand that he simply could not act this way. Out of control! Yelling at me. Exactly like my sister! And then, in a moment of fury, I did hit him. A slap across the cheek. Convinced this would teach him a lesson. Even though I sensed I was merely being vindictive.

For a brief second, it worked. Lucas staring at me wide-eyed in disbelief, holding his palm to his cheek before his face crumpled with fear and he started to scream, "You hit me!" Lucas now curled up into a ball on my kitchen floor, crying inconsolably, saying over and over again, "You hit me." His voice tinged with disbelief and hurt. My heart breaking at his inconsolable fear and sadness. Unable to believe that I had caused this terrible state. Desperate to hug Lucas and say I was sorry. Lucas pushing me away as I came close, then running, screaming, to his room, repeating over and over again, "You hit me!" at the top of his lungs, his voice carrying up the spiral staircase and through the cavernous rooms of the house. Shutting my eyes, ashamed and remorseful, grateful that at least Josh was at the Weinbergers.

After a good long while I went upstairs and knocked lightly at his door before letting myself in. Lucas was curled up under the comforter on his bed, his face buried beneath the blanket.

"Can I come in?" I asked from the doorway, knowing I had no right to assume he wanted to see me.

No answer from Lucas.

"I'm going to come closer unless you tell me not to," I said, inching my way carefully toward his bed.

When I was next to him I peeled off the comforter and said, "I was wrong," which only caused Lucas to turn away from me and start crying again.

"I'm afraid of you!" he screamed, then buried his face in his hands again. My heart clenching up as if it were a fist, squeezing the air out of me, making me remember all the times I'd cried on my own bed as a child.

"I was totally wrong," I said again, wishing I could make this all go away. Wishing I could punish myself and make myself disappear. Give Lucas a better mother. Someone he deserved, who knew how to handle him.

More whimpering from Lucas.

"I can't take it back," I said. "But I can promise never to do it again," I said, praying this was true.

"How can you promise?" Lucas asked, his voice muffled beneath the covers.

"Because I'm the adult. And I can make those promises and keep them," I said, nervous that I couldn't but also certain that by saying it I could at least try. Which would have to be good enough, not just for Lucas but for both of us. Which terrified me almost as much as hitting him had. How uncertain the future was; how I might not be good enough.

* * *

"No kid wants to see his mother out of control," Jay said that evening when I told him about the slap and my horrible remorse about it.

"I know. I know! I feel sick about it," I said, getting out of bed to get socks, my toes suddenly numb.

"You have to be the adult," Jay continued, his slender shoulders and thick curly hair just visible above the top of the sheets.

"That's easy for you to say," I retorted, putting on my socks and then sitting on the chaise longue. Jay a good and loving father, but shockingly absent when it came to anything difficult. Jay an expert at setting up complicated Hot Wheels tracks, or teaching the kids to ride a bike without skinning their knees, but quickly excusing himself if the boys started bickering or needed discipline. Jay's own father equally passive and not even present for the fun stuff. Saul Westerhof working long hours as a scientist at the local glass company, his free time spent sequestered in his basement workshop.

"Can we please go to sleep now?" Jay called from the bed into the dressing room, refusing to engage with my parry. Which only made me madder.

"I want to talk about this!" I insisted. Which wasn't at all what I meant. I wanted him to excuse me and also compliment my parenting. I wanted him to reassure me that I was nothing like my own mother, who had or hadn't mistreated me.

Sighing from Jay. Then, "Look, just move on and try not to get so angry."

I let out a groan. This was Jay's answer for anything. Not to feel things. His own mother a mean and difficult woman who held grudges against him from the time he was seven. For forgetting to turn off the television set. For not holding her hand at a mini mart.

I hugged my knees tighter, furious that Jay couldn't give me the love and reassurance I so desperately needed. Even though I knew he was merely afraid. Possibly more afraid than even I was. Of the things he couldn't name. Of the forces he claimed had no effect on him.

SLEEPING

I CAUGHT PAIGE IN public and in a good mood. Paige scrubbing her yoga mat when she looked up and our eyes caught. Paige in brightly colored tights, a white tank top spotted with sweat. The studio heated to ninety degrees in contrast to the cold October air.

"You told me about this place!" Paige said, sensing my confusion as I stared at her slicked-back hair and hollowed-out face.

I had?

"I love it here!" she continued cheerily, standing up with me to return our mats, walking blithely past the shrine with the Buddha and candles and carefully coiled prayer beads.

"How are the kids?" I asked, not wanting to call attention to the strangeness of running into each other in a place like this. The strangeness of running into her, period. I never ran into Paige!

"Great," Paige said. "Did I tell you Cameron's in a play?"

She hadn't told me. When would she have told me? I hadn't seen her socially in nearly five months. She never came out of her house except to wave and hurry away again. Although obviously she did.

"*Cinderella,*" she continued. "He's the prince! They actually wanted him to play two parts, but some of the other mothers protested."

I listened. I murmured surprise and then support, catching a glimpse of my face in the studio mirror, disturbed by how odd my expressions looked with my hair pulled back. My dark roots glaring beneath the blond. My nose too big for my face.

When Paige had finished, I said, "You must be driving a million carpools!"

"Too many," she agreed. Even though I doubted she drove any carpools at all. Was convinced Yazmin did everything for her except attend yoga class.

"Well, if there's an afternoon when Winnie's just sitting at home and Cameron's at play practice, I'd be happy to take her," I said as we walked into the vestibule. Very carefully. So as not to make it sound like I liked Winnie too much. Adding, "I'll take Cameron, too, if he's home."

"Winnie would love that," Paige gushed.

"I'll text you," I said, eager to leave before it became awkward. Eager to leave before I was compelled to ask what she was doing with herself. Not eager to hear her half-truthful answers. Not eager to pretend I believed them.

* * *

I was writing an e-mail when the appointed day came. A note to my old boss asking for freelance work. Even though I knew that she judged me for leaving my job. For having children to begin with! My old boss going so far as to ask why I was having two of them.

I wrote one more sentence about my volunteer work. Deleted

it. Wrote it again. Finally closing my computer and walking over to Paige's house. Thrilled when Winnie saw me and reached her arms straight up to hug me. Hugging her back and forgetting all my misgivings. Paige reaching down to smooth Winnie's hair, to remind her to be good. Paige telling me not to be surprised if she couldn't follow directions. Which annoyed me even as I accepted it. Aware that I probably sounded the same way when I sent my boys off with someone else. Eager to control things from a distance, to avoid being embarrassed.

In the car, Winnie was quiet, looking out the window, saying nothing. Tiny in my booster seat, barely filling it up. I tried to make conversation with her, looking into the rearview mirror to see if she could understand me, but without the eye contact it was harder than I had anticipated.

"Do you like stuffed animals?" I asked, unsure where to start.

"Yes, please," she said.

"Are you comfortable, or is there too much air blowing on you?" I asked.

"Yes, please," she answered. Which made me sad. Which made me worried. Was this what Paige demanded of her—constant agreement? Or was this all she was capable of—limited conversation? How much had I really talked with her in the ten months I'd known her?

When we got to the Build-A-Bear store, the clerk told us what to do. Where to pick the furry skins, how to stuff them, what special things we could bury inside to make them feel more real, or at least personalized. Winnie silently nodding, her hands behind her back.

"Did you understand?" I asked, bending down toward her.

Winnie nodded some more, but I wasn't certain. I took her hand

and together we walked to the wall where stuffed animals were perched on shelves, bins below them with the plush fur to make one. We walked slowly down the row, eyeing the white floppy bunnies, the beige bears with big, puffy noses, dark spotted monkeys, purple dinosaurs, black-and-white cows. Winnie walking slowly, examining each piece with her eyes, careful, never touching anything without asking. When she wanted to see a particular animal more closely, she pointed and turned to me, saying, "Please?"

I lifted each one up—the frog, the rainbow bear, the monkey—all of which Winnie would consider for a moment before turning to me with her impish smile and saying, "Not that one!" And I would put the stuffed animal back, amazed by her determination, her discrimination, and her patience.

Finally, after what seemed a long time, Winnie picked out a white dog with floppy brown ears, the dog larger than most of the other stuffed animals, somehow cuter and more lifelike. "I like it!" I said, pulling the stuffed animal off its perch and hugging it to show her I meant it. Winnie reaching out her arms to take the animal from me, then hugging it close to her chest as well, rocking forward and back with pleasure before settling back down on the soles of her shoes and saying, "I make it."

"Yes, you make it," I said, putting the dog back where it belonged and reaching into the bin to pull out a fluffy skin. Winnie eyeing the fur skeptically, taking a step back, uncertain what she was supposed to do with it.

"It's like magic," I said, smiling broadly, amazed myself the first time I'd come here with Josh and discovered that the stuffed animals really did come out as well as the ones you bought premade in a store. Even if they looked so sad and empty when you saw how they had begun. The lifeless patch of fabric. The depressing "stuffing" station.

Winnie seeming to accept my promise, or at least my enthusiasm. Taking the limp material from me and skipping toward the corner where another clerk was working the loud fluffing machine. Winnie greeting the girl with a smile and a hello, carefully standing on the pedal like the girl showed her to, turning to me and saying, "I like that!" when the machine began to churn and the dog became more believable. In another moment, the girl handed Winnie a red gingham heart and told her to put it through the open hole in the back of the dog.

"Why?" Winnie asked, smiling toward me, her fists beneath her chin, tilting her head to one side so that she almost looked like she was posing. I imagined it was the look she'd used in the orphanage. To get what she needed. To convince people to like her. Which didn't make it ineffective. Even if there was the hint of artifice.

"It's the dog's heart. So he's real," I explained, smiling back at her. Wondering if I was confusing her. Of course the dog wasn't real. Of course the heart was a made-up contrivance. And yet I wanted her to play along. To understand the pleasure of a make-believe world.

Winnie nodding enthusiastically and saying, "I do it," taking the small cotton heart and sticking it where she was told. The girl telling her to push it through the stuffing to the front, so that it was in the right place. Winnie nodding, looking at her blankly, going along with it when the girl put her hand over Winnie's and showed her how to maneuver it. Which meant what, exactly? That she was slow? Or that this particular activity didn't make sense to her? I wasn't sure. I tried to think about it, comparing her to Josh at that age and realizing how much more advanced Josh had been. Josh unnaturally verbal. Josh planning out the animal and all of its clothing before he even started stuffing the skin. Which could have been a function of being American, I told myself. Even though I doubted it.

When the heart was in its proper place, the clerk asked us if we would like the dog to make noise. I looked at Winnie, expecting a blank face. No comprehension. But she nodded enthusiastically and said, "Yes, my dog talk."

I smiled. Pleased that she'd understood. Pleased that she was enjoying herself. Wandering over with her to the touch screen in the center of the floor. Winnie touching the buttons and grinning loudly at the animal sounds and pop music tunes that came spewing forth. Insisting I touch some of the icons, asking me, "Do you like?" when a loud, syncopated beat came on.

"No, I do not like!" I said, "But do you like?"

"Yes, please!" she said, rolling forward and backward on her feet again, a sort of rocking that I hadn't noticed before today.

We picked out the sound chip and put it in the dog, then asked the lady at the stuffing machine to sew the hole in the animal's back. Winnie hugging her dog to her face as we walked toward where the clothing was.

"Is it a boy or a girl?" I asked.

"Is dog!" Winnie said, lowering her animal from her face so I could see how smart she was.

"I know, silly. I mean a boy dog or a girl dog?"

"I love my dog!" Winnie answered me, either not comprehending or not wanting to. I took a deep breath and said, "Do you want clothing?" holding up a white karate suit that I thought might fit her dog, then a tuxedo that looked too small. Rummaging around the rack to find a ruffled brown skirt in case she thought it was a girl.

"No, thank you," Winnie said, hugging her dog back to her face.

"We can put it on the dog," I said, not sure she understood. Widening the waist of the skirt and showing her how we would slip it on.

"I love it," Winnie said, her voice muffled, her mouth on the fur.

"Okay then, no clothes," I agreed, bending down to give her a hug. Thrilled when she reached her arms out from around the stuffed animal and tapped me on my neck. Pulling away from her and telling her, "Winnie, you're the best." My eyes unexpectedly teary. Blinking a few times to clear them before approaching the register. At the checkout, Winnie lifted herself on her tiptoes and placed the dog on the counter, smiling and saying, "My dog go home with me," to the woman who was waiting on us.

The woman smiling. The woman turning to me and saying, "Your daughter's lovely," in such a way that I could tell she meant it. Winnie was lovely. We were lovely together. Already I had a fantasy about all the wonderful memories Winnie would have about me when she grew older.

"She's not my daughter," I said to the cashier, glad for the mistake but feeling the need to correct her. The woman looked confused. Not charmed. Like she wanted to understand the situation more concretely.

"But you have the same smile."

We did? I hadn't considered it. I was thrilled. Even though I knew I shouldn't encourage this fantasy.

"She's adopted," I said.

The woman looked confused.

"So she is your daughter, then?"

"No. I mean, she's a friend's daughter. A friend's adopted daughter," I felt the need to add. Stupidly. The woman looked more perplexed, pushing her wire-rimmed glasses back up on her face, nodding her head like now she knew something she hadn't known before. But what?

"I like spending time with her," I explained, hoping to turn things around. Hoping to inspire praise. But the woman merely handed me my change and a coupon for 20 percent off my next purchase. The conversation over. Her opinion of me now skewed in the wrong direction. Which was so frustrating. The way you could be so completely misunderstood and not able to explain yourself. The way you had so little control over the way people saw you.

On the way home, I gave Winnie a Ziploc Baggie of chocolate ginger cookies. A handful of mini bears and cats and dogs from Trader Joe's. Winnie daintily pulling the cookies from the bag one at a time and munching on them, occasionally making funny faces in the backseat and calling out to me to look at her. She was a cat with whiskers. She was a dog barking at the cookie.

She was funny. She knew she was cute. I smiled and told her to keep going—to try being different animals. Not just cats and dogs but a monkey, too. Then an elephant. She obliged with a long "trunk" made with her arms. Scratching her head for the monkey. Which was rather advanced. Had she seen monkeys at the zoo with Paige? I hoped so. Even though I couldn't imagine her at the zoo with Paige, the smells and the crowds, the heat and the cracked asphalt.

"Try a giraffe," I suggested.

"What's that?" Winnie asked, twisting her mouth into the sign of universal confusion, nearly resting her cheek on her shoulder as she gazed up at me in the rearview mirror.

I explained about the neck and the spots and the big mouth that liked to eat leaves.

"Aah!" she said, her face suddenly animated as she began to

wave her neck back and forth as if trying to stretch it. I smiled and nodded encouragement. Amazed by her ingenuity. Amazed by her will to be admired and understood. Aware that this was the thing that had drawn me to her always. Her will to succeed at the business of love.

Paige was home when we returned. I saw her white Lexus in the driveway. The model she'd claimed she hated and traded in for an Audi, which she claimed was defective. Now she was back to square one with a new version of the car she'd disliked and was starting to complain about again.

"My mommy home!" Winnie said as we pulled up.

I was happy that she was happy. Grateful that she was. Winnie's love for her mother something positive I couldn't deny.

We parked in my driveway and then walked to the Edwardses' house hand in hand. Paige had told me to text her a half hour before I was ready and she'd send Yazmin to my house for Winnie, but this seemed silly and unnecessary. Why not just drop her off?

On Paige's front stoop, I rang the bell and waited, but there were no footsteps. I tried the door to see if it was locked. A stiffness greeted me. Where was Cameron? Where was Paige? I waited a minute, then two. I rang again. Knocked with the knocker, a loud, foreboding sound that reminded me of a black-and-white horror movie. Still no answer.

"Mommy's probably outside," I explained to Winnie, not wanting to alarm her.

We walked to the back of the house and opened the gate in the hedge, calling softly, then louder, "Paige? Paige?" Nothing. Silence. Just the sounds of some men on the golf course, their cart whirring past. Walking up the bluestone steps to the stone terrace, peering through the French doors and into the Edwardses' great room. The leather couches draped with fluffy white throw blankets. Paige's horticulture books stacked neatly on the oversize coffee table. The room completely empty. Where the hell was Paige? And how could I rouse her if she was sleeping?

From the dead suddenly popped into my head, which was ridiculous. Why would I imagine Paige dead? I pulled out my cell phone and dialed her number but the phone range straight through to voice mail.

"Winnie, Mommy's not here; let's go to my house," I said, turning to take her hand, to lead her out of the yard. My hand was shaking. Slightly. It gnawed at me, this total absence, as if Paige had chosen to leave their life, abandon Winnie. Why was I thinking this? I had no idea. It didn't make sense. She had simply forgotten to be home. Or the babysitter had. There were dozens of possibilities, none of them scary. And yet my arm shook and my heart raced.

We went home. I called Lorraine. I hated that I was calling Lorraine! It made me feel like a gossip and a troublemaker. But I had to call Lorraine. She knew everything about everyone, her phone calls peppered with news from every suburb west of Boston. Her nanny Beatriz filling her in on whatever she missed in the neighborhood. Lorraine answered on the first ring. "Thank God you have Winnie!" she said as soon as I finished my story.

"What does that mean?" I asked, my heart beating faster, my hands shaking with adrenaline and excitement and fear.

"We were looking for her."

"Who was?"

"Beatriz. And the other mother who dropped off Cameron."

My fingers were turning cold. This was not going where I wanted it to go. Where I needed it to go. Somewhere mundane and uneventful. I needed to make it more mundane. Less eventful. I took out the metal mixing bowl, the one I used for baking and sometimes for cooking, and dumped in a package of raw chicken. I cradled the phone beneath my chin and listened to Lorraine as I added pepper, salt, garlic, some lemon. Winnie quietly drawing at the island, watching me.

"Cameron had play practice, and I guess Paige arranged for another mother to drive him home. Beatriz happened to be in the driveway and saw the mother standing at Paige's front door with Cameron, looking sort of tired and frustrated. Paige's car is in the driveway, and the other mother is ringing the bell and looking out toward the neighborhood like, 'Will someone come help me?' So Beatriz called me. And I told her to go over and offer to help out."

I nodded, carefully cradling the phone beneath my neck and washing the raw chicken remains from my hands, pulling back the skin from my fingernails to get the bacteria that I feared had settled there.

"The other mother's name is Grace Keenan. She's one of those perky blond women from Cameron's private school. I've played tennis with her before."

"Where's Paige?" I interrupted, knowing full well what the mothers from Cameron's school looked like and not caring. "I mean, how did this resolve itself?"

"Beatriz put me on the phone with Grace and after reassuring her about twenty times that I really was Paige's friend, she let Beatriz take Cameron."

"My God, Grace Keenan is going to have a field day with this at drop-off tomorrow!"

"Obviously!"

"But where's Paige?" I repeated.

"We don't know! We called the house and the cell but it just rings straight through to voice mail. You don't think she did something crazy, do you?"

My heart, which had slowed to a drumroll, started to beat wildly again, like a fluttering bird trapped in too small a space. "You mean you think she's in there?"

"Well, her car's there!

"Maybe a friend picked her up."

"And she forgot about Cameron coming home? No sitter? Nicole, think!"

"Someone should call Gene."

"That's what Drew's doing."

"What does Drew think?"

"He thinks Paige took some pills."

"Jesus Christ!" I muttered. Impressed by Drew's street smarts. Even if you didn't have to be a genius to come up with something like that. Just brave enough to imagine it. Or admit it.

"Why do you have Winnie anyway?" Lorraine asked.

"It's a long story," I said. Even though it wasn't. I just didn't feel like getting into it with Lorraine. Hearing her ponder my reasons for wanting to spend time with Winnie, which were amorphous, or dissect the fact that I'd run into Paige at the yoga studio. But Lorraine murmured something and let it drop.

"You don't think we should call an ambulance, do you?" I whispered. Embarrassed to even suggest it. Even though I feared what could happen if we didn't.

"An ambulance? Now? Today?" Lorraine shouted rather than asked.

"I just thought…" I began, not sure what I thought. Hadn't

Lorraine just implied that Drew was worried about suicide? Or had I misunderstood something?

"Someone's clicking in," she said. "I'll call you right back."

I hung up. I put oil in a pan and placed the chicken cutlets in the oil. The oil jumping up and burning the corner of my chin. Fingering the skin as I leaned against the island and thought about making a salad. Setting the table. Cleaning the counters! But I couldn't do anything but stare at the chicken. Aware that I should act, call the police, make a move to help Paige, to help Winnie and Cameron. Not just from this moment, but from a lifetime of moments. But I had to wait for Paige, hopeful that if she did emerge, she wasn't sick, wasn't in trouble, didn't have a problem. Or that she could convincingly pretend that she didn't. Hopeful, as I always was, that the very act of being alive and able to cover something up made you someone to believe in once again.

In a little while—five minutes, ten—my phone rang. It was Lorraine. "Paige was asleep!" Lorraine said.

"How do you know?" I asked, already unsure whom to trust, which version of this story would go on the record, which one would be correct.

"Paige just called me panicked. She said she'd meant to close her eyes for a minute but had fallen asleep. Something about not sleeping well the night before."

"And she didn't hear the phone or the bell?" I pressed, imagining a yellow pill bottle near her bed, fearful that she'd taken too many.

"She's fine!" Lorraine said. "Her bedroom door was closed."

The chicken was finished. I lifted it out of the oil and placed the pieces on a paper towel to drain. Did Lorraine believe this? Did I? In the end, did it matter what we believed?

"So anyway, she said she's sending Yazmin over to get Winnie. That's how she woke up. Yazmin was running errands and came home to find Paige in her bedroom."

Yazmin to the rescue, I thought, wondering what it was that she knew.

"What did Gene say?" I asked, curious and nervous about this last bit.

"Drew never got him on the phone. He left him a message. Then Paige woke up."

I was adjusting something. My perception. My version. This wasn't an incident. There was nothing dramatic about it. It was a misunderstanding. In a minute Yazmin rang my doorbell, even though the door was open, my welcome sign to all that they were free to rap on the glass and enter at will. I went to the door and looked out at Yazmin's smooth brown face for some hint of alliance or knowledge or cover-up. But she merely looked back at me with neither fear nor knowledge. A studied look, I was sure. Practiced and perfected after many years. A look I couldn't penetrate.

LEFTOVERS, AGAIN

LORRAINE STARTED AN E-MAIL chain about the leftovers party, insisting that we reserve a different cabin at a different park. Insisting that our kids couldn't really enjoy themselves without Wi-Fi or a television set. Which was ludicrous. Wasn't that the point of renting the cabin in the first place? To remove them from their creature comforts? To get them out of the house and into a different setting?

Nobody agreeing on a new place or even on the ongoing benefit of our nature experiment, causing me to suggest that we simply move the party to December and I'd host it at my house. Everyone agreeing to a Saturday night in the middle of the month. Or at least most of us did. Nela a maybe, and Paige not responding to any of the e-mails. Which irritated Lorraine—who said that no matter what you had going on, you should have basic manners—but didn't bother or surprise me at all. Of course Paige wouldn't respond. The nonresponse the perfect response. So she could decide last minute whether she was up for it. The sleeping incident no doubt embarrassing her. Nela merely more obvious in her desire to not commit to us. Nela claiming she had a half dozen work and family commitments that hadn't been firmed up yet. And it was only October!

But now that our gathering was on the calendar, it was the perfect excuse to do some early holiday baking with Lucas. Eager to find a way to connect with him. Eager to do something other than discipline and lecture him.

It was a Sunday. Josh and Jay at some mini soccer academy when I suggested we make cookies and freeze them for the party. Lucas enthusiastic about the idea. Getting out the flour and the sugar, laughing when I told him to smell the vanilla, then taste the bitter difference.

I let Lucas measure. I let Lucas pour. I let Lucas hold the electric mixer, my hands over his. Thrilled with our progress. Thrilled we were enjoying ourselves. Lucas in green overalls I adored, their old-fashioned style making him appear younger than he was, innocent and easygoing.

When the eggs were cracked and the sugar added more or less correctly to the butter, I let Lucas hold the mixer by himself. Aware of how much he loved electronics. Aware of how much he would love the whir of the spinning beaters. But almost immediately, Lucas turned the mixer to high speed, ignoring my calls to turn it down. Lucas lifting the blades into the air to show me how slow they were going, flinging batter across my kitchen cupboards. I grabbed the plug from the wall and wrenched the mixer away from him. Furious and frustrated as I explained about the importance of following directions.

Lucas was silent.

"Let's begin again," I said, trying not to notice the splotches of batter that surrounded us, handing him the bowl of dry ingredients and asking him to pour it slowly into my mixing bowl. Lucas pouring the first bit out slowly, then growing impatient and dumping out the whole bowl into the wet batter.

"Do you like cookies?" I demanded, shutting off the handheld mixer and putting it down on the counter. Aware that I should have purchased an expensive Mixmaster long ago, but still insisting on making do with this one.

Lucas wouldn't look at me.

"If you like cookies, and you want them to taste right, then you'll listen to me," I said, my voice rising.

"Why does it matter if the flour's added slowly?"

"Because it's hard to blend this way," I insisted.

"It's not hard for me. I'll blend it."

"How do you know it's not hard to blend? You've never done it before!"

Lucas stepped off the stool and started to walk away from me, heading for the dining room with his powdered, sugary hands.

"Stop!" I commanded him.

Lucas kept walking.

I ran after him, grabbed the back of his shirt collar and turned him around. Furious at how defiant he was being! I took a deep breath, Lucas staring back at me with his chapped cheeks and giant brown eyes.

"Don't leave the kitchen without washing your hands," I said gently yet firmly.

Lucas went back to the sink, got on the stool, and washed silently, not using soap, which infuriated me all over again.

"How many times have I told you to use soap?" I demanded.

Lucas ignored me. I wrapped my arms around him and squirted the soap on his hands, then rubbed them together under the warm water. Feeling his thin body press against mine, breathing deeply and nuzzling his neck as I calmed down and asked, "Why don't we try again?"

"I don't like making cookies," Lucas answered, starting to squirm.

"But you agreed you wanted to cook for the party," I reminded him. Shocked by how changeable he was. Disturbed by his lack of focus.

"I want to make the *meal* for the party!" he whined.

"That's not realistic," I chided.

"Why not?" he said, stomping his foot on the stool and then turning to stare at me.

"Well, for starters, we'd have to cook on the day of the party and there won't be enough time."

"There'll be enough time. Don't worry."

"And it has to be something special," I said, trying to reason with him. Which I knew was idiotic. He was eight. Wasn't I supposed to be the one in charge?

Lucas oblivious. Lucas saying, "I know something great!"

I closed my eyes and sucked in my breath.

"What?" I managed to ask.

"Noodles and butter. Everyone likes noodles and butter!"

I sighed and then said, "Let's make noodles one night for dinner and if it goes well, maybe you can make it for the kids' meal at the party."

"I want to make it with toppings," he said, smiling and jumping off the stool. "With sprinkles and maybe pieces of peanut butter."

"Toppings like cheese could work," I suggested, trying not to sound as frustrated as I felt.

"Tonight?" Lucas asked, hopping from foot to foot, thrilled that he'd gotten his way.

"Yes, okay, tonight," I agreed, knowing I'd have to finish the sugar cookies on my own. Clean up the batter and the dishes and put up with another mess for Lucas's dinner preparations. Disappointed and frustrated that this was who he was. Disappointed and frustrated that this was who I was! Someone weak and also bossy. Someone who didn't have a handle on good parenting. Even though I sensed we were making progress, both of us finding our way.

* * *

Six weeks before the party, I decided to purchase a shimmery silver tablecloth to match my dining room décor, an idea that felt inspired and glamorous as soon as I thought of it. Even though I hated the mall. Even though I hated shopping for my house. Never able to shake the feeling that decorating was beneath my intelligence, despite the fact that I was bad at it. That it was challenging! The tablecloth proving to be no exception. Arriving at Crate & Barrel to discover that you needed to know the exact measurements of your table to get a proper fit. Realizing I had no clue how long my table was. Staring and standing and trying to venture a guess until I finally gave up and wandered over to the Mixmaster display. Certain that this was something I couldn't mess up, even if I was shocked by how expensive they were. Deterred by how much space they took up. Jay talking me out of it for our wedding registry for the very same reasons. Lingering anyway, thinking about where I could put it, when my phone started to trill, my sister's name flashing on the caller ID. Deciding after a calculated pause to answer it.

"I got you!" Penny said by way of greeting.

"Here I am," I said, relieved to walk away from the appliances and out toward the lower-level atrium. Relieved not to have to make a decision about spending too much money on baking equipment.

"I have good news," Penny told me, and then launched into a story about running into some girls she'd gone to college with who said online admission to Ohio State was super lenient and that she had nothing to worry about.

"Wait, aren't you enrolled already?" I asked, wondering where the money I'd lent her for tuition had gone.

"I applied. I'm waiting to hear. I used your money for the deposit, don't worry!" she said.

I was worried. How could she use half the tuition for a deposit if she hadn't gotten in yet? Wasn't she supposed to start next month?

"Nicole, it's under control. I paid off some money I owed my old boss, and he got me some students so I'm not working at night, like you cautioned me about, and I'll have plenty of money for the tuition."

I rolled my eyes. I hoped this was true.

"Seriously, Nicole. I called the school and they said it's a mere formality, the application. I should know for sure by the middle of the month."

I breathed a sigh of relief. So she wasn't manipulating me. She just had a complicated situation with a lot of different balls in the air. I understood. It was how I had lived before I'd married Jay. Working hard as a copywriter and still behind on credit card debt. Stretching for a bigger apartment and then getting in over my head on the rent. It was expensive to be single. And taxing. And here Penny was doing it for the first time in many years. As if reading my mind, Penny said, "I have a date."

"You do?"

"Yeah, sort of. We're calling it a date."

"How'd you meet him?"

"I gained a little weight. Maybe you can lend me some old designer thing you're not using?"

I paused, confused and slightly guilty. I did have a few designer things, but they would never fit my sister. Penny a size two. I was more like an eight pushing a ten.

"Who's the date with?" I asked, ignoring the dress question.

"It's more like a party than a date," Penny said, starting to mumble.

"What does that mean?" I asked, suddenly wary.

"What do you mean, 'What does that mean?'"

I held my breath, refusing to answer her.

"I'm hosting a get-together with Bob. At our old house. Okay? Happy?"

I was silent. Furious. How dare Bob waltz back in when I was helping my sister to get back on her feet? How dare Penny lie about it, or attempt to? Even though I knew how much she missed him. How much she wanted to believe he was the solution to her backlog of problems.

"Penny, I just want to say something about Bob," I began, uncertain what I would say. That my sister was better than him? More intelligent and also harder working, if she could just kick the drinking? Aware the drinking was a part of her. My image of her at a piano recital in an embroidered white dress forever frozen in my mind, but not necessarily realistic. Not who she was. Not even relevant.

"Aren't you having a holiday party this year?" my sister asked. Unaware of my musings. Or else well aware of them and not willing to go there.

"Yes," I said, confused about how she knew about it. Had I told her about the leftovers party changing into something more formal? Immediately full of guilt about how much money I was spending. The silvery tablecloth just the tip of the iceberg.

"Thanks for inviting me," she said, then hung up on me.

I stared at my lap and then out at the bright lights of the stores. Suddenly sickened that I'd even considered spending $350 on a Mixmaster. To make cookies! Deciding to buy my sister a Chanukah card at the Papyrus shop instead. Writing her a check for $350 and slipping it inside.

*   *   *

A week before the party, Paige sent me a text. *I'm looking forward to your party. I already bought and wrapped the presents!*

The presents! I couldn't believe it! She'd actually gone out and bought the kids presents again without even discussing it with us? But what could I do? Complain to Lorraine, who hated her presumption more than I did? Of course I couldn't. Of course I didn't. Instead I sent Paige a text in return. *Can't wait! Thanks for helping out! Let us know what we owe you.* Hoping that my enthusiasm would make her feel welcome and that by feeling welcome she'd act normal. Or at least not paranoid and defensive about the past six months. Paige quickly texting me back a smiley face and a photo of her purchase: a miniature fir tree with beads around the branches and a gold star on top. *It's a Chanukas bush*, Paige insisted. Which meant what, exactly? That those were stars of David on the tops?

The day before the party, Paige texted *Do you mind if I bring my cousin? Honestly, you can say no.* Which was ridiculous. Why would I mind? Did I expect her cousin to sit home? But how rude! Did Paige really not know her cousin was visiting until the night before my party? As it was, Drew was bringing his brother Malcolm, technically a white-collar felon. I doubted I'd have room at my table for the two extra guests. Even with two leaves and the ugly kitchen chairs as extras. But I told Paige to bring her cousin. I told Paige I'd love to meet her cousin!

Lorraine arrived first, at six o'clock on the dot. Not even with Jeffrey and the kids. By herself, in a navy sweater dress and pearls with a bottle of vodka in her hand, ready to talk to me. Why did she always do this? Show up early. Or at least not appropriately late. My hair was wet. The centerpieces not ready yet. Lorraine didn't notice. Or she did notice but didn't care. That my hair was wet. That she shouldn't have come yet!

"You need anything?" she asked, setting down the vodka on my island, intent on unscrewing the lid.

"Want to make drinks?" I asked lightly, knowing that she would, knowing I was supposed to be grateful for it. Her bartending skills. Her coming on time to help me. But who came on time to a dinner party?

The doorbell rang again, Nela and Drew with Sophia, Sebastian, and Matias. Sophia's hair in one long braid down her back, adorable and serious.

"We saw Lorraine walk over, so we figured it was time to come," Nela said, her face smiling, more welcoming than I'd seen it. Handing me an expensive-looking gift bag. A first for Nela. To bring a hostess gift.

"It looked like something you'd like," Nela said when I'd unwrapped the blown-glass platter. "I got it when I went to Portland on a business trip," she added. Which surprised me more than the gift itself. That she'd bought it in advance.

Lorraine making everyone drinks while Nela and I complimented each other's outfits. Me in my customary A-line dress, a sea green that accentuated my eyes and hid my waistline. Nela in gray slacks with a burgundy silk blouse. Which I thought showed a certain lack of imagination. To wear corporate attire to a Saturday-night holiday dinner. But at least she wasn't in her usual fleece jacket and slippers!

And then, the doorbell ringing again. The sounds of people calling and converging. Drew on my front porch with his brother Malcolm trailing hesitantly behind him. Jeffrey shepherding Lorraine's kids in the side door with Gene and Cameron right behind them. Cameron in an expensive striped button-down, the cuffs turned up to reveal a yellow checked pattern. Which was stylish and handsome, but also a tiny bit ridiculous. Cameron so much more dressed up than all the other kids in their sweatpants and T-shirts with logos on them. A few minutes later Paige calling, "Can I come in?" from my open front door and then, not waiting for an answer, emerging into my kitchen carrying a platter of bûche de Noël.

"My mom's recipe," she said, her pale face glowing.

"Wow!" I said, thrilled that she'd made the effort. Hopeful that this meant she was all better. Which was ridiculous and simplistic but also possible, in my mind.

Paige put the dessert on my granite counter and then introduced her cousin Anne, who had come in behind her. Anne a chubby blonde with crooked teeth, her crepe pants slightly wrinkled. Which was not what I would expect from a relative of Paige's. But then, what did I know of her family, really? Paige hugging Anne's shoulders, telling us that they were like sisters. Which was sweet. And reassuring. That Paige had someone like that she could turn to. Someone unassuming and unpretentious. Even if I had no way of knowing this about her cousin. I'd met her less than two minutes ago!

Jay shaking Anne's hand, kissing Paige hello, offering drinks, taking coats. Both of us convincing everyone to move into the living room, the noise levels rising and falling as we made our way through the front hall, past the tall branches I'd arranged there. The children shouting and laughing in the basement as we passed, causing me to remember the thing I'd meant to ask when Cameron had first come in. Where was Winnie? Was she coming late? The question nagging at me as we settled ourselves around my cheese platters and hot hors d'oeuvres. Aware that I couldn't ask it just yet or I'd risk ruining the festive mood. Joining Paige on the velvet sofa, Drew's brother and Paige's cousin on the adjacent couch, neither one talking to the other or to us, which was awkward. Which was something I needed to address as soon as possible.

"Can I get either of you a drink?" I asked Anne and Malcolm. Malcolm pointing to his scotch on the table, while Anne said, "Just a beer, if you have one."

"I'll get us both something," Paige said, rising from my couch and going to the bar in the corner.

"Paige, I have wine," I said, eager for her to have a drink, to loosen up.

"I'm fine," she called over her shoulder, returning a few moments later with a ginger ale for herself and a bottle of Amstel Light for her cousin. Was Paige really not going to drink anything? She was uptight normally, no doubt even more so now from having to act normal after not seeing us for so long. And she wasn't going to have one drink? Before I could fully contemplate this, Gene joined us near the couches, handsome in his blue dress shirt.

"What's this?" he asked, pointing to my stuffed pumpernickel loaf.

"Artichoke spread," I said, watching him move slightly away

from it. He never ate anything exotic. Artichokes apparently falling into that category for him.

Paige said, "You always make the best spreads." Even though I'd never made a spread before. But this was Paige in party mode. Complimentary bordering on obsequious. And nervous. If only she would have a drink! She looked gorgeous in her pink tweed jacket. Narrow white pants that only she could pull off.

"What's in it?" Gene asked, still referring to the spread we both knew he wouldn't eat.

"Artichokes," I said, hoping for a laugh. He gave me a smirk instead. My comments somehow always offensive to him. His dislike or distrust just beneath the surface. Or maybe this was merely how I felt about him, the feeling bouncing back at me the way it can between two people who don't say much. Gene cut himself some cheese, then joined the men, who were merging toward the bar in wordless agreement that group conversation was over. Drew in a narrow black dress shirt that was too tight on his tall, husky frame, leaning in to join them, even though I could tell he didn't care about their conversation, something no doubt about money or business or how to improve their already stunning standard of living. Malcolm still on the sofa. Not eager, I suspected, to talk business, given that he'd been convicted of fraud, or was it embezzlement?

"I wish Winnie could have come," Paige said to the rest of us, crossing one thin leg over the other, her raw silk capris flattering her small, delicate ankles.

"What happened?" Lorraine wanted to know, nonchalantly piling her cracker with artichoke dip as though she weren't asking anything threatening.

"She had a stomachache. Poor thing," Paige said.

Across the room Paige's cousin nodded and said, "It's common with adopted kids." All of us smiling in her direction. Obviously she was here to help Paige. To offer moral support. Maybe insight. Which was reassuring, even if I doubted that she knew much of anything about adopted kids. Hadn't Paige said she was a paralegal? Anne smiling blandly in our direction while next to her, Malcolm stared at the modern painting above my fireplace. Not joining the conversation, obviously nervous or possibly embarrassed that we knew the thing about him that we tried to pretend we didn't. His criminal past. His current unemployment. Which was fine with us. His absence from the dialogue. We had our hands full with Paige. Eager not to let her take over the floor with a diatribe about Winnie, especially if she was going to be negative.

But already Paige seemed to have decided something, sitting up straighter on my couch and taking a deep breath as she said, "Winnie was all dressed tonight, standing with us in the foyer, ready to go out, when she says, 'Mommy, I have accident,' and guess what?" Paige said, her voice rising in faux humor. "She pooped in her pants!" Paige's voice brittle and giddy as she described Winnie's embarrassing accident. As if she were laughing at her. Which I suspected really wasn't the case. Which I suspected was Paige's attempt to appear festive instead of upset. I was a master of the dark story told for comic relief, but Paige wasn't very good at it. The story making her appear unkind instead of vulnerable. Which I knew was how Nela was interpreting it. Nela staring at Paige with her smoothly blank look, the one she adopted when she was seething, or at least judging. Lorraine oblivious across from me, loading up another cracker with artichoke dip and asking, "So is she coming or not?" before popping it in her mouth. Lorraine mainly interested in the food and drink, which I had to admire about her.

"It's too much stimulation for her," Paige offered. "She's not a good listener and she can't regulate her food intake, so no," she said. Clearly frustrated by Winnie's limitations. Still not hitting the right note to elicit sympathy. Even though I could tell that was what she was going for. That we should feel sorry for her but not necessarily for Winnie. Which irritated me, but I tried to understand. Paige naive and not used to dealing with a child who had issues. I myself furious with Lucas half the time for being clumsy and argumentative. And I myself was clumsy and argumentative!

"Thank God we had the weekend sitter with us," Paige continued more cheerily. "I told Camille to put the dress in the machine, throw out the underwear, and get Winnie ready for bed!"

"Poor Winnie," I said, trying to let Paige know that Winnie deserved sympathy. "She's missing the party."

"Don't worry!" Paige said with a wave of her hand. "Winnie doesn't even know the difference!" Laughing a little. Her cheeks turning pinker. I hoped she didn't mean this, even though it bothered me that she kept insisting on it. That Winnie didn't need or want the same things the other kids did. Or that she didn't deserve them.

"Are you guys going away for Christmas?" Lorraine asked, looking from Paige to her cousin, desperate, no doubt, to change the subject. She didn't want to hear any more about Winnie's poopy pants. She didn't want to have to contemplate whether it was right or wrong to leave Winnie home. She wanted to enjoy the party. She wanted us to have a festive evening with memories and laughter that could be documented in Drew's end-of-year video. The one we watched every January. The one that was proof of our friendship and our shared happiness.

"She will probably have digestive problems for the rest of her life," Paige said, not taking the hint, or taking it and shoving it aside.

Paige a marathon talker when she wanted to be. Or maybe she was just determined for us to understand something about Winnie.

"Winnie had giardia when she arrived, which is why she's so skinny," Paige continued, her cousin nodding in agreement. "It may affect her learning and development long term. We can't know yet," Paige said, sadness and defeat creeping in beside her anger and frustration. Finally.

All of us murmuring support. All of us telling her, "It will work out," while next to me, Paige started to cry. Lorraine rising to hug her. Nela's face softer as she caught my eye. Nela's five-year-old Sebastian full of delays himself, rarely speaking on his own, his twin, Matias, seeming to do everything for him. Nela denying every diagnosis she'd ever been given—about apraxia and selective mutism—telling us she hated the experts and was convinced that kids grew out of things. Which didn't mean she wasn't terrified.

Paige wiping at her eyes with a cocktail napkin, then telling us, "You guys are like family."

Which I knew she meant and which I wanted to be true for her. Eager to forgive her earlier callousness, even as I told myself there was nothing to forgive.

*　*　*

At dinner, Paige's cousin said she loved my china. "Do you mind that I'm looking up the label?" she asked, laughing lightly as she turned over my grandmother's salad plate, the bone white complemented by a burgundy border and small flecks of silver.

"Of course not," I said. Proud of my grandmother's Noritake china. Pleased I'd brought one beautiful thing from my past life into this one.

"Are you planning on buying it?" Paige called down the long table, suddenly aware of what her cousin was doing, laughing lightly, embarrassed but not really. Her spirits higher than they were in the living room. Her mood relaxed and more carefree than I'd antici-pated. Was she enjoying herself? I hoped so. I couldn't tell for certain. There was too much commotion. Next to me Anne put the plate down while Drew's brother started to tell a story about a trip to Punta Cana with a girlfriend who dropped dead in the morning. Which morning? Of the trip? This morning? Why was he telling us this?

Drew appearing to understand it, rubbing his beard, smiling like it was an amusing anecdote and not a dark one. Children run-ning in from the living room, where the sitter was supposed to be containing them. Lucas proclaiming that everyone loved his noo-dles and asking if it was time for dessert yet, a sugar cookie in each hand, which infuriated me and caused me to snatch one of them from his fist. The cookie crumbling and dirtying the table in a way that made Lucas start crying and me feel ashamed of my aggres-sive demeanor. My festive mood temporarily spoiled as I reached for more wine and tried to forget about my poor parenting.

Paige at the head of the table, telling a story now. Paige explain-ing about all the holidays she'd spent in Los Angeles with her fam-ily. "I don't think I saw a white Christmas until we moved to the East Coast. Remember, Anne?" she asked. "All those suites my dad got at the Peninsula?" Anne nodding next to me. Paige smiling happily toward her cousin. Relaxed and nostalgic. Even though Paige had once told me her parents spent too much. That her father had had to keep working as a lawyer long after age sixty to pay for their extravagant lifestyle. The fact popping into my mind unbid-den, then shoved aside just as quickly. Why couldn't I un-know the things she had told me?

We drank more wine, helped ourselves to seconds. Stories were told or retold. The first time Paige met Gene's parents; how she'd made cookies with salt instead of sugar. The time Drew's mother insisted on hosting thirty-four cousins for Thanksgiving in her one-bedroom apartment. Jay relaying the first time he met my mother, how he accidentally elbowed her in the eye, causing a shiner by morning. My mother coming down in the morning with an eye patch, pretending to be a pirate, making French toast and insisting he walk the plank for his breakfast. The promise of a new chapter hovering with the idea of a new family member. The happiness of that visit rising up like a swarm of mosquitoes. Almost painful.

Around me, people continued to compete for air, for attention, for the most humorous anecdote. I got up to check on the warm apple compote. Arranging dessert dishes. Pressing coffee on people even though no one really wanted it. The dessert soon finished. Lorraine's son Jesse asleep on my carpet. Drew capturing all the kids in the family room on his video camera, then snapping photos in my kitchen while I doled out leftovers in Tupperware containers. The kids whining in my overly bright kitchen, tired, refusing to leave even though they were sagging, barely able to keep their eyes open. Jesse hunched over in his down parka like an old man. Only Cameron alert. Cameron protesting loudly that Sophia had said the Chanukas bushes were ugly. Sophia looking exactly like Nela, her dark brows furrowed, her face closed off, silent.

We said our good-byes. The kids suddenly rushing out into the night air, shouting to each other, eager to make their words soar over the frosted lawns and quiet houses, their voices pure and loud beneath the dark and cloudy sky.

HIDE-AND-SEEK

As soon as the party was over, the food complimented and the quantity groaned about, things returned to the way they had been before. Paige hiding out. Paige ignoring us. Paige busy or else resting while Gene ferried the kids about on the weekends. Gene, Cameron, and Winnie sometimes walking around the neighborhood on Sundays. Happy to join us if we invited them. Which I did whenever they passed by my kitchen window. Eager to engage with Winnie, to draw with her or bake something simple. Lucas willing to participate so long as the dessert contained chocolate. Josh and Cameron happy to decorate. Winnie always saying, "Yes, please," and "Thank you," as I handed her a wooden spoon or lent her my apron. Her personality lovely to be around, even if it was troubling to contemplate. Her seemingly endless desire to please. Her inability to more fully communicate. Gene never acknowledging Paige's absence or how much I obviously enjoyed his new daughter. Even though I sensed that it weighed on him. His easy jocularity more muted. His body sometimes resting on our kitchen stools while his eyes looked outward, seeing nothing.

* * *

Soon it was March. The ground frozen but snowless. Cameron not around; Winnie joining the boys in a game of hide-and-seek. Josh and Winnie crouching behind a thin, wintry bush in the backyard, obvious, fully in sight. Somewhere in the front yard, Lucas was counting loudly. His voice shrieking as he got closer to twenty, the numbers climbing faster and louder. He was at eighteen, then nineteen, then twenty. "I'm coming!" he hollered, shouting out toward the bare trees, mottled grass, and cool white air that surrounded him.

I grabbed Josh's hand, motioned to Winnie to follow us, then raced with them toward the corner of the backyard, pointing to the shed where we stored our bikes and balls and lawn equipment.

"Here, squat down," I said to Josh behind the shed. "Winnie, come look," I said, pulling her next to me. "He won't think to look here," I whispered to her, squeezing Winnie's narrow shoulder and kissing her downy cheek. Winnie adorable in her purple quilted jacket, the color bringing out the pink in her complexion. Her beauty and grace fulfilling my exact fantasy of how it would be to have a daughter: easy to love, a pleasure to influence. Already imagining myself like a favored aunt to Winnie. Someone who would be there for her always.

"Don't make a noise," I whispered, smiling at Winnie and Josh crouched down in total seriousness, their heads bowed, their legs like haunches. I dashed out from behind the shed and walked toward the driveway; I'd rightly guessed that Lucas was making his way from the front of the house to the back.

"Tell me the truth. Where are they?" Lucas asked when he saw me walking toward him.

I smiled. I laughed. I held my palms up and said, "I have no idea!"

"I know you do!" Lucas insisted, stomping his foot. "Why won't you tell me?"

I laughed again. Lucas knew me so well. That I loved to keep a secret. It was one of my best traits, I had once told him, even though I doubted he knew fully what this meant.

"Give me a hint!" Lucas whined, stomping his foot some more, balling his hands into fists, his cheeks flaming with cold. I made the zipper sign across my lips and walked away to join Gene and Jay at the end of the driveway, leaving Lucas to pout and then continue his uneven, rocking gait toward the back of the house. In the driveway, the men were talking about Gene's business. They were always talking business; there was nothing else between them, really.

"How long you think before Lucas finds them?" I interrupted, not caring whether a credit line should be refinanced, what the company's current receivables were.

"Never," Jay said absentmindedly, no doubt still trying to figure out how he could shave a half point or more off an interest payment.

"Not much of a seeker, but then, Winnie's not much of a hider," joked Gene, no doubt done with the refinancing question or just not that interested in it to begin with. Gene's role in the business murky to me, which always made me wonder if he even understood a word Jay was saying. Which was unfair and unkind, and which I tried to cover up by asking, "Where are Paige and Cameron?" Realizing as soon as I'd said it that this was the exact wrong thing to bring up.

"School uniforms," he said. Too quickly? I sensed he was uncomfortable and wished I hadn't asked it.

"Makes sense!" I said, hoping to stop him from straining further. Wondering how to change the subject when I heard Gene's cell phone ringing. Gene holding up a finger, answering his phone, talking in his businessman voice.

"I'll watch Winnie," I mouthed after a minute, motioning for him to go take the call in the privacy of his home, to leave the hide-and-seek and mothering to me.

A hesitation. A pause. Then finally nodding in my direction and walking toward the end of our cul-de-sac, his head bowed, the phone pressed close to his ear.

Almost immediately, Jay asking, "Can I be excused?"

I rolled my eyes. I said, "Why?"

"To read," Jay said, referring no doubt to his doomsday websites: the ones that said the recent recession was just the beginning of the soon-to-arrive end. The ones that said the government was colluding against its citizens, threatening to deceive them.

"Why do you want to read all that stuff?" I asked, already exasperated.

"Because this country is completely fucked up, and the government is lying about it!" Jay said, predictably.

I rolled my eyes. His extremism irritating. Even though I knew it was how he made his money. Being the contrarian. Recommending original investment strategies.

"You're going to wake up one day and it's going to cost two thousand dollars to buy a hamburger," Jay insisted. "And believe me, you'll wish you'd listened then."

He was quite possibly right. He was quite possibly wrong.

But what was it he proposed that I do about it? That any of us do about it? There was only so much you could control. So much you could plan for. The rest, most of it good, some of it awful, was up to chance. You had to assume that something horrible was going to happen to you someday—likely soon, definitely not never—and that when it did, you would have the brains and the fortitude to survive it. It was Jay's great good fortune and colossal naïveté that had prevented him from knowing all this already. Even though at another level, he'd known it his whole life and was forever trying to guard against it. The unfairness of the world. The way the people who were supposed to protect you and love you could let you down.

"Well?" Jay asked, as though his statement about economic collapse wasn't merely rhetorical but demanded immediate action by me. With a furrowed brow I prepared to say something demeaning. About how he didn't know anything about politics. Or world history. Which I knew was ridiculous. We'd met in a foreign policy class at Amherst! But before I could speak, there was shrieking followed by laughter. We both turned and saw Winnie running across the driveway, Josh behind her, followed by Lucas, who was chasing them both, shouting something unintelligible and vaguely threatening about getting them. Jay turning to watch, wondering, no doubt, whether there was any way that Lucas could catch Josh. Lucas older, but Josh already swifter. All of it on account of some amorphous developmental delay we still couldn't figure out.

"He's never going to catch up," Jay muttered, stuffing his hands in his pockets, his own body lean and athletic.

"It doesn't matter," I said, glad they were running, hoping they might be tired by bedtime. More shrieking. Then something louder. A cry. Jay and I running toward the corner of the front yard just in time to see that Winnie had tripped over a branch, falling into a tree trunk. Lucas falling on top of her, his head tangled near her knees. I ran toward them, Jay behind me, my heart racing, terrified of what I would find. Did Winnie crack her skull? Break her neck? And then, there it was. The blood. Winnie's mouth gushing it.

I must have stood in the spot and screamed. Clutched my hair. Done nothing but make noise and create more chaos. I couldn't think. I was terrible with emergencies. Jay was terrible with blood, even now standing with his back toward me, saying, "I can't look!"

"Go get towels!" I finally screamed at Jay, turning toward Lucas, who was already disentangling himself from Winnie, his body upright and seemingly unharmed while Winnie lay on the ground mewing like a cat. Josh standing over Winnie, his eyes wide with wonder and fright.

"I think I stepped on her," Lucas said, then started to cry.

I didn't want him to cry. I didn't want to console him at a time like this. I wanted him to be quiet for once. To not be needy! Which was ridiculous. He was eight years old. I couldn't help it. "Go sit on the steps!" I yelled.

"Take your voice down," Jay said gently, squeezing my shoulder, telling the boys to go sit on the porch, handing me the napkins he'd gotten instead of the towels. Which was infuriating! I squatted down beside Winnie, smoothing her hair and placing the napkins gently over her mouth, telling her to hold them there and press a little if she could, doubting that pressing would do much good. The blood was copious, mottled, and thick. The napkins soaked and useless almost immediately.

"Call Gene!" I yelled over my shoulder, knowing my voice was too loud, that I was scaring Winnie, but unable to control my hysteria. Jay dialing Gene, waiting as it rang and rang. Where was he?

"Do you think we should call an ambulance?" Jay finally asked.

There was silence while we thought about it. The embarrassment of calling 911. The shriek of the sirens and the commotion on our lawn. Doors open. Families on stoops and in doorways. But I didn't feel comfortable driving her to the hospital, either. What if she bled to death from her mouth injury?

Jay called 911. We waited.

"Winnie, you're going to be okay, do you hear me?" I asked, my voice cracking, tears working their way into it.

Whimpering from Winnie, who was still on the ground.

"Winnie, I want to take you to the doctor. To make it all better. Okay?" I said, rubbing her arm, squeezing her shoulder gently toward me. Now that help was coming, I felt less scared and hysterical.

Winnie seemed to nod or at least fall in closer to me. I held her like that, half hugging, half leaning, until the ambulance came and we loaded her up, me riding with Winnie, Jay staying behind with the boys. Which seemed unfair and stupid to me. Given how bad I was with emergencies. Which made perfect sense to Jay, who couldn't deal with the blood.

* * *

"Two chipped teeth, a cut to the gum, a pretty big gash in her lower lip, but no head injuries," the doctor, or the doctor's assistant, said, mumbling into his clipboard, not bothering to introduce himself to me or to Winnie when he entered our cubicle. Which annoyed me. I was standing at the side of the bed, holding Winnie's hand, the nurse already having taken her temperature and blood pressure and assuring me that she wouldn't bleed to death.

"Can you tell me again how this happened?" the man continued, mumbling, then looking up at me in a way that made me nervous. As if he thought I did this to her!

"I'm not her mother. I'm the neighbor," I said, as if that explained everything.

The man shrugged and continued to stare at me with his pudgy, bearded face, his demeanor young and boyish. He was, I suddenly realized, at least ten years younger than me, which for some reason only stoked my frustration. I doubted he was even a parent!

"Do you want the whole story?" I asked, my palms starting to sweat with indignation and fear.

He nodded and kept looking at me blandly, like he was interrogating me while trying to seem like he wasn't interrogating me. I wanted to bash him with something hard and plastic, with the phone handset or the remote control, both of which were directly within eyeshot. I breathed deeply, then glanced toward Winnie, who was involved in a TV show. I tried to smile politely and then told him the story about the hide-and-seek and the tree trunk. About Gene taking a cell phone call and not being reachable. All of which he wrote down with quick flicks of his pen as if he knew shorthand.

"And the mother?" he asked, looking up momentarily from his clipboard.

"She's shopping," I said. Which sounded inane, even to me. "For school uniforms, with their son. The one who's not adopted."

Why did I say this?

The man nodded in a way that revealed nothing and then put down his clipboard and approached Winnie, turning down the volume on the TV and explaining that he was going to examine her. Lifting her shirt to place the stethoscope on her chest and along her back, then lifting her sleeves to peer at her wrists and tapping her knees with his little hammer.

"I'll be back," he said to me, exiting quickly through the parted curtain.

A nurse came in, took Winnie's temperature, checked her blood pressure again, and said, "A social worker's on her way. We're going to need to talk to the little girl privately."

"Why?" I asked. "Is that normal?"

"In these cases, yes."

"Because I'm the neighbor," I said, suddenly panicking. Did the man tell them I'd done something to her?

"It's because of the scratches," the nurse said, raising Winnie's purple sleeve to reveal faint red lines along her forearms. Not ugly lines, but lines nonetheless. Some of them scabbed over a bit; others fresher, like they'd been drawn with a nail just that morning.

I felt my chest tighten and tears well up behind my eyes.

"Are you her legal guardian?" the nurse asked, lowering Winnie's sleeve.

"No. Not at all," I said, relieved that I wasn't and therefore couldn't be accused of this. But also disappointed as the nurse nodded curtly and pulled another, smaller curtain around Winnie's bed, forming a circle that wouldn't include me.

"I didn't see the scratches when she fell. I was, you know, focused on the blood," I said, trying to insert myself into the narrow enclosure.

"Please wait in the waiting room while we talk to her," the nurse said, unimpressed by my explanation or simply uninterested in my version of events.

"She's only five," I said. "She can't speak that well. She's Russian. I mean, she's adopted. Her language skills are a little, you know..."

I stopped. What was I trying to say? That I didn't want Winnie talking to them? Why? I couldn't think of a good reason. And yet it still didn't feel right. This interrogation. This separation. I had no choice. I wasn't even on the right side of the curtain anymore.

I went to the waiting room and sat stiffly in one of the orange molded chairs they had lined up there. A tired-looking kid sitting in the middle of the white linoleum floor playing with a spiral maze and some balls, his weary parents eyeing me, then returning their attention to the wall-mounted television set. I couldn't watch the set. The screen was hard to see, faded out where the sun came in through the half-drawn blinds. I picked up an old, wrinkled *Newsweek*, its cover torn, and tried to read, but the words kept blurring on the page. I didn't care about how GM was faring. I didn't care about a new lobby aquarium being built in Las Vegas. Why was Winnie being forced to answer questions she had no words for? Why did she have scratches? I was worried, even though I told myself a lot of people had scratches. I had terribly dry skin in the winter and was a constant leg scratcher, my nails going up and down my calves, seeking relief for the dryness even though I knew I'd be better off using lotion. I pushed down thoughts of the other scratches I had; the kind I'd made with my nails when I was furious with my mother. When I was frustrated with Penny. The marks visible only if you knew where to look for them. The faint lines attributed to a friend's cat whenever someone asked about them. A fact I half believed whenever I told it. Careful to not look at my wrists now, to not damn myself by observing them. I gave up reading just as I saw Gene open the waiting-room door and look around.

"I've already been with her," he said immediately. "They let me in through the main entrance."

I nodded like this was important. The logistics of things. The way he had hurried to get here! Which of course he had. But where had he been? And where was Paige?

"My phone was on vibrate. I didn't know what had happened until Jay came back and banged on my door," Gene continued.

"I've done that a million times!" I insisted, eager to reassure him that I wasn't judging him. That I was a good friend—not a total failure as a stand-in parent. Which he was no doubt thinking. Which was unfair, given that I suspected him and Paige of something. Even if it wasn't necessarily the scratches, but something harder to pinpoint.

"Paige's home with Cameron," Gene added. "I mean, no use dragging him here," he said, waving his arm toward the dirty linoleum floor, the lurking germs, the desperate tediousness. Gene himself appearing deflated, as if it were he who had been trapped in the waiting room, not me.

I nodded and tried to smile. Then I got up to follow Gene back to Winnie's enclosure, the inner curtain open now, Winnie's bottom lip stitched together with ugly black thread, gauze stuffed under the top lip to protect her damaged gum. Winnie waved when she saw us.

"Dathy!" she said through the gauze, her voice muffled, her cracked teeth barely visible beneath the giant, puffy lip. I bent down to kiss her cheek, to smooth her hair, then turned to Gene and said, "I'm really, really sorry," hoping Winnie couldn't see the tears in my eyes, not wanting to worry her, but hoping Gene could see them as proof of my sincerity.

"It's not your fault, Nicole, seriously," Gene said. "It could have happened to any of us. Remember when Jesse fell off our swing set and broke his wrist last fall?"

I remembered. I'd thought Lorraine was reckless to let her two-year-old swing unattended and Gene foolish to have allowed it on his property, on his watch. Was he thinking the same of me now, that I should have intervened when I saw the chase, should have removed the fallen tree branches? Probably, somewhere in the back of his mind.

"In case you're wondering about the scratches," Gene continued, sitting down next to Winnie on the bed, leaving me standing awkwardly across from him, "Winnie has a bit of a problem, don't you, honey?" he said, turning toward her, rubbing his palm against her long, thin arm.

Winnie wasn't paying attention anymore, her head swiveled toward the TV set hanging in the corner, SpongeBob having been replaced by a cartoon rocket ship and a boy with funny, upswept hair.

"She scratches herself," Gene continued, looking back at me. "It's common with adopted kids."

I nodded. I didn't know what to say. This made sense. Sort of. That an adopted child might do things you didn't expect.

"She obviously couldn't explain herself with the cracked lip," Gene continued. "And even if she could, I don't think she's aware of the fact that she does it," he said, folding his hands in his lap and looking just past my shoulder.

"Okay," I said, starting to chew on my nails, nervous to be alone with Gene, to be having this sort of conversation.

"Winnie has a lot of issues. Things we weren't expecting," Gene said, looking at me briefly, then hanging his head to stare at his lap as he said, "Paige is struggling, as I think you know." I held my breath and waited for him to go on, wishing he would, even though I was embarrassed. The pause elongating, the silence ballooning in front of us.

"I understand," I finally said.

Gene kept his head down, sighed once, then looked up toward me, blinking his eyes rapidly as he ran his fingers through his once lustrous hair. I doubted he saw me. I doubted he saw anything. His stare seeming to go internal, into some dark recess I didn't want to plumb and didn't know how to.

"I'm so glad her lip's going to be okay," I said stupidly, eager to make the awkward moment disappear. To bring him back into the room with me.

"Everything will be back to normal in a month or so," Gene said, suddenly looking me in the face. Smiling. A certain confidence and authority returning to his body.

I was relieved even as I was disturbed. By Gene's changeable nature. By Winnie's mysterious personality. But I needed to believe him. To believe that everything was going to get better, not just the lip and the broken teeth, but the rest of it: Paige's struggles, Winnie's scratching.

"If you've got everything covered, I guess I'll take off," I said, backing away so that my body was now pressing the curtain outward, away from the enclosure, away from the bed and the chattering television set.

"Thanks again, Nicole!" Gene called after me as I waved good-bye to Winnie, relieved to escape from the fluorescent lights and the strange beeping noises of the hospital. Relieved to call a taxi and avoid having to travel home with Gene and with Winnie.

THANK YOU FOR THANKING ME

THAT NIGHT I LOOKED up "adopted preschoolers" on the Internet. The list of results massive and confusing. The list as much about American foster children looking for homes as it was about foreign children with adjustment issues.

I tried to search for something more specific that might pertain to Winnie's situation, typing "foreign children with adjustment issues" into the Google search bar. Almost immediately I found what I was looking for in the form of a lovely story about a Korean three-year-old who was adopted by a Midwestern family. In the beginning, Hak-Kun was homesick not just for Korea, but for the foster family with whom he'd lived for a short while. He cried and couldn't sleep, which sounded a lot like Winnie. He refused to eat and then ate nonstop, which the family had to quickly limit because he was always having diarrhea. I was fascinated and amazed. Clearly Winnie was a lot like other adopted children. I read on, quickly scanning the page for how things had turned out. The boy rejecting his parents' attempts at giving him love, ignoring them, not following simple rules, testing them, according to the article, to see if he could trust them. Maybe this was what Winnie was doing now and what Paige was so sorely struggling against? Paige not someone who liked to be tested. Paige someone who liked to have everyone do exactly as she said.

By the end of the article, the mother wrote lovingly of her son's transition from grief to acceptance, from rebellion to love. The whole thing was over in less than a year, which meant Winnie should be pulling out of it. She'd been adopted just over a year ago. I felt so relieved, so full of hope and happiness for Winnie's future that I realized for the first time that I'd been truly worried about her. Or at least nervous that things were not going to work out as perfectly as I'd imagined when I'd first heard about the adoption. The idealized picture of the situation I had painted in my mind at the leftovers party so embarrassing to me now. Picturing Winnie as if she were a doll or a puppet.

I was so relieved, so ready to close my laptop and resume my normal life, that I almost forgot about the scratching. About the marks on Winnie's arms that Gene said were common for adopted children. I searched again. I typed in "foreign adopted children who scratch themselves." The search came up with children who scratched others. A few children who hurt the family pet. Children who kicked and screamed and mistakenly scratched their new parents when their new parents reached out for a hug. But even in these more extreme cases, there was no mention of self-mutilation. No scratching, as Gene had indicated. Which meant what, exactly? That it was a problem specific to Winnie, not to adoption in general? It certainly could be. I tried not to think about my own scratching. Ashamed and embarrassed that I'd been so angry, so out of control. Aware that Winnie might feel the same way.

*   *   *

The day after the hospital visit, I found a letter in my mail slot. An ecru card inside an envelope lined with pale blue paper. Tiffany's, I realized as I pulled the card out of the envelope. It was handwritten in neat, thinly shaped cursive. Penmanship obviously Paige's strong suit.

> *Dear Nicole,*
>
>   *I just want to say from the bottom of my heart that we are so grateful to have friends like you and Jay. Thank you so much for taking such good care of Winnie yesterday. You are truly like a second family to us and I don't know what we would do without you.*
>
> Love, Paige

I turned the card over, hoping for more, perhaps a P.S. or something extra she couldn't fit on the front. A continuation of the flowery, half-true feelings. There was nothing written on the back, which made me embarrassed to be looking for more. I flipped the card over and read the front again, my heart swelling with pride and gratitude, wanting it to be true. Wanting to believe that I'd created an extended family for myself here, amid the towering oak trees of our cul-de-sac. Wanting to believe that Paige would be there for me if I needed her. Knowing that she would bring Lucas or Josh to the hospital. Would stand with the doctors and get all the proper diagnoses. Even though I would never turn to her for sustenance. I would be suspicious of her decisions, and doubt any story she might tell me. Pushing this thought away as I stored the

ecru card in its envelope and placed it in a narrow slot in my secretary desk. The slot a resting place for past wedding invitations and
small, slippery photos from when my kids were younger. Items you
couldn't throw out and didn't have an exact place for yet.

I pulled out a card and began a note back to Paige. Explaining how sorry I was about Winnie's accident. How relieved I was
that it wasn't something more serious. How I should have written
to her first! Then I thanked her for all the kind things she'd said
about Jay and me and told her we felt the same way about her and
Gene and their kids. I signed the note with a flourish using my
good silver pen, a gift from Jay one Mother's Day. I knew the note
was ridiculous and old-fashioned. Insincere and overly formal. But
it seemed exactly right for the occasion, acknowledging something
deep yet untrue between us, something delicate and easily broken if
we didn't do this thank-you thing just right.

I put on my coat and walked the card over to Paige's, eager not
to run into her, unable to say any of these things face-to-face. Certain that I wouldn't have to, because Paige didn't want to see me,
either. Even though she was no doubt able to chart my progress if
she was looking out her bedroom window. My hurried pace as I
descended the narrow slope of my yard, my head turning from side
to side in an effort not to look directly at her Tudor. Taking in the
Guzman-Venieros' ranch, the Weinbergers' weathered gray colo-
nial. Finally ascending the Edwardses' long bluestone walk and
slipping my card through their mail slot. Paige's bedroom curtains
just visible out of the corner of my eye, the flutter of an object at the
window causing me to look up against my will, to squint against
the weak winter sunlight, then jump back when I thought I saw
a shadow just next to me. Clutching my heart, breathing deeply,
embarrassed to be imagining things.

A NEW BEGINNING

Winter drizzled out the way it always did, with fits of warmth followed by long stretches of numbing and miserable cold. The weather always about to deliver a new season, then failing in its promise. My mother calling to inform me that she was sick of waiting out the cold Midwestern winter and had finally saved enough to go on a warm-weather vacation.

"Don't tell your sister," my mother warned me. "She'll just be jealous of me!"

"Lucas made corn tamales," I said, hoping to change the subject. Our monthly conversations lately limited to the weather and the boys. Both of us eager to pretend there wasn't something vibrating between us. Penny's struggles, our helplessness to make everything better.

"Your sister told me I'm the reason she stayed with Bob for so long. That she had no male role model!" my mother hissed, starting to cry. I closed my eyes and tried to think about what to say that was fair and wouldn't cause trouble.

"You hate me," my mother sobbed before I could come up with a suitable answer. As if there could ever be a suitable answer to such a murky and explosive accusation.

"I don't hate you," I pleaded, bending down to clean one of the cupboard doors, to wipe away the dried food remnants and smudges of grease that seemed to forever accumulate there. Wondering if you were supposed to use a special wood polish, wondering if my mother knew what it was.

"Then why won't you say I was a good mother?" my mother demanded while I scrubbed.

"I have. You were!" I said. Wishing we didn't have to talk about this. Aware that Penny's unhappiness weighed on my mother more than she let on. Aware that it would weigh on me, too, if I were in her shoes.

"You blame me for the past!"

"I don't blame you for the past," I insisted, exasperation creeping into my voice. Wishing that I could tell her the truth. Deciding to try it and bracing myself for the worst. I walked outside where the boys couldn't hear me and said, "I blame you for the present," waiting for my mother to start screaming, aware that if she did, I would hang up on her. Not willing to console her any longer.

"What? That I wouldn't help Penny with the bedding? Is that it? I should enable her the way you do?"

"I'm helping her with tuition!" I retorted, resisting the urge to pull my hair or dig my nails into my wrist. Determined to be different, as if standing beneath sky and trees on the lawn of my home could make it so. Aware that it could and that I planned to make it true.

"You want money from me?" my mother asked, starting to cry again.

"I want you to stop destroying yourself," I said softly. Aware that I hadn't been thinking this until the words were out of my mouth.

"Your sister is killing me!" my mother began to wail, crying uncontrollably now.

"Penny is a smart girl," I said. Something I hadn't fully given her credit for until I was saying it on my lawn.

"So why does she drink? Why is she so moody and difficult all the time?"

"Mom!" I shouted, staring up at the canopy of barren branches just above me.

"What?" she shouted back.

"You can't change other people," I offered, knowing this was inane and also simplistic. Something I no doubt got from some self-help book about men I read in my twenties. Or from the one time I'd gone to Al-Anon.

"So what should I do? Watch her drink herself to death?" she asked. "Give her money whenever she asks for it?"

"Is she asking you for money?" I asked, shocked.

"I don't want you bringing wine coolers to my house again!" my mother retorted. I breathed deeply, not willing to take the bait. Instead I asked, "Mom, remember when you first met Jay? When he came home with me from Amherst senior year?"

Unbelievably, my mother started to laugh through her tears. "I asked him to take down the lightbulbs from the hall closet and then stood directly behind him."

"Exactly. He had no idea you were there and clocked you with his elbow!"

"Typical Phyllis!" my mother admitted.

"Remember, the next morning, you wore the pirate patch!"

"I did! With that hat with the feather from the dress-up clothes in the attic."

We were both silent, remembering the aura of happiness. The creeping hint of the start of something new.

"You seemed so much happier then," I prodded softly. Even though it was possible this was just my reimagining of the situation. Wanting to believe my mother had had the chance to seize her future once Penny and I were out of the house.

Silence from my mother, who seemed to be considering what I was saying.

After a moment, she said, "I was younger then. And thinner. And I didn't have diabetes!"

"Well, go to the gym," I persisted.

"Do you know how much a gym membership costs? I'm living on a fixed income!"

"How about a Jane Fonda video? Or whoever the new Jane Fonda is. It's fun. The music really gets you motivated," I lied. I hated working out at home.

My mother paused as if considering it, then said, "Nobody loves me!" and started crying again.

"You're mad at yourself. You're killing yourself!" I insisted, eager to say it as much for myself as I was for her. Aware that my sister's suffering had both nothing and something to do with her present condition.

My mother still sobbing as I walked back into my kitchen, examining the cupboards I'd recently cleaned. The same streaks of oil and old food still visible in the sunlight if you knew where to look for them. Pleased that I'd at least tried. Determined that next time I'd have the right vinegar or Murphy Oil Soap solution to remove the food without stripping the finish. My mother eventually calming down enough to tell me that she'd found a cute sundress at T.J.Maxx that she planned to bring on her trip. As if we'd been talking about her vacation the whole time.

"It covers up everything and I bought shoes to go with it," she explained.

I nodded even though she couldn't see me. I asked detailed questions and made kind, empathetic noises, trying to actively listen and understand her, as if by understanding her, I could give her what she was craving.

*　*　*

My sister called the next day to report that Phyllis was going on a Beaches vacation. "Did you know that already?" Penny demanded. I wandered into the mudroom, sponge in hand, prepared to wipe the random specks of dirt and ink off the walls.

"She mentioned it," I offered, unsure if this still counted as breaking a confidence and furious with myself for caring.

"Do you know I haven't been on vacation in over ten years?" Penny demanded.

I sighed. I rubbed harder at the wall and said, "Maybe when you finish your course, we could go on a girls' weekend together." Cringing as I said it. Aware that Penny and I weren't exactly suited for laughter and confidences.

Deep sighing from Penny. As if she were considering the logistics of a trip. Or maybe she was just smoking. Then she said, "Yeah, about that..."

My body growing tenser as I stood on my tiptoes to swipe at a cobweb, waiting expectantly for her to go on.

"I'm a little behind," Penny finally said.

"What does that mean?"

"Look, I didn't write all the papers I was supposed to, but the professors are cool. I'm going to take two incompletes, then finish over the summer. By the fall I can enroll in the teaching certificate classes, if I still want to."

"What do you mean, if you still want to?" I asked, suddenly furious that she was so changeable. That I'd lent her money for something that might not amount to anything.

"Did I tell you about my idea to start a music school for under-served communities?"

I gritted my teeth, got down on my hands and knees, and scrubbed the mudroom baseboard as Penny explained about a woman who worked specifically with communities of color and was always looking for new programs. She planned to meet with her as soon as she'd finished a business plan, which she couldn't do because she'd lost the power cord to her laptop. Which was why she hadn't finished the papers, by the way.

"Are you finished?" I asked when she'd finally stopped talking and the baseboard was as free of dust as I could make it.

"Go ahead!"

"I want to say something and not have you respond, okay?"

Silence.

"Penny, you can do whatever you want with your life—take the incompletes, finish in the fall, blow it off completely. It's your life. I'm not standing in judgment. But I'd be a shitty person if I didn't tell you what I really thought. And what I really think is that something else is clearly going on here. And you don't have to admit it to me. But I seriously suggest you admit it to yourself and get the help you need or you are never going to have any of the other things you want and, by the way, deserve."

Silence. Inhaling from Penny. A hiccup. Aware she was smoking and probably drinking. Imagining the row of wine coolers surrounding her bed. Wishing I had a cigarette, even though I'd long ago quit. Remembering the times Penny and I used to sneak them together at our grandmother's cottage in the summertime. The dock long and rickety. The setting sun casting its bright alley of light across the nearly smooth water. Our favorite part of the day. The humidity like a blanket of calm. Penny dangling her feet off the end of the dock in her bikini while I sat cross-legged, embarrassed of my body in my hooded terry cover-up. Aware that Penny was "the pretty one" in the family and I was the less attractive "smart girl," according to my mother's mother, who often spoke of us in loud stage whispers. My mother's cocktail of bossiness and neediness no doubt brewed in that cauldron of maternal deficiency. All of us part of some thin, knotted chain stretching backward and forward through time. I wondered how you ever escaped it, or even what "it" was, exactly, as I waited for Penny to respond. Her silence enough of an acknowledgment that I'd said something she was considering.

After a while, Penny sighed and said in a low, serious voice, "You know how most people are afraid of being unhappy?"

I nodded, even though she couldn't see me. My every moment of every day filled with plans and goals and chores so that I wouldn't have to feel the thing she was conjuring: sadness and dread. Loneliness and loss.

My sister not waiting for a response. Or else well aware of what my response would be.

"Well, I'm afraid of being happy. Of being a success. I purposely fuck things up."

"Why?" I asked, shocked and not able to believe the possibility she was presenting me.

"Because when you're happy, you have so much more to lose."

I felt something thick lodge in the back of my throat, the hard ball of a truth I'd failed to imagine. Aware I'd been born lucky in my disposition, determined in my optimism.

"Are you there?" Penny asked, her voice still low, the hint of embarrassment in her tone, or was it relief?

"If you know this about yourself, can't you undo it?" I asked, aware this was simplistic but determined to make her see the possibility. That she could change. That she could risk it.

"Maybe," she said, not willing to commit to my optimism, my insistence on forward momentum. Which I tried not to judge. Aware for the first time of just how different we were. Of how different we'd always been.

* * *

Within a month, the freesia turned yellow against our fence posts, and tulips started to sprout in their thinly mulched beds. There were demands to throw off sweatshirts. To have naked arms, open shoes, to bask in the warmth and promise of spring. The green and the birdsong awakening something in Paige, who suddenly emerged, standing on her stoop in her brightly colored espadrilles. A stylish scarf knotted at her neck. Her body frail and thin, her arm lifted in greeting as Drew or Lorraine or I walked by.

We waved. We called our greetings in kind. We stopped and walked up her path to chat with her. After a few minutes of chit-chat she'd look nervous, like she'd been out too long or had had too much interaction, and she'd excuse herself just as quickly as she'd appeared, saying she had a load of wash to do or something burning on the stove, even though we knew Paige didn't do the wash, wasn't cooking anything on the stove.

By May, she seemed like an almost complete version of her previous self, setting up Drew's croquet set on her lawn, making lemonade for the kids, yelling at dog walkers to clean up after their pets. Laughing at her own bossiness. Calling herself the neighborhood dog warden. Which reminded us why we'd liked Paige in the first place: because she could occasionally make fun of herself.

Drew remembered, too. Or I assumed he did. Why else did he suddenly suggest it? That we all take a vacation together.

"It'll be great!" Drew said, more to Nela than to me, the three of us gathered around their dining room table after it started to rain on the kids, the table covered with their ugly brown vinyl table protectors. Nela's legal files spread from one end to the other.

"I'm not going if Paige goes," Nela said, raising her head from the file she was scanning. It was a Sunday afternoon, Nela in sweats with a pot of coffee beside her.

"It could be okay," I said, willing her to drop her protest. Did she think she was the only one with misgivings about Paige? It was ridiculous and sanctimonious and served only one purpose—to divide us. What was the point of that?

Nela sniffed. Then pulled her file closer. Bending her head to examine the fine print, running her crooked finger under a highlighted section. Which was so Nela. Buried in her work on a Sunday! Which just went to show you. That we didn't judge her, at least not openly.

"She's too nutty," Nela said, putting aside her file suddenly and staring up at me.

"Absent's not nutty," I protested, wishing Nela could be a little bit empathetic. A little bit realistic! Everyone had their issues.

"It's her whole uptight white-girl shit that drives me bananas," Nela said. "We went over there for dinner last Sunday, and it was like crazy time," she continued. "She monitors Winnie down to the second: what she eats and in what order. She had half a hot dog and no bun and a glass of milk. And she had to drink the milk first. I mean, what the fuck is that?"

"It's an adopted-kid thing," I said, trying to imagine in what circumstances Nela and Drew would be invited to the Edwardses' for dinner without Jay and me. Wondering if Lorraine and Jeffrey had been there, too. Ignoring the unwanted bud of jealousy as I plowed on. "Remember, Winnie couldn't come to the holiday party? She had an accident?"

No response from Nela, who merely tapped her cheekbone with her finger and stared at me; Nela beautiful and poised even when she was disagreeing with you.

"I read that a lot of adopted kids overeat. Something about not getting enough food when they're in the orphanage," I said, queasy at the thought of it. All those starving children. Neglected and unloved.

"Do you know I bought Paige a book about parenting an adopted preschooler?" Nela asked, ignoring my story completely, pausing to take a swig of water from the giant water bottle she always carried around with her. Purple with ribbed sides, which I found so ugly.

"That was really nice," I said, averting my eyes from the plastic jug and hoping to encourage Nela to go on with her story. Even though I sensed where this was going. Overt judgment. A preconceived idea about Paige that she'd no doubt had before she gave her the book.

"Well, when we went over for dinner I asked her about that

book, and you know what she said?" Nela asked, raising her eyebrows for emphasis.

"What?" I asked with dread, knowing I wouldn't like the answer.

"She said, 'What book?'"

I paused. I wished someone had offered me coffee. Or at least water. I shifted on the dining room chair, ran my fingers through my curls, and said, "Well, why didn't you remind her? Maybe she forgot." Pleased that Nela had cared enough to do something helpful for Paige, but annoyed that she'd stopped short of going the extra step. Namely, figuring out whether the book had been lost or misplaced and then making sure to get it into Paige's hands so she could read it. Wasn't this the way to make a lasting difference? To really go the extra mile? To not assume or judge? Maybe Paige read a different book, for all we knew!

Nela merely looked at me and shook her head like I was naive. Which infuriated me. The way Nela didn't know the first thing about me. About how much savvier I was about life than she could possibly imagine. Not that I cared to correct her. My appearance as someone without a care in the world was exactly what I had tried to cultivate my entire life. Even though it suddenly felt hollow. To be so little known.

"I know something isn't right," Nela said, folding her arms over her chest and staring at me as if she dared me to contradict her. I stared back at her for only a minute before dropping my eyes to the ugly brown table protectors. Furious with Nela for her superiority. For her failure to understand the true nature of difficult people! You didn't try to reason with them. You didn't expect things from them. You certainly didn't waste your time judging them! You took what you could get and you survived them. Because the good outweighed the bad. Because to do otherwise merely sank you.

* * *

Paige loved the idea of a group vacation. "I've never been to Bermuda!" she said when Drew suggested a cruise the following weekend. Drew insisting that his college friends had done it with their neighborhood friends. Drew insisting it wasn't as cheesy as we imagined it would be.

"Definitely, let's do something," Lorraine said, stirring her drink with her finger. It was Sunday. Five o'clock. We were in Lorraine's living room. We were always in Lorraine's living room now that she'd redone it, changing it from the formal style her ex-husband preferred—flowery walls, a grand piano—to some sort of pleasure den: boxy green couches, Lucite side chairs, a funky brass chandelier with arms like an octopus. It reminded me of a hotel lobby.

"Whatever you guys say; we're good with it," Gene said, jovial, eager to please. Gene in a lime green golf shirt and plaid shorts that only he could pull off. Even though the clothes hung on him. His frame inches smaller than it once was.

"Jay won't go on a cruise," I said. "Too cramped," I explained. Certain he didn't want to go. Certain he didn't want to be trapped on a ship with all of our neighbors.

"So you get a stateroom with a balcony," Lorraine said, shrugging off my concern like she did any problem.

"Jay?" I asked, looking toward where he was lounging in a swivel chair, his long legs crossed at the ankles, his entire demeanor silent, as was his nature in a group. Was he even listening? Jay shrugged good-naturedly. Which for Jay was almost an approval.

"Looks like it's happening," Lorraine said, raising her highball glass and telling Drew to get his video camera ready.

Everyone laughing. Everyone relaxed. Everyone talking over one another about the possibility of a new summer tradition. I sat back in my chair, excited and eager. Even though I thought a road trip would be easier. Even though I thought any trip could be disastrous. How well did we know each other, really? But I wanted to go, too. Even with Paige. Especially with Paige! Eager to be what we'd set out to be: close friends. Family friends. People who had each other's backs.

ALMOST PERFECT

WE DROVE TO BOSTON Harbor, stowed our bags, then met on the pool deck. The children running off to play on an oversize Twister board while the rest of us smiled and tried to be enthusiastic. Taking in the giant waterslides, the loud, annoying DJ who was calling out colors and goading the children into ever more complicated positions. The July sun already hot, the music deafening. All of us astounded that Drew had picked this ship and trying hard not to say anything. Had his friends really done something similar?

Questions about the rooms ensued. Whether they were bigger or smaller than they had seemed in the pictures; whether the balconies were worth the extra money. You couldn't fit both a table and a chair out there!

After a while the men wandered off toward a bar in the corner, eager for some shade and refreshment, the women going to stand on the edge of the deck, looking down at the port and ocean below. We were hot. Our faces shiny with sweat. The screams of the DJ interrupting what we'd no doubt hoped would be a silent or at least peaceful reverie. For a long while no one said what everyone was thinking.

Finally Nela said, "Drew's friend is pretty tacky," twisting her mouth from side to side in a way that let me know she was embarrassed. That Drew had picked this ship based on a friend's recommendation. That he hadn't even apologized.

"It's fine," Lorraine insisted, not bothering to turn away from the ocean. Shifting from side to side as if she were contemplating something. Or maybe she was just practicing her tennis stance. Nela looking at me for my input.

"I insisted we were on the wrong boat!" I admitted, hopeful that Nela could take the gentle ribbing.

"You did not!" Nela said, *tsk*ing and shaking her head from side to side, but smiling.

"Well, when I saw the other ship docked next door I was certain we were meant to be on that one instead," I said, jerking my head toward the larger and seemingly statelier ship in the next berth over, embarrassed now by how uptight I'd been. I'd literally been shouting at the steward to double-check our tickets.

"Well, what does Paige think?" Lorraine asked, turning in search of the Edwardses, who hadn't yet appeared. And then, as if on cue, there was Paige, rounding the Twister board with Cameron. Winnie not with her. Winnie no doubt taking a nap. This despite it being only eleven o'clock. This despite the fact that Winnie was five years old and too old for naps already! Paige still insisting Winnie had sleep issues. Even though I feared she was lying. Or at least exaggerating. Paige just wanting a break from her. Who took a nap on the first day of vacation?

"Do you hate it?" Nela shouted toward Paige, the wind pressing Paige's face into distorted relief. Her silver-white hair blowing messily around her face.

"It's terrible!" Paige said, laughing.

"There were used, dirty glasses in our bathroom!" Lorraine admitted, turning to face us. We all moaned, cringing. I tried to picture it. Worried that the same dirty conditions existed in my room that I just hadn't discovered yet.

"Not like we're going to be in the rooms that much," Lorraine added, shrugging and trying to make the best of things. Which I appreciated.

"Whatever—we'll be fine," Paige said gamely, more gamely than I'd ever seen her act. I wondered, was she on something?

"I want a picture," Lorraine said, obviously pleased that Paige was pleased, gathering us together and motioning Drew to come over with his camera. All of us near the deck railing, our faces tilted inward, our bodies blocking the long, precipitous drop behind us.

* * *

In the morning Drew organized our pool chairs in a circle, laying out the ship's thin white towels to save a spot near the shade, paying a deckhand twenty bucks to stand close to the pool and keep an extra eye on our children. All of us amused by his ingenuity. All of us astounded when he insisted on a round of piña coladas. The drinks cold and refreshing. The drink making me feel like a torpedo had lodged itself between my eyeballs. It was only ten o'clock in the morning! We'd all just gotten up. Not that any of us slept. The beds lumpy. The ship's nighttime rocking causing us to complain that we felt hungover already.

Meanwhile, all around us, groups of revelers were also saving lounge chairs, also drinking, a few men with large, greased bellies settling across from us with plates of food resting on their mounded stomachs. Which was rather embarrassing. To be here among them with our morning cocktails. To be acting just like them! But I sensed that we liked it, too. All of us more relaxed than we'd ever been with each other. All of us teasing Drew and Gene about how quickly they finished their drinks, laughing as they made their way to the buffet. Jay and Jeffrey getting up to join them while the women proceeded to take off our cover-ups and subtly check out each other's bodies. Me in my navy one-piece with strategically placed shirring. Nela in a simple black bikini that looked better than it had any right to, given that she worked in an office all week. Lorraine in her typical sports attire, a high-neck racing suit that accentuated her muscled biceps and was no doubt ideal for distance swimming. Was she actually planning on swimming amid the waterslides and flapping banners? Or was there a lap pool somewhere, away from this madness?

Before I could ask, Paige announced, "I love how much fun the kids are having!" adjusting her yellow-striped bikini and checking that her rear was covered. Paige thin but lacking any muscle tone, the result of good genes and never working out. Even if she'd gotten too thin in the months since she'd adopted Winnie. Her face increasingly ferret-like.

"I've heard Bermuda's gorgeous," Paige added, beginning to slather herself with sunscreen, oblivious to me sizing her up.

A conversation ensued about which islands were prettiest. Where we'd traveled when we were younger. A comparison of romantic weekends with our husbands. Lorraine had been to Bali. Also Seychelles. We listened to her recite descriptions of hotel rooms she'd stayed in. A certain elaborate suite with its own plunge pool on some island in Greece that she'd secured last minute using membership rewards points. Lorraine famous for her travel savvy. Lorraine dispensing her travel advice as freely as her career tips.

Nela was silent. Listening. Not commenting. Was she judging? She waited until Lorraine had finished and then told us a story about visiting family in Puerto Rico. Something about being left there for the summer with her two brothers and no real supervision. An uncle who may have been a pervert. Spying on him through the keyhole as he talked intimately with the maids. I suspected there were things she wasn't saying. The story not exactly funny. The story sad and a little forlorn. But it was funny the way she told it. Wistful. For a certain lost innocence. Or innocence she'd never been able to have. And the shrewdness it had left her with.

"My sister and I once got left in a hotel room when I was fourteen and she was sixteen," I finally said. More for Nela than for Paige or for Lorraine. Because I wanted Nela to understand something about me, too. Even though I was nervous that Paige and Lorraine wouldn't get the point exactly.

"You have a sister?" Lorraine asked.

"Yes, I have a sister," I said, annoyed and nervous that now Lorraine would feel the need to ask me a lot of personal questions. Already anticipating the short and half-truthful answers I would give her. Willing to dole out information when I was ready to, not on an as-asked-for basis.

"Let the girl finish," Nela said, looking at me with mirth in her eyes, which I appreciated.

"So anyway, we went to this wedding with my dad. And the next day my dad must have forgotten he'd taken us to the wedding because he checked out of the hotel and drove back to Pepper Pike without us."

Everyone nodding. Their faces sufficiently bland to convince me they weren't judging me. Or that I wasn't saying anything outlandish. Even though I knew it was outlandish. What father left you in a hotel room?

"So anyway, we called the front desk, and my dad had indeed

checked out. We thought about calling my mom, but we knew that she'd do something nutty like try to have my father arrested. So we sort of walked around downtown Akron for a little while and met these two guys, boys really, maybe around our ages, I guess. They were skeevy in that skinny, shifty-eyed way. But they were sort of interested in us, and we had nothing better to do than talk to them. After a little while, they asked us if we wanted to get high. So we invited them back to our hotel room. Which was sort of stupid, in hindsight."

"I'll say!" Lorraine interjected, laughing.

"So we went back to our hotel room and smoked a couple of bowls, and afterward things got weird. I realized that the guys were sort of menacing. Not toward Penny and me, exactly. It was more like they thought we were rich and were casing the room, looking for stuff to steal."

At this Nela laughed out loud and said, "Word!", an expression I hadn't heard since I was about the age I was in the story. The expression causing me to smile, to meet Nela's eyes. To feel brave about the rest of my anecdote.

"So just when I'm trying to figure out how to get rid of these two greasers, there's a knock on the door and guess who it is? My dad! We hid the pipe but he knew something wasn't right. He sort of looked around laughing and then reached out his hand to shake with the boys in this really faux formal way that made me laugh and that the boys didn't get and that made them nervous. They left pretty quickly after that, and my dad told us that he'd just gone to run some errands, which was obviously a lie—it was two in the afternoon, well past checkout—but he didn't question what we'd been up to, so that seemed like a fair trade-off."

When I had finished, I took a deep breath and then quickly flagged down a waitress, anxious for another drink. The drink suddenly essential for maintaining my equilibrium. My memory of the story funnier than it was in the retelling. The idea that I could have been raped or killed by the two teenage boys suddenly occurring to me more powerfully than when the story had been a distant, untold memory. The idea that my dad hadn't been disturbed by that so unsettling to me that I gulped some of Lorraine's drink before saying cheerily, "Anyone else got anything?" as if I weren't upset. As if I hadn't just told them the whole of my childhood in one small snapshot.

Nela looked at me, raising her eyebrows and giving me a sly smile. Which made me happy, glad to have an ally. Even if I wasn't convinced she could be fully trusted yet. Hadn't she seemed supportive of Paige when she'd announced she was adopting? Her support unfounded and then withdrawn suddenly and without warning?

Lorraine said, "I got caught after hours on a golf course once," and proceeded to tell us about senior prom and sneaking into her country club with a case of beer and some boys. Which was really nothing at all like my story but more a story about being a certain kind of upper-middle-class kid who was a certain kind of popular. Paige jumping in with a story about how she'd almost gotten kicked out of Catholic school because she was caught smoking in the girl's room repeatedly.

The conversation now turning fully to bad teenage behavior: pool hopping and shoplifting, stealing from our parents' liquor cabinets. Stories that I suspected were meant to convince one another that we weren't always the good girls we now seemed to be. Even though I knew this was false. All of us patently good girls who merely did a few bad things to test the waters. Even Nela and me. Especially Nela and me. Being good the fastest way out of a bad situation. Which Lorraine couldn't possibly understand. What rebellion could cost you. Paige neither a good girl nor a bad one, but rather in a bubble of her own making. Paige not like any friend I'd ever had before, and yet more familiar to me than anyone else in our beach chair circle. A fact I tried to forget about as she launched into an unrelated story about traveling through Canada with her mother and three sisters in an old silver Airstream. The story seemingly invented on the spot, as I suspected a lot of Paige's stories were: bits and pieces of fact woven together with imagination and exaggeration to create an image she wanted us to have of her. Of someone who had had a happier and more carefree childhood than the one she'd hinted at on other, less guarded occasions. The light and the sun seeming to stream right through Paige's thin, delicate frame, illuminating for me what I'd known all along about her and had handily chosen to ignore: namely, that I hardly trusted a word that she said.

* * *

In Bermuda, the sand was pink, the water warm and translucent. The kids wading in the shallows, or else playing in the sand, digging for treasure and seashells. They wove in and out of our field of vision, asked anyone's mother for money, permission, towels, more sunscreen. Gene tan and a little bit handsome again. Even if he was still too skinny. Paige happy, or at least not uptight and yelling.

All of us shopping for trinkets in the boutiques that lined the harbor, eating out in a restaurant that was too fancy for children. Waiters forced to bring extra baskets of bread. More butter. Round after round of Shirley Temples even though we knew so much sugar was dangerous. The children running around the town square as soon as they'd finished eating—red sauce dotting their lips and chins from their child-size ravioli. The kids playing freeze tag while the adults drank vodka and made toasts to each other. Certain that our kids were having the time of their lives. Convincing us with their smiles and their laughter that this was the best vacation ever.

And then, all at once, it was Wednesday night, the final night and the fireworks night. The ship announcing there would be a beach party on their own private island before we sailed for Boston Harbor. Paige eager for us to gather on the Verandah Deck before heading to the party. Paige surprising the children with goody bags: star-shaped sunglasses, sailor hats, and beaded necklaces.

"When did you do this?" I asked.

"From the gift shop," she admitted, sticking her hands in the pockets of her maxi dress and leaning back slightly.

I couldn't believe it. That in the midst of the swimming and shore excursions, the mealtimes and the chaos, she'd thought to buy all of the kids presents. To make the vacation a little more festive. A little more memorable. Which reminded me of why I liked her to begin with. Because she cared so much. Because she really did try. Even though I thought goody bags were completely wasteful. The ridiculous piles of junk they generated. One whole drawer in my playroom devoted to balsa wood airplanes, purple stretchy men, candy-colored noisemakers.

As soon as the bags were distributed—the contents spilled clumsily on the tables and the carpet—the children grew clamorous, running up and down the long glassed-in lounge area, shouting to each other, begging to make their way to the party or whatever occasion it was for which they'd been given the presents. The goody bags like a signal, a Pavlovian command, to start running, shouting, anticipating fun.

We told them to be quiet! We told them to calm down! We told them, "Walk slowly toward the elevators." The children flinging themselves at the double glass doors that separated the lounge from the open-air deck, waving their flags, shouting too loudly to be considered acceptable, even here on this tacky ship, at least for our standards. Our standards having fallen with each day of the trip. The children barefoot, still in wet bathing suits, not even changed after a day in the sun. All of us trailing after them with armfuls of sweatshirts, bug spray, and water.

We neared the gangway and descended to the pier. Already there were dozens of families gathered on the beach, Chinese fire lanterns with the ship's insignia bobbing from brightly colored beach chairs, kids running wildly between groups of bonfires. I stood for a long moment on the pier, taking in the calls of laughter and obvious displays of happiness. The sheer volume of the revelers. It was like a dream. An act of imagination of what a vacation could be. Pure joy. Innocence.

But when we got closer, it was nothing like it seemed from above. There was too much smoke! There were too many kids! The fires dangerously close and unprotected. Jay and I standing up and down like prairie dogs trying to find our children, to warn them to be careful. I was so engrossed in the action that I didn't notice her at first. Paige, standing a few feet in front of us, berating Winnie. Jay nudged me.

"Where's your goody bag?" Paige asked sternly. More than sternly. With a hint of malice. Winnie seemed to not understand the question. She stood staring up at Paige, a look of worry crossing her face.

"Where?" Paige demanded, jutting her jaw out a little so that her face looked contorted with, what, rage? Or was it power?

Winnie hung her head, her dark hair blowing in the wind, and Paige pointed to a spot on the sand. "Sit!" Paige commanded.

"If you can't keep track of your things, we won't give them to you, do you understand me?" Paige asked, still standing, her body towering over Winnie. I couldn't see Winnie's face. I hoped she wasn't crying. I feared that she was.

"Where do you think you lost the other items?" Paige was demanding. The question impossible to answer.

"Since you can't answer me and you don't have the things that you were given, I think you know what's going to happen to you," Paige continued, folding her thin, papery arms over her chest and shaking her head like she was disgusted with Winnie.

After a minute, Winnie reached inside her shorts pocket and pulled out a bouncy ball and some red tinsel pieces that had obviously fallen off something else, showing them to Paige as if they were proof of something. That she wasn't careless? That she had some toys that she hadn't lost or broken?

Paige took the ball and the tinsel from Winnie's hand and then yanked her to her feet in a sharp, jerky motion.

"Apologize," she commanded.

I heard Winnie say something, her voice slurred and whiny.

"Stand up straight and speak clearly!" Paige commanded. "No baby talk."

I hung my head away, desperate not to witness Winnie's humiliation. Straining to hear Winnie say "Sorry" more clearly. Her voice barely reaching me and not reaching Paige, at least not in the timbre and tone that she wanted.

"You're out of here!" Paige said angrily, pulling Winnie to a standing position as she marched her toward the pier, shouting, "Gene!" into the wind. "Gene!" The words harsh and demanding. The words getting washed away almost before they reached us. My ears straining to hear them long after she was gone. Hoping she would find him. Hoping Gene could help them.

When they were gone, Jay and I stood up silently. Eager to get away from the smoke, which had made its way over to us. Eager to get away from the acrid residue of Paige's anger. Not talking about it. Both of us no doubt considering what we might say about it. But before we could decide how to begin, we heard it. The booming, cannonlike sound, the sky suddenly brilliant with beaded pellets. Everyone shouting, pointing, dropping to the sand to stare up at the starbursts and glittering, flowerlike patterns of fireworks. In another moment, Paige was forgotten. The sky dazzling with color, grabbing our attention with its audacity and boldness. It never failed to amaze me. The beauty and the pageantry. The sense that everyone on the beach was in on it together. This was what mattered. This was why I'd come. For the magic and the mystery. For the memories and the happiness. I hoped my kids would always remember this. Already I was remembering it for them.

* * *

Later, in our stateroom, the kids asleep in theirs, Jay brought it up first.

"She's not a nice mother," he said, not bothering to define whom we were talking about. Who else could we be talking about?

I agreed. I said it was awful. I said it was worse than awful. It was disgusting and deeply disturbing.

"She should never have adopted," Jay said, lying back on the bed in his T-shirt and boxers, his long, lean legs making him look like the fencer he'd once been.

"What does that mean?" I asked, hopeful he knew something I didn't. Hopeful that together we could see this thing more clearly. Jay's insights usually surprisingly accurate, even if I thought they were harsh sometimes. Jay lifting his hands in a shrug, reaching for the remote.

"Tell me," I insisted, a whine creeping into my voice. More shrugging. Jay unwilling or merely unable to articulate this thing that he felt. Which made it seem more true, not less.

"Paige isn't always nasty!" I said, suddenly desperate to make Paige less bad and therefore not an obstacle we'd be forced to contend with later, when we wanted to go on vacation again or celebrate Leftovers Day. Jay not bothering to answer me, his face closed, no longer listening to my interpretation. Which only made me speak louder.

"I've lost my temper with the kids. That doesn't make me a terrible mother, does it?" I asked, my voice rising in a way that I knew Jay hated.

"Sometimes you're a little mental," Jay said matter-of-factly.

"What, now you think I'm like Paige Edwards?" I demanded.

"You just said she's not that bad!" Jay reminded me, beginning to flip through the channels on the tiny, old-fashioned television set.

I wanted to kill him. I wanted to hug him. I wanted him to hug me back and say I was nothing like Paige Edwards. Even though I sensed we were more alike than I cared to acknowledge. Both of us vulnerable. Both of us eager to cover up the things we didn't want known about us. I sat down next to Jay on the bed and asked more gently, "Did you like the fireworks?"

Jay shrugged. "They were all right."

"The kids loved them," I continued, my voice rising with manufactured enthusiasm. "Not just the fireworks, but everything. The beach. Running around the ship with all their friends. You have to admit, this was a great trip!"

More shrugging from Jay, who seemed unwilling to commit

to the topic of our shared happiness. Surfing through the limited TV channels for another minute before turning to me and saying, "Let's just say I'm not eager to go on vacation with everyone again. Paige is crazy."

I stared at him, stunned, then got up and locked myself in the bathroom with a paperback. Furious. Frustrated. Flipping through the pages of my novel without really reading them. My head roaring with confusion and irritation.

*　*　*

On the way home from the port, Jay was unaccountably cheerful, mainly, I knew, because he'd gotten his way and we were practically the first ones off the ship, the highways clear as we drove west out of the city. It was going to be an easy ride home. Which made me happy even if it made me sad. Happy that Jay wouldn't complain about traffic, but sad that he was desperate to get away. Already he was whistling. Already he was asking the boys if they'd like to stop for pancakes, which they screamed yes to. Jay laughing and full of plans for next summer as we got back in the car after breakfast. About how we'd go with the neighbors to the Cape or Ogunquit like normal people did. About how we'd never let Drew be in charge of reservations ever again.

I agreed! Someplace classier, but also fun. Happy that Jay wanted to vacation with everyone again. Thrilled that the trip had meant something to him. Paige's bad behavior something we could overlook. Which meant it wasn't really that bad. Not something we had to make a big deal about. Which I appreciated about Jay. The way he could understand nuance after all. Even if I wasn't entirely sure I understood it myself. The difference between imperfect and totally unacceptable.

DRESSES

THE LEAVES TWIRLED DOWN and the weather turned cooler. Sweat-shirts were stuffed into backpacks along with homework and lunches. Oh, how I hated the homework. The lunch packing. The daily routine of it. It was so much worse to be the parent than the kid. To supervise all of it! Not that I could tell my kids that. They hated school. Complained about their teachers. The difficulty of so much writing and arithmetic! But at least they did it. Nela admit-ting that Sebastian was struggling with simple directions. Lor-raine claiming that Gabe refused to write anything. Apparently he'd folded his arms during language arts, not even picking up a pencil. Which was brave, when you thought about it. Lorraine had been forced to think about it! She'd already had a conference with his first-grade teacher, and it was barely October. She called me constantly. About tutors. About books on tape. About whether I knew anyone who would read to Gabe nightly. I understood her. I consoled her. I told her under no circumstances to hire a part-time reader! But I didn't want to talk to her daily. Especially now that I was finally working again. I had started freelancing for my old company. Which was like running into an old boyfriend. The rush of it. To be admired still. Even if I knew what was coming. The rejection all over again. By me, who had quit to begin with. By my boss when she discovered I was no longer the person she hoped I was. Someone wholly focused on work. Someone without a personal life.

I told myself it didn't matter. I told myself I could do it. I *was* doing it. Every week another writing project. Every week another feeling of accomplishment. This despite the constant interruptions from Lorraine, who didn't get the fact that I was working.

It was Tuesday. I was finally into the rhythm of my latest assignment—updating the bank's educational web page about personal credit. And now Lorraine was calling. She'd called twice in the morning. Which I had ignored. But if I didn't pick up, she'd call me after dinner with that hurt voice, the voice that sounded accusatory and slightly injured. Like I wasn't being a good friend.

I picked up. I tried to sound like I was trying not to sound aggrieved. Lorraine didn't notice. Or else she noticed but didn't care.

"I have to tell you something," she said, as if that could explain her hounding me.

"Okay," I said, standing up from my cluttered desk to look out my side window, hoping for some relief. Disappointed by what greeted me there. My deer-eaten hedge. My droopy forsythia bush that needed to be staked or replanted. And of course the empty flower beds I'd been talking about filling for more than four summers!

"We went to Paige's for dinner last night," Lorraine said, pausing dramatically. As if this were news in and of itself. Which it was. Sort of. The air around Paige's house charged since we'd returned from our trip. The particles clanging together with anger, or at least upset, whenever Paige lost her temper with Winnie, which was frequently and over nothing. For not saying please and thank you. For not asking permission to leave the stoop and play in the yard, even if Cameron was already playing there.

"She had Yazmin waiting on us like it was the queen's dinner," Lorraine continued.

I said, "Paige always does that," not really caring about how tense the dinner was or how badly Paige had acted. Wondering instead if I should cut down my hedge or spray it with deer repellent and see if it could flourish. Which I always thought about, every single time I looked at the property line from above.

"No, I mean it was embarrassing," said Lorraine. "She was shouting orders to Yazmin like, 'Hurry up and don't forget!' I had my head bowed! I couldn't look at Paige. I mean, it was just the two of us and four kids eating chicken nuggets. Why did she have to shout at Yazmin to clear the plates?"

"Because that's what Paige does," I said, relieved that this was all Lorraine was telling me, turning away from the window.

"Wait, there's more," Lorraine continued, her voice growing slightly scratchy, as if she'd choked on a cracker. Getting up, no doubt, to close her office door.

"Go on," I said, returning to my own desk with its clutter of birthday party invitations and school notices.

"Well, you know the big third-floor bonus room Paige has?"

I knew it. I'd been amazed by how large it was the first time I'd seen it. Paige and Gene bragging that they'd designed it with their architect. Half of the elaborate space devoted to Paige's wrapping projects: a giant Parsons table on one side, surrounded by bins of expensive ribbons and exotic silk flowers. The other half lined with closets for off-season clothing and a wooden rod for gowns and formal wear. Not to mention the built-in bookshelves with rows of holiday decorations. Easter baskets and miniature ceramic bunnies. Halloween skeletons and Fourth of July banners. And, of course, Christmas wreaths and baskets of handmade ornaments. I told Lorraine I definitely knew it.

"Well, she went up there to show me this old sweater of her grandmother's—don't ask me why; it's a long story—and while I'm standing in the entrance I see a row of like twenty girls' dresses in plastic dry-cleaning bags along the wall. I'm like, 'That's a lot of dresses, Paige,' and she laughs a little and tells me they're designer dresses from Gene's sister. She handed them down to Winnie. Apparently Paige can't give them to Winnie because she doesn't take care of her things. I mean, Winnie's five and a half. How's she supposed to take care of her things?"

"Well it's not like she's poorly dressed," I said, remembering Winnie's colorful leggings and quilted fall jacket. Her pretty bathing suit at the beach in Bermuda.

"I know, it's true. So I was prepared to let it drop, but then Paige just stands there looking tired and annoyed and she says, 'You have no idea how destructive Winnie is.'"

I closed my eyes, not wanting to hear this. Even though I knew that I should.

"She says she can't let Winnie play in the basement anymore because she's breaking all of Cameron's toys. According to Paige, and this is a quote, 'the playroom reminds Winnie of the orphanage in Russia'!"

We were both silent. Speechless. Unsure how to proceed. Or at least I was. Should we believe this? And what was Winnie supposed to do while Cameron played down there? Wouldn't she feel excluded, or worse, like a second-class citizen?

"Well?" Lorraine pressed, her voice nearly jolly, as if she was keeping herself from laughing. Which I understood. The impulse to pretend this was kooky and not disturbing. The sudden release it was offering us if we both just gave in to it.

"That's craaaazy!" I said, my voice dramatic and full of playful emphasis. Leaning back in my office chair to fully embrace the mood of it.

"I mean, how does she justify it?" Lorraine persisted, chuckling a little, relieved, I could see, that this was the direction we were heading in. The entertainment value of Paige's strange parenting.

Suddenly I was eager to hear the whole story again from the beginning with greater detail and more questions answered. What did the dresses look like? Why did Gene's sister dry-clean them? Did Paige plan to give them away or keep them forever, a shrine to Winnie's misbehavior? And, of course, one last sweep through Lorraine's memory to justify the basement comment. Couldn't the babysitter just supervise the kids in the playroom?

When every dress and basement toy had been mentally picked over and examined by us, the truth of the story obscured and no longer relevant, I asked, "What about Gene?" wondering if Lorraine thought he loved Winnie, as I thought he did.

"Gene!" Lorraine said, and I could imagine her flinging her hands up in tired acceptance.

"No, seriously. Doesn't he seem to love Winnie? Or at least spend time with her and seem proud of her when Paige isn't around?"

"But it's just dresses. And toys. He's not going to get involved at that level."

I wondered if Lorraine believed this excuse, or if this was just another example of her insistence on denying anything difficult. It was true that Gene was traditional, certainly not the kind of father to get involved in day-to-day parenting. And yet. He had to know these decisions weren't normal. Certainly not kind or generous. Which made Gene seem suddenly worse to me. Fully aware and passive. Willing to just let things happen.

When we finally hung up, I went back to my assignment: writing about credit reports and credit scores. Which was so boring! But also fascinating. The nuance of the thing. The way that everyone in America was rated and scored based on their purchases and loan history. But your score was constantly changing, so you could go from being a good risk to a bad one by making very simple mistakes. Or by making no mistakes at all, just failing to understand the system. Of course, the formulas were all secret. And each credit organization rated you differently. Which made the whole process more maddening, more confusing, and impossible to understand. But I didn't need to understand it. Not fully. I just needed to explain it, which was different.

In a little while I no longer remembered Winnie and the dresses. Thrilled instead with my progress. With my output and accomplishment.

A DISAGREEMENT

THE BOYS WANTED NEW Halloween costumes. A karate suit for Josh. Some sort of ghoul mask for Lucas. I said maybe. I said, "I doubt it." I said we had plenty of old costumes already to choose from! The entire mess of hand-me-downs and gently worn purchases piled in my front hall vestibule as I looked for something suitable. Aware I was being overly practical. What kid didn't want a new Halloween costume? Remembering the time Penny and I had dressed up as Charlie's Angels when we were both in high school. Me as Farrah Fawcett and she as Kate Jackson. Both of us buying wigs, high boots, ugly polyester blouses. Which had seemed funny to us then. Which seemed funny to me now. Deciding on impulse to call Penny. The apartment phone ringing and ringing with no answer. The cell phone temporarily out of service. Which wasn't entirely unusual. My sister sometimes late on bills. Penny's absence from the apartment easily explained by the fact that she often went to the library on weekends to finish the teaching certificate. Which I was thrilled about. Even as I worried that things weren't exactly as she reported them. What if she was passed out somewhere from binge drinking?

I dialed again, which I knew was obsessive, going back downstairs to stare at myself in the hallway mirror. My green eyes staring back at me. Wishing I had some sort of answer. Aware I couldn't go on staring and dialing. Returning to my costume pile when the phone suddenly rang. My mother on the other end asking me if I'd talked to Penelope lately.

"I have," I lied impulsively, not eager to create a crisis if there wasn't one.

"I can't get a hold of her. We're supposed to go to a jewelry-making class tonight," my mother said. "At the new bead design store."

They were?

"I told her no drinking when she was with me. That's my iron-clad rule!" my mother said, her voice rising.

"I'm sure they don't want alcohol in the store," I joked, hoping to appease her before she got started. My mother ignoring me. My mother saying, "If she stands me up, I'll be furious."

"Why would she stand you up?" I asked, beginning to get worried that my mother knew something that I didn't.

"Well, as long as you talked to her, I feel better," she said. "I've called her every day to confirm the workshop and she hasn't called back. It's not cheap, you know."

"Someone's at my door," I lied. Eager to get off the phone with her. To stare out the window and contemplate whether something was actually wrong with Penny, if both my mother and I had had the same hunch. Aware this was nonsensical, even though it also made sense. To have sudden inexplicable feelings that were more often right than they were wrong. The ones you loved tied to you forever by some invisible cord of electrified knowledge. Staring out the window at the Edwardses' yard, at the ghost dangling from their maple tree. Wondering how they hoisted it so high. Imagining Gene leaning out the third-floor dormer, walking gingerly across the roofline.

* * *

My sister called me the next day to tell me she was in Wheeling, West Virginia.

"West Virginia?" I asked, astounded that she had traveled three hours from home without telling our mother.

"I came with another substitute teacher," she said, her voice booming with enthusiasm. Or was she covering up something?

"Does Phyllis know where you are?" I asked, settling back down into our hall vestibule. Avoiding the mirror, even though I couldn't help but glimpse the ugly downturn of my mouth. The look of disapproval. Even if I wasn't disapproving. It was just what my mouth looked like!

"Do you tell Phyllis everyplace you go?" my sister asked me.

"She thought you were going to a jewelry-making class with her!" I exploded.

"I didn't say yes. That was her interpretation of events. You know our mother. The world according to Phyllis!"

"We were worried!" I said, wishing I had some corner of the house to clean, aware that my housekeeper was doing it right then. That I couldn't jump up and do it, too.

"Because I wasn't in my house? I do have a life, Nicole. Or did you forget that?"

I closed my eyes and sucked in my breath.

"Is this trip for any special occasion?" I finally asked, trying to sound supportive, even though I worried there was something she was hiding. That Bob was involved somehow.

"It's a meditation retreat. They had a sliding scale and my sponsor paid the fee. I just had to pay transportation."

Sponsor? Was that AA speak? Was there more to this weekend

away? I was afraid to ask. Aware I wasn't supposed to bring up drinking with someone who drank. The other tidbit I'd gotten from my single visit to Al-Anon.

"So anyway, I'm in the countryside. It's gorgeous. I feel so much better about myself. About everything. I'm not with Bob, in case you're wondering."

"Okay," I said. Wishing to believe it.

"I know what you're thinking. That this won't last. It probably won't. That's one of the things I love about it. The idea of impermanence. I'm not even arguing with Phyllis. You should try it. It could really help you come to terms with your anger issues!"

"I'm not angry!" I said, clenching my jaw and beginning to wander around my house, wishing it were bigger, that I could get exercise while talking to her. Even though it was plenty big.

"Anyway, I know you won't want to do this, but I'm calling to ask you a favor," she said, her voice suddenly low and serious.

"Okay," I said noncommittally. Assuming it was for a large sum of money. Not that we couldn't afford it.

"I would love you to spend a weekend here with me sometime. Next month they have family weekend. They have therapists on hand to do, you know, family therapy stuff. We could even ask Phyllis to come."

I opened my mouth. Too shocked to speak.

"Nicole?"

"I'm in Massachusetts."

"You could fly out here," she said quietly.

"Let me think about it," I said, squeezing my eyes tight, wishing I wanted to go. Aware I had no intention of confronting my sister about how she had hurt me—and that I didn't want to be confronted about how I had hurt her, either.

Penny sighing. Penny saying, "I totally understand. You're not into it."

"I didn't say that," I protested, aware I should grab the out she'd given me but not willing to give up so easily. Not willing to let her down. Or myself.

"Nicole, stop. I don't think it's right. I don't want you to come here. This is actually a really special place for me and you have a tendency to overshadow things."

I swallowed. Aware that she was hurt and felt rejected. Aware that I was. Wishing there was a way to make it right between us before we got off the phone with each other. "Do you need any money?" I offered, knowing this was an easy out and hoping she would give it to me.

Penny sighing deeply. Penny saying, "I'm all set, but I want you to know how much I appreciate everything you've done for me."

I felt my sinuses flare. "I know you do," I said, my voice husky, pushing back tears. Both of us promising to try to get together when the time was right. Aware that moment was elusive and impossible to predict.

* * *

Nela invited us all to her backyard for a pre-Halloween party. The party just pizza and candy, which Lorraine was miffed about when Nela first announced it. Lorraine boldly suggesting that Nela hire a guy she'd heard about who could barbecue and wait on us. Which Nela pointedly rejected before asking me if I wanted to help her with the setup. Nela friendlier to me since our return from Bermuda. Which made me nervous even as I embraced it. Uncertain we'd learned the same life lessons from the childhoods we'd both survived and chosen not to talk about directly. But I was happy to help her. Nela standing at the end of her driveway wearing a sexy Catwoman outfit as I approached for my duties. Drew next to her, dressed as a motorcycle guy, or maybe that was just his outfit. Both of them looking intently at Paige and Gene, who were standing in the street in front of them. I waved and called to everyone, wearing my Charlie's Angels wig and ungainly seventies style boots.

No one seemed to hear me. Or see me. Or they heard me but seemed determined to continue to stare at one another. Gene without a costume, in his customary loafers and a cuffed sport shirt. Paige dressed as a dogcatcher in high boots and a short pleated skirt, a shiny black cap resting atop her silver-white hair.

"You look great," I called to Paige, determined to make someone notice me. Confused about why they were all in the street when the party didn't start for another half hour. But already Paige was saying something to Nela that I couldn't catch. When I was a few yards away, I heard Paige say, "She's a child. How can you defend a babysitter over a child?"

I stopped in the road, not wanting to get closer, feeling suddenly ridiculous in my Farrah Fawcett wig and boots. Nela shook her head like she couldn't believe what she was hearing, and then a red head bobbed into vision. It was Nela and Drew's babysitter—Colleen. She was standing behind Drew, crying, rubbing her eyes with her fist like a child.

Nela turned toward Colleen and said something softly, and Colleen walked up the path that led to the Guzman-Venieros' glass sunroom. We all watched her leave, as if she were on TV or in a movie.

When the door shut behind Colleen, Nela crossed her arms over her chest and said to Paige, "You have no right to talk to my babysitter like that," her voice full of attitude and more Spanish accent than I'd ever known she possessed. Like she was back in East Boston, where I knew she'd grown up.

Paige spluttered for a minute. Uncertain, I could tell, how to proceed. She didn't know this side of Nela. Clearly didn't know anyone like this version of Nela. A woman who might swear and call her a name. Who might even hit her if provoked.

Gene, suddenly aware that Paige was out of her league, or perhaps just used to defending Paige whenever she got into these situations, stepped in front of her as if both protecting Paige and making her irrelevant. He looked at Drew instead of Nela and said, "Let's be reasonable," his red face betraying his anger, his voice steady and confident. "Colleen was one hundred percent wrong. You don't say to a child, 'I don't know how you have any friends left.'"

Drew rubbed his hands up and down over his eyes and his beard, obviously trying to figure something out. I sensed he was angry. But clearly in a bind, too. He liked Gene. Watched baseball with him. He couldn't yell at Gene. He couldn't dismiss what he was saying. But you could tell he wanted to. Or rather, he wanted Gene to dismiss it, to drop the protector routine and be a normal guy friend to him. Which clearly Gene was not going to do.

Finally Drew said, "Look, it was probably a little insensitive, but c'mon. Cameron kept swinging the baseball bat around. And Colleen kept telling him not to. And after the twenty-seventh time, Colleen lost her patience. We all would have lost our patience after the third time, or even the second."

"I will not stand for this," Paige said, stepping out again so that she was in her dogcatcher suit alongside Gene, a fact that was at once both disturbing and silly. Did she have any idea how ludicrous she appeared?

Paige said, "I want Colleen to come out here right now and

apologize to me and apologize to Cameron, and then I want you to send her home. I am not coming to a Halloween party with an abusive babysitter who is unkind to my son!"

I waited to see how Nela would get out of this. Would she walk away and let Drew settle it? Have Colleen apologize and get Drew to talk to Gene, who would talk Paige off the ledge? That was the only way. Silent surrender. Compromise. We needed to have the Halloween party. We needed a babysitter to handle all of these children!

Very, very quietly, Nela said, "You're the one who should apologize. Number one, you screamed at Colleen without giving her a chance to explain herself," she said, holding up her thin, crooked finger and pointing it at Paige. "And number two, you're the one who spoils Cameron and lets him disrespect the babysitter," she said, pulling out her second finger. "And let's face it, *you're* the one who's abusive. You treat Winnie like a second-class citizen. You didn't even buy her a real Halloween costume!" Nela said, her voice finally rising as if to make her point more believable. The argument about the Halloween costume thin and insubstantial as soon as she said it.

And yet she'd said it. Had attached the word *abuse* to Paige, and Paige was immediately taken aback, then stricken.

"How dare you!" Paige said, her face crumpling, then openly crying, shaking her head like she knew all along that Nela wasn't her true friend. Then turning and running toward her lawn in her high boots and short skirt, the cap obviously pinned to her head, teetering but never falling as she ran up her front path.

I knew I should leave then, get away from the ugliness and pretend I hadn't seen this. I could hear Jay's voice urging me to. But I was rooted to my spot, determined to see how it would play out, already thinking how I might salvage it. The hurt feelings. The group. How I might maneuver everyone's interpretations slightly so that no permanent damage was done.

In front of me, Gene suddenly stood up straighter, took a deep breath, and started counting on his own fingers. "One, you are never home," he said, looking meanly at Nela. "Two, you have no idea what goes on with your kids. And three, Sebastian's got massive issues, and you are in complete denial about it!" And with that, Gene calmly swiveled on his foot, turned his back to Nela, and started to slowly walk back to his own house, his brown loafers shiny in the late-afternoon sun.

When Gene had gone inside, Nela and Drew both looked at me, their faces contorted with anger and fear. Clearly concerned about Sebastian. Clearly looking for me to take their side. It was true that Sebastian had delays. He was six and still didn't speak much or seem to be able to follow a simple board game. It was something we had all tried to ignore and had never mentioned directly. Even if we all thought it and subtly alluded to it. With eye movements and furtive glances. And now everything was laid bare. Our fears about Sebastian. Our misgivings about the Edwardses' parenting. How could I support one and not the other? They were either both true or both false. And it was important—for their feelings, for the future of our neighborhood, and for the peace in which we coexisted—that they both be untrue. Patently false.

"Sebastian is fine," I said, a tightness in the base of my throat as I tried to make my words sound felt and not forced.

"I know he's fine," Nela retorted, not looking at me, looking up toward the blue sky and thick, leafy branches that hovered beautifully above us. Willing herself not to cry, I suspected. Willing herself not to let her tough-girl persona be deflated by some asshole's comment. She had told me that this was her motto that day we'd traded stories on the cruise. That the shit people said to her didn't bother her, and that she had taught her kids the same thing. To be proud. To be confident. To do what they saw fit and not to worry about what anyone else thought.

"I think you may have been a little bit harsh with Paige," I ventured, worried that Paige was watching me, peering through her bedroom window and judging me for talking to Nela. I didn't want to take sides. I didn't want there to be sides! I needed us all to get back to the place where we accepted each other's imperfections and kept our worst opinions to ourselves. It wasn't like Nela was anyone's role model for perfect motherhood. She worked sixty hours a week in her office and did paperwork at home over the weekend!

Nela looked at me and said, "I know about the dresses."

Drew said, "Nela doesn't put up with child abuse."

"Child abuse?" I asked, incredulous. How was it that we were seriously talking about child abuse? Even Nela had to know that withholding hand-me-down dresses did not constitute child abuse. Nor did her failure to buy Winnie a store-bought Halloween costume. Wasn't Paige letting Winnie dress as a farmer? In overalls with a bandanna around her hair. Which was not nothing!

Nela shaking her head at me. Nela chewing her cheek like she wanted to say something but wasn't sure that she should. But already the kids were flying at us from all directions, Lucas shouting, "I brought ghost cookies," while Josh yelled, "I made them, too!" and tried to grab the plate from him. The plate toppling as Jay ran to catch it, the platter saved but the cookies sliding out onto the sidewalk.

"It's okay. They're ghosts," I said, rushing over to reassure Josh, who was already crying. Lucas oblivious to the upset he'd caused, walking blithely into the Guzman-Venieros' backyard while

Sebastian rushed out to compare eyeballs with Gabe, both of them dressed in identical yellow Minion suits.

Nela forced to change gears, to welcome everyone, forcing me to act normal, too, joining the stream of children as they pushed and shouted their way through Nela and Drew's back gate, the folding tables uncovered, the packets of tablecloths and plates still in their shrink wrap. Which embarrassed me. How ugly everything looked. How I'd failed to help Nela set up.

Nela unaware of how messy it all appeared, or else not caring. Nela telling the children that the limbo was a Puerto Rican Halloween tradition. Cuing the music and lining everyone up to try it. Asking me to demonstrate, which was fine with me. The limbo one of the few physical pursuits I was naturally good at. Nela laughing after my first success. Nela lowering the bar just inches from the ground and goading me to try it again, forcing me to fully arch my back, to stumble and fall, even as I insisted I could do it.

* * *

Later that night, the kids stuffed with candy and watching TV in the basement, Jay long since gone home to peruse the Internet and make overseas phone calls, Nela recounted the story about the babysitter to the rest of us. Omitting the Sebastian comment, but not the accusation she'd made about Paige being abusive to Winnie.

"How are you going to resolve this?" Lorraine wanted to know, certain it would be resolved. Determined to not let something as stupid as a fight with a college-aged babysitter derail the closeness of our friendship group.

Drew looked surprised. He gave Lorraine a squinty-eyed look

before saying what he'd already said without saying it. "Are you crazy? We're not resolving it."

"And what, now you're officially not friends with them?" Lorraine asked, her mouth hanging open in disbelief.

"They're mad at us, too. About not firing Colleen. So it's mutual," Drew said, standing up to refill his wineglass, grabbing a handful of M&M's from the plastic pumpkin as he went.

"You're going to end a friendship over a fight with a babysitter?" Lorraine half shouted at his back. "I mean, c'mon. That's not even the truth of it."

Drew stopped halfway to the bar, turning to face us. "Yeah, well, exactly. That's not the whole truth of it. The whole truth of it is that we think they're mistreating Winnie. I know you're worried, too. Nela's more convinced of it than any of us."

"If you just stop talking to them, you won't have accomplished anything," Lorraine protested. "If you really think something's wrong, you should talk it over with them. Help them."

Nela rolling her eyes, ignoring Lorraine's suggestion.

"What do you think about this?" Lorraine demanded, turning to me for my input.

I thought Paige was difficult in general and not that kind to Winnie in particular. I thought Drew couldn't care less about how Paige treated her daughter, but was trying to please Nela. I thought Nela was determined to grab the moral high ground for some reason. Which was infuriating to me, even though a piece of me admired her. For making a decision. For not being afraid of the consequences. Even if I was determined not to let her destroy things. Not to abandon Winnie.

"I think it will blow over," I said, looking toward Nela for confirmation she refused to give to me.

PRAYERS

LORRAINE PRETENDED NOTHING HAD happened when she saw
Paige the next morning, which gave Paige the courage to pretend
the same. Both of them friendly, according to Lorraine, who called
to tell me about it as soon as she got to her office. Nela left for work
by eight most mornings, and wasn't back until nine in the evening,
a hardship for her family but a convenience when it came to ignoring people. I knew she would ignore Paige and Gene indefinitely.
And Drew was a guy, which excused him from nearly everything.
At least in his book. He practically told me so when he drove by
on the way to the gym Monday morning. Drew rolling down his
window to complain about the Williamses' lawn, which had gone
to weed, then shrugging his wide shoulders when I asked whether
he would ever come to a group gathering again. Which left the true
work of reconciliation to me. I knew I should call Paige, text her,
tell her something untrue and reassuring, something that would
maintain the facade of our friendship without promising anything
too taxing. But instead I avoided her. I didn't walk near her house to
gather up my boys from their street games, didn't slow my car and
roll down my window to chat as we drove by each other. Although

I did wave with extra enthusiasm. To be sure she knew I wasn't mad at her. To convince her not to be mad at me!

And then, two weeks after the Halloween incident, there she was: on the sidewalk, impossible to miss when I stepped out on my porch. The late-autumn sunshine making us both squint as we waved to each other. Paige in a navy peacoat, ankle boots, a pretty midcalf skirt.

"Hi, hon," Paige called. Wanly. Nervous, I could tell, about where she stood with me. I walked down my front path and gave her a hug, both of us placing our arms carefully around each other's shoulders and giving a little squeeze. When we separated, there was a strange awkwardness, both of us no doubt recalling the fight and wondering how to spin it. If I mentioned it, I'd have to tell her how wrong I thought Nela and Drew were. Which I couldn't do. But if I didn't say anything supportive, she'd know I agreed with them—which I didn't want her to think, either. It would prevent me from helping her, which I believed I could do, especially now that Paige was looking at me hopefully, like she knew she'd been wrong and wished to make amends. Or at least that's how I took it.

"You and Gene and the kids should come to lunch this Sunday," I said, the idea popping into my head unbidden. The idea taking form as soon as I'd said it. Hopeful that if we had lunch, just our two families, we'd share the kind of intimacy we used to share. Which wasn't intimacy at all but a kind of effortful joviality. Paige on her best behavior. Paige willing to listen.

"We would love that!" Paige said, her face lighting up, turning pinker at the cheeks, reassuring me that I'd done the right thing. Reassuring me that the other Paige, the one who made an effort, was ready to make a comeback.

* * *

Jay shrugged when I told him what I'd done and then reminded me to order Gene's favorite sandwich. The one with the roast beef and the thinly sliced Swiss cheese. The deli sandwiches still wrapped in wax paper in their bakery boxes when the Edwardses arrived on the dot of twelve o'clock, Paige in a long, pleated skirt and white blouse, Gene in a blue gingham oxford shirt that was far too loose around the collar, the skin of his face strangely rubbery, nearly masklike.

When the kids were sent to the basement to play, the sandwiches unwrapped and the pickles still gleaming in their plastic tubs, Paige began to talk in a stream of rushed emotion. "As you know, it's been really tough. Or maybe you don't know. But the thing is, Winnie is not who she seems to be. She certainly isn't the kind of child we were expecting," Paige began, not reaching for the food, sitting at the head of my kitchen table as if she'd been invited here to give some sort of lecture. Which I did not want. I wanted a conversation!

"We told the authorities, 'We do not want a special-needs child.' And guess what? The adoption agency lied to us. The social worker lied to us. The orphanage lied to us. Winnie has a lot of special needs! The lazy eye was the least of it. She doesn't listen. She has no idea how to be part of a family. She does deliberately mean things to Cameron and blames everyone else for her behavior. We kept thinking it was us. What were we doing wrong? But guess what? It's not us. We're doing everything we can to love a normal, well-adjusted child. But Winnie's not normal. She's not well adjusted. So everything we're doing doesn't work for her. Get this: she has oppositional defiant disorder."

"What does that mean?" Jay asked doubtfully, reaching for his sandwich before anyone else had taken theirs. Which annoyed me to no end. His lack of manners. His belief that he could actually get to the bottom of things!

"It means that at home, Winnie can't be part of our family. She seems okay one minute, listening to music, even dancing. But in the next, she's angry. Resentful. If I ask her to clear a plate, she'll throw a fit, become destructive," Paige said, unaware of Jay's skepticism, relieved that she was being allowed to steam on. "It seems like Winnie is fine, which is why you think she's cute," she said, looking pointedly at me. "But it's fake. It's manipulative. In a house, alone with her family, she can't control herself."

I nodded. I thought it strange that the syndrome would be limited to just one setting, but then anything was possible. "I was a psych major," I said, hoping this would make Paige see I was on her side. Or could at least buy into some of what she was saying.

"She will likely have problems the rest of her life," Paige said gravely, as if I hadn't spoken.

"Have you ever heard about reciprocity theory?" I asked, pulling up a long-ago memory from a class on parenting theories.

"She will probably be promiscuous," Paige added, nodding her head solemnly. Gene reaching for a sandwich and nodding along with her.

I took a deep breath and said, "Reciprocity theory is fascinating. It's the idea that a mother and child read each other's signals and reflect them back to each other. Like if a baby is colicky and crying and the mother reacts with irritation when she's holding the baby, the baby will cry more," I said. Hopeful Paige could hear me. Hopeful she wouldn't feel judged by me. I'd purposely said "colicky." I'd purposely made it about a baby. But Paige could draw parallels. Paige could be introspective when she wanted to be. She'd gone to a support group, hadn't she?

Across from me, Paige's face was growing narrower, as if she was clenching her jaw in an effort not to talk over me. When I was through, she merely shook her head and said, "Look, there are things with adoption that you can't understand. That we didn't understand until we found this specialist who diagnosed Winnie's condition. These kids who have been institutionalized are highly manipulative. They make it seem like they're normal in public, but in private, they're a nightmare. You can never really understand it until you've lived it!"

"It's true," Gene said, jumping in.

"Like if I had a birthday party for her, she'd ruin it!" Paige said.

"When's her birthday?" I asked, stunned that I didn't know this. Realizing suddenly that I'd never been to a party for Winnie. She'd been here nearly two years already. Surely she'd had a birthday.

"It was last weekend. It doesn't matter. She doesn't even know," Paige said dismissively, finally reaching for the container of coleslaw and helping herself to a serving. Wasn't she going to eat a sandwich? Meanwhile, Jay was fishing in the plastic container for another pickle, holding it up, motioning for me to get something to cut it with. Thank God he wasn't saying anything!

I stood up. I got the knife. I asked, "So where are you guys going for the holidays?" eager now to move the conversation away from Winnie's disorders. Away from the narrative Paige was spinning. That the unrest at home was all Winnie's fault. That she, Paige, had nothing to do with the situation.

"Nevis," Paige said, looking at Gene pointedly. "It's the one Caribbean island I've always wanted to visit."

"Pip needs a break," Gene said, tilting his head in sympathy toward Paige before taking a bite of his sandwich.

"Never heard of it," Jay commented drily.

I shot Jay a look. I didn't want a confrontation. Even though I knew he was thinking what I was thinking. That these people were fucked. That we were fucked for having them in our kitchen. The way they spoke about Winnie deeply disturbing. Even if it was all true.

Jay smiled his sly smile at me, neither agreeing nor disagreeing with my unspoken edict to please behave.

Gene said, "I booked the Four Seasons," looking at Jay and nodding his head slightly to imply how much it had cost him.

Jay said, "Awesome," in a flat way that clearly meant he was judging Gene. At least to me, who knew he hated beach vacations and especially hated anyone who bragged about how much money they were spending.

And then, before I could speak, change the topic, make things more normal, there was Cameron. He'd climbed the basement steps and now stood at the corner of the table, the sunlight falling on his golden-blond hair.

"Hi, Cameron," Paige said affectionately, reaching for his arm.

"Mom, Winnie's ruining our game!" Cameron whined, the whine of older siblings everywhere when they are used to getting their way and aren't getting it.

"Do you want me to go down and referee?" I offered, eager to escape the kitchen. Eager to see what the actual situation was.

"No, no, sit. Let Pip handle it," Gene insisted.

"Send Winnie up," Paige said, and Cameron raced off to the basement.

"Mommy says to go upstairs right now!" Cameron shouted, his

voice trailing up the steps behind him. In another moment, Winnie appeared. She was smiling as always, but nervous, too, her eyes darting from Gene to Paige.

"Now, Winnie," Paige began. "It's not nice to interfere with other people's games."

I looked down at my half eaten sandwich. This was wrong. Didn't Paige possess even the most basic parenting skills? She hadn't asked Cameron what specifically had happened. And she didn't bother to find out from Winnie if it was even true.

Across from me, Winnie nodded her head in agreement, her chin staying dipped, not looking at Paige.

"Winnie, look at me," Paige commanded.

Winnie raised her eyes to meet her mother's. Reluctantly. Nervously.

"What do we say when we've done something wrong?" Paige demanded.

Winnie started to fidget with her hands and wiggle her hips from side to side. Clearly afraid. Or at least nervous.

"See, she's manipulating you right now," Paige said, turning to us. "She's trying to be cute and make you feel sorry for her and take the focus off what she's done wrong."

I wanted this to stop. I wanted Paige to leave. For Paige to cease being my friend and therefore my responsibility.

Paige said, "Winnie, what do we do when we get fidgety?"

Winnie continued to stand there looking at her mother, smiling faintly. Nodding in agreement like she didn't understand what was being asked of her. Or preferred not to. I felt like crying.

"We pray for forgiveness, remember?" Paige asked, pulling out one of my kitchen chairs and motioning Winnie to kneel on the floor, positioning her hands together on the seat. "Pray with me,"

Paige said to Winnie, and together they chanted faintly, "Oh father in heaven, lead me, guide me, walk beside me. Help me find the way."

When they were through, Paige turned to us, Winnie's hands still clasped in piety, and said, "They told me she's never going to be okay, but I think prayer goes a long way."

I felt my mouth go dry, the taste of something sour at the back of my throat. Aware that Paige wanted me to say something supportive of her recent demonstration. I rose from the table, clearing the dirty dishes, refusing to give it to her.

A GIFT

JAY CAME HOME THE next day with two large rectangular gift boxes, each one wrapped and tied with a ribbon, even though it was nobody's birthday and not even close to our anniversary. Not that Jay necessarily gave presents on holidays to begin with. Jay once surprising me with a sapphire bracelet because another guy in the office had dragged him to Fortunoff to get his wife a birthday present. Forgetting Mother's Day two years in a row after that.

The kids jumping up and down when they came into the kitchen to greet their father and saw the presents on the island, asking if they were for them and could they please open them immediately. Lucas going so far as to remove the yellow ribbon before Jay grabbed his hand and said, "Stop!" and "Please learn to control yourself." Which wasn't the mood I was going for in such a festive moment, even if I was glad Jay was stepping in for once.

"First," Jay said, after he'd herded the boys to the kitchen table, "I want to tell you that it's nobody's birthday, it's not Chanukah, and we don't celebrate Easter."

"But the Edwardses do!" Josh chimed in. His eyes serious, his full cheeks slack as he waited for Jay's reply.

"Yes, some of our friends do," Jay said, cringing, I knew, at the mention of their name. The memory of the lunch like a bad odor that suddenly wafted into the kitchen. The children unaware and focused solely on the boxes.

"Is it candy?" Josh asked, his face growing more animated.

Jay held up his hand for silence. "The point is, it's not a special occasion exactly, but we did have a special thing happen today." And with that, Jay reached into his suit pocket and pulled out an orange-and-white ticket, saying, "We had a winning lottery ticket!"

The boys started to shout, jumping out of their chairs to grab the ticket Jay was now dangling above them, my own heart starting to pound as I came close and snatched it from him, studying the numbers and squinting at the front and then the back, disappointed it didn't say what it was worth, feeling giddy that we just might have won a seven-figure jackpot.

"It was for five dollars," Jay said, laughing.

I hit him on the arm and the boys grabbed his legs and then his waist, trying to push him to the ground, to grab the ticket away from him. Jay laughing and feigning a fall and then gently peeling Lucas and Josh off of him.

"Okay, so it's not a lot of money," he said, herding the boys back to their seats at the table, "but it got me thinking about the time I won five dollars at a fair once, and how I spent it right away on some model rockets. That money was the sweetest money I ever spent."

"Are you sure we didn't win a million dollars?" Lucas asked. "Is this a trick within a trick?"

"Even though we didn't win a million dollars," Jay said, "I left work early and went to a hobby shop in the city and bought a present for us to work on together as a family."

"Are both boxes for us?" Josh asked, his brown eyes growing wider.

"And while I was at it, I got a present for Winnie, who had a birthday recently but didn't have a party."

I swallowed, feeling tears rise in my throat and behind my eyes.

"Maybe Mommy can open it with Winnie this week," he said, not looking at me, which I appreciated. Not sure I wouldn't burst into tears if he did.

"But tonight, we're going to open our present," Jay said, lifting the larger box off the island and bringing it to the table.

The boys pulled off the thick yellow ribbon and ripped into the royal-blue wrapping paper. Inside was a model sailboat, a picture of the finished product in pale balsa wood on the cover. There was silence as the boys considered it, then Lucas said, "Oh."

"Boys?" I prompted. "What do you say?"

"Thank you," they both said. Weakly. With no enthusiasm. Both of them staring glumly at the box. The cover said there were more than two hundred pieces, and they'd never so much as built a LEGO spaceship before. But I knew Jay wanted to teach them this thing that he had so enjoyed doing as a kid. Aware that our little tête-à-tête with the Edwardses over lunch had no doubt triggered something deep within him. Even though he would deny it.

In another moment, Jay got out the scissors and carefully opened the box, showing the boys the instructions and pointing out the different steps they'd have to take. Josh leaning over to examine the tiny paint bottles and brushes, excited, I could tell, that the finished product might include some decorative touches. Lucas silent, focused on the manual, more focused than I'd ever seen him. Studying the blueprint for the ship, nodding his head and looking at the pieces like he wanted to understand something about them.

"Should we start tonight?" Jay asked. The boys nodding solemnly. I was relieved to escape and leave them to their building.

"We can't let Mommy go, can we?" Jay asked, causing me to roll my eyes and keep walking toward the living room. Desperate to relax.

"Do you guys think I'd buy something for everyone and not for Mommy?" Jay asked loudly as I was just about in the hallway.

I turned around and went back to the kitchen, hands on my hips, smiling, asking, "Where is it?"

Jay going out to the mudroom and coming back with a giant white box with handles attached, the box heavy when I tried lifting it.

"You got me a bowling ball?"

Josh and Lucas jumping up and down, desperate to open another present, which I let them. The boys disappointed when they couldn't lift the machine out of the box and then confused by what it was when we set it down on the island.

"It's a Mixmaster," I explained, beaming at the red color, the splash of brightness in our otherwise brown and gray kitchen.

"But we have a mixer," Josh said.

"This is the one Mommy wanted," Jay explained. Which shocked me. That he'd remembered my hesitation from that long-ago day of our gift registry. That he knew I still wanted one.

"Thank you," I said, reaching up to hug him, resting my face against his neck and breathing in the musky smell of his skin. The kids coming in to hug our legs, all of us locked for a moment in an awkward, many limbed embrace.

A STORM

AN ICE STORM DESCENDED over the holidays: high winds, sleety rain, the branches covered with slick, icy remains. We couldn't go out. The kids couldn't play. Power was out for three days and we all bemoaned the fact that we hadn't gone away. The holiday party canceled. Nela claiming she had a family conflict, no one eager to get together given our misgivings about one another.

The absence of company leaving me too much time to think about the situation just down the street from me. My mood shifting violently whenever I thought about the Edwardses—which was often. My head full of ideas about what I could say or do to help improve things. My conviction strongest in the gray light of dawn, when I couldn't sleep, my body turning ceaselessly, my heart beating wildly.

And then, toward the end of winter vacation, the Edwardses due home any day, the roads finally cleared, Lorraine stopped by after work to tell me she'd spoken with Paige. Lorraine always adamant that everyone keep up with her, even while they were away. Hurt and insulted if you didn't call her at least once, which clearly Paige understood.

"She said the hotel was worth every penny. They have waiter

service on the beach and a private plunge pool in their room," Lorraine reported as soon as her car had rolled to a stop in front of my driveway. Lorraine's face in shadow inside the dark interior of her Range Rover.

"That's great," I said listlessly, leaning into the car with my neck and shoulders so that I could see Lorraine more clearly. Lorraine wearing her customary black suit, a strand of pearls resting on her silk collar.

Lorraine nodding. Lorraine saying, "She said Winnie loves the ocean. She's taking swimming lessons at the kids' camp every morning."

I smiled. Happy for Winnie. Happy for Paige. Happy they were enjoying their time as a family. Lorraine eyeing me carefully. Waiting for me to say something. What was she expecting?

"She told me she had a great lunch with you and Jay before they left," Lorraine said. Obviously fishing. Obviously peeved I hadn't told her about the date to begin with. Lorraine interested in everyone's get-togethers. Especially this one, apparently. Convinced I'd hidden it for a reason. Which wasn't false, exactly.

"Yeah. We invited them for sandwiches," I said, not sure I felt like getting into my true intentions, aware that I'd failed. Aware I'd quite possibly been misguided to begin with.

"She said that it was a relief to tell you guys everything. That they feel so much better that you're not like Nela and Drew. That you listen!"

I felt a sudden shakiness in my body, my adrenaline rising. Disturbed that Paige was spinning this story for me. Disturbed that I'd been weak enough, or uncertain enough, not to share it with anyone else.

"It was okay," I offered, feeling the shaking growing stronger.

"Did she seem good? Did Gene?" Lorraine pressed. Obviously wanting my answer to be hopeful. Conciliatory. Wanting, no doubt, for me to tell her that next year we'd definitely have our holiday party again. That everything was moving in the right direction.

"Do you realize that Paige and Gene have never had a birthday party for Winnie?" I blurted out, guilty for repeating it but relieved to be sharing it. Uncertain whether this was backstabbing or necessary.

Lorraine shutting off her engine. A single line appearing between her eyebrows, which I'd never noticed before. Lorraine fiddling with her car keys for a moment before saying, "A lot of people don't have parties for their kids when they're little. They think it's a waste of money."

I sighed. I knew this. But did Paige and Gene ever worry about money? And besides, this wasn't their excuse. I closed my eyes, then opened them, determined to make Lorraine believe me. That something was wrong. That something didn't sit right.

When I opened them, Lorraine was staring at me quietly. Not trying to change the subject for once.

I told her about the oppositional defiant disorder. I told her how Paige claimed that Winnie didn't have any symptoms in public, which was why we hadn't seen the problems. That Paige said I didn't know the real Winnie. That she was manipulative. Falsely cute. Hoping I was capturing the flavor of the conversation, not putting my already biased spin on it.

Lorraine listened intently, fingering her pearls and occasionally looking over my shoulder, taking in my porch and my walkway, like she was preparing to comment on my new low-level lighting. Not that I blamed her. Not exactly. The story about the Edwardses stifling. Claustrophobic. The story without beginning or end and certainly lacking any concrete conclusion. But I forced myself to continue. Forced myself to describe the praying routine. To try to explain how uncomfortable it had been.

When I finished, there was a long and awkward silence. Both of us no doubt trying to sort out fact from fiction. Aware we knew next to nothing about adoption. Even less about childhood psychiatric disorders. Even if we thought we knew a lot about Paige. Her tendency to blame other people for everything. Her increasingly unkind demeanor toward Winnie.

"They found a babysitter for Winnie. In Nevis," Lorraine finally said.

I stared at her. Waiting for her to go on.

"She said the trip's so much better now that they don't have to revolve their day around Winnie."

I felt like crying. Pinpricks pushing at my eyes. Not wanting to cry in front of Lorraine, who would no doubt think I was overreacting. Maybe she wouldn't think that, but I couldn't imagine crying in front of her. Showing her how helpless I felt, how cruel I believed the world could be. Lorraine, who believed every problem had a solution. Lorraine, who devoted her entire waking life to telephone calls with clients and friends. To planning her social calendar and offering people advice about where to go on vacation. All her actions and reactions merely proof of what I knew and wished I didn't about her: that she refused to deal with the truly tragic and completely unfixable. Disturbed by Lorraine's complacency, still unsure whether Winnie fell into that category.

"Maybe she'll bring the new nanny home with her," I joked. Willing myself not to let my voice catch. Not to let Lorraine know how upset I was.

Lorraine laughed, adding, "Or maybe she'll leave Winnie there with her."

The air suddenly prickly between us. The joking abruptly over. Lorraine aware that she had crossed a line, spoken a fear that neither of us had ever acknowledged. That Paige seemed not to love Winnie like a real daughter, that she might regret her decision to have adopted her. The harsh possibility making my chest hurt, my breath catch.

I looked toward Lorraine to see if she would add anything. When she didn't, I asked, "Now what?" not because I expected Lorraine to have a solution—I knew there was no solution—but because I knew that Lorraine would still think there was one.

Lorraine swallowed, then looked at me seriously and said, "Remember when you took Winnie to that Build-A-Bear place? Maybe you could do that again. Or something like that."

I breathed deeply, disappointed that this was all Lorraine could come up with. Even though I appreciated the sentiment, the simplicity not entirely without merit. Nodding my head as I considered it. Hopeful that giving Winnie some love was better than nothing. Remembering the rocks I'd picked up on the beach in Bermuda last summer. The single streaks of white in their dull gray backgrounds making the stones something to collect, something to cherish.

A VISIT

PAIGE CALLED ME BEFORE I could call her. The day after she got home from Nevis, her name flashing on my caller ID. Staring at the phone while my hands turned clammy—not yet ready to talk to her. To be fakely nice to her! Lucas shouting, "It's the Edwardses!", picking up the receiver before I could stop him. Lucas saying, "My mommy's right here" and handing me the phone, which made me want to slap him. For being so impulsive. For not letting me be the grown-up and answer my own damn telephone! My temper roaring in my head. Resisting the urge to squeeze his arm in punishment. Trying to breathe deeply, willing myself to say, "Hi, Paige!" with friendly enthusiasm.

"We're back!" Paige cooed into the phone.

"You are!" I said. Trying to sound as enthusiastic as she did.

"It was amazing. The hotel was incredible."

"Lorraine told me!" I said, hoping to cut her off at the pass. Hoping to find out what she was calling about! Paige launching into the story that I'd already heard from Lorraine. About the plunge pool and the waiter service. About the swim lessons and the babysitting amenity. I murmured surprise and then pleasure. I murmured support and agreed it was fantastic. Forced to pretend I was interested.

"Anyway, besides my blah, blah, blah, I have a favor to ask you," Paige said when she'd finally finished her story. "You can say no. But I know you once said you wouldn't mind taking Winnie. And you have such a nice way with her."

"Anything, Paige. You know that," I said. Meaning it. Which was so confusing. How well I lied. How I still sort of meant it!

"Would you mind taking Winnie this Thursday while your boys are at soccer? I have Cameron's dress rehearsal for the school play, and for once it would be nice to not have Winnie ruin something."

"Of course I don't mind," I assured her. "Drop her right after school," I offered, hanging up the phone with a mixture of disgust and fear.

*   *   *

On Thursday, Paige dropped off Winnie at my house, obviously in a hurry. Starting to back out of my driveway before Winnie had even reached my porch steps. Waving at me on the porch and saying, "Thanks!" and "Talk to you soon" as she rolled down the street and away from me.

I thought about getting out the gift that Jay had bought for Winnie, a giant dollhouse that required minimal assembly. But already I was worried we couldn't build it in the time allotted to us. Aware that if I gave it to Winnie in the box, she might never see it again. That Paige might keep it away from her, insisting she didn't take care of her things. Instead, I led Winnie upstairs to Josh's room to pick out a book, pointing out the shellacked cardboard covers with the frogs and the mice, the lions and the chipmunks. We sat cross-legged on the carpet, Winnie next to me even though

I wanted to put her in my lap, to hug her and kiss the top of her head. But I couldn't. It felt wrong, like promising more than I could give her.

Instead, we sat knee to knee, the sunlight falling on us, the books scattered in a half circle in front of us, the chosen book stiff and sleek in my hand, the cover nearly new. Josh and I had read it every day for two weeks one summer and then forgotten about the book completely. It was about Rabbit and Froggy. I remembered the story instantly. How Rabbit lived alone and liked it that way. How slowly Froggy had eased his way into Rabbit's life. As I read, I told Winnie she could play the part of Froggy. She should knock on the hardwood floor next to the rug whenever I said, "Knock, knock, knock, it's Froggy!"

She knocked. Sometimes. Usually I had to remind her. She seemed happy in a distant, confused sort of way. Like she wasn't sure what was happening in the story. Or what to do about the knocking. Which surprised me. I thought she was more aware than this. Understood more. Had I made all that up? Was there something to what Paige had said about her disabilities and limitations?

I tried to push Winnie. Just a little. "You say, 'It's me, Froggy,'" I suggested. "After you knock." Winnie nodded. Cautiously. As if I were giving her a test she was uncertain she would pass. I turned the page. Froggy was at Rabbit's door again.

"Knock, knock, knock," I read, looking at Winnie expectantly.

Winnie smiled. Her giant American smile that split her face in two. Her smile telegraphing something pure and joyful from the inside. I was certain it was the smile that had gotten her adopted, or at least to the top of some list.

"I like that!" she said, nodding her head and smiling emphatically now.

187

What did she like? Was she following along or just trying to please me?

"Do you remember the knocking?" I asked.

She nodded some more, tilting her head sideways to smile up at me, almost posing. Wasn't that what Paige said she did? Pose? Act one way in public and another with her family? It unnerved me. Did she understand the story?

"Do you remember what you're supposed to do when I say, 'Knock, knock, knock'?" I asked in my gentlest, most encouraging voice. If she couldn't remember, I would understand something about her. That she had limited short-term memory. Her cognition most likely impaired. Winnie looked at me blankly, the smile fading slightly.

"Let's knock!" I said, desperate for her to catch on.

Winnie knocked.

"And now what do you say?" I asked.

"I say, 'It's me, Froggy'?" Winnie asked, her voice faint, uncertain. But right. She was right. She had remembered. She could be taught! I thought, Screw Paige! Even if Winnie was nowhere near where she should be for her age. She was six—she should be nearly reading by now.

We finished the story. Sometimes Winnie knocked, but mainly I did. Sometimes I would ask her to repeat something, make the voice of Rabbit, say the lines for Froggy. And she said some of them. Would get halfway through a sentence before she forgot the rest of it. I could see it was an effort. That it didn't necessarily make sense to her. And I felt bad for pushing her, exposing her in a way that clearly made her feel embarrassed, or if not embarrassed, then at least less animated. Less sure of herself. Her smile diminishing as she struggled to speak, struggled to remember the steps I was suggesting to her.

When we were through, I closed the book, set it down on the rug, and asked her if she wanted to read another. Winnie shrugging her shoulders and smiling broadly, tilting her head again to peer at me in that Disney-like gesture.

"Is that yes or no?" I teased.

Shoulders up, then down again. Still smiling. Still somewhat posed.

"I have a better idea," I said, suddenly pushing myself up from the rug and taking her hand to pull her along with me.

We went into my bedroom. I told Winnie to sit in the middle of my bed, surrounded by my dozens of throw pillows, the ones Jay hated and I loved, their colors and textures and patterns so pleasing to me that sometimes they seemed the whole point of the bed—to display them. I retreated into my closet and pulled out a cigar box stuffed with old costume jewelry. Beaded necklaces. A spoon ring from my grandmother. Geometric earrings from an old boyfriend whom I'd never loved. The earrings not my style. But I couldn't part with them, either.

I kept rummaging through the box, pulling out pieces for Winnie to try on, to play with. Winnie loved it. I loved it. Winnie draping the jewelry from her wrist, her neck, even around her knees and ankles. Standing up on the bed. Laughing as the too-large pieces came shooting down her limbs. Only one item fitting her properly. A pale pink-and-green friendship bracelet I'd acquired in my late twenties.

"I like," Winnie said, holding up her wrist, posing with her hip out and her head tilted. She was manipulating me. A little. I knew that she knew I would give it to her if she smiled like that. Which annoyed me a little. That she wasn't guileless. That she wasn't as innocent as I'd hoped or once imagined. But so what? So what if she was working me over, trying to get her way? I was glad she was at least capable of manipulating me. Glad she was a survivor.

"You can wear it when you're here," I said, not wanting to give in to her, not completely. Teaching her, I suppose, that she couldn't manipulate me like she did other people. Or else afraid of what the gift might cause. Paige claiming the bracelet made her look cheap, or that Winnie had somehow begged for it. Paige's coldness toward Winnie so much worse than her frustration with her. Even though I knew it was all part of the same mess, the beginning hard to tease out.

"Okay," Winnie said in that singsongy voice of hers. Okay with not getting the bracelet. Which was astounding for a kid that age. That she accepted my refusal so easily. Or maybe she'd already forgotten about the bracelet request? Winnie's cognitive delays no doubt driving Paige crazy, filling her with fear that her daughter would be slow and require care for the rest of her life. Which I sort of understood, if I squinted and tried. But didn't Winnie's personality count for anything? Couldn't Paige taste this? Feel this? How Winnie was such good company?

I glanced at the alarm clock. It was nearly five o'clock. Time to make dinner. Time to return Winnie. Worried that I'd kept her too long. Gently removing the costume jewelry from Winnie's dainty limbs before walking her back to the Edwardses' property. Ringing Paige's doorbell, readying myself to be nice. And then, the door opening not to Paige but to a brassy-haired middle-aged woman with a large mole on her cheek.

"Well, well, well," the woman said, smiling like she'd discovered a treasure, bending down to hug Winnie.

"Come, come," she said to me, motioning me inside. Her accent heavy, possibly Greek. Reaching out my hand to her. The woman's handshake limp but warm. The woman saying, "I'm Lydia, the new nanny."

Where was Yazmin? I wanted to ask, was trying to think how, when I heard a car door slam behind me in the street. Was Paige parking on the curb in front of her house? I braced myself to greet her, turned around with my lips stretched into an almost smile, but there was no white Lexus at the curb. No silver-haired woman in elegant clothes hurrying toward the house, irritated and pretending to be happy. Instead, a tiny blue Chevy was parked in the street. Its paint faded. Two women in skirts and coats coming up the walk. Church ladies with slow, careful steps.

"Excuse me, ma'am?" one of them called.

"I don't live here," I said, hoping this would cut them off, excuse me. I didn't want to be pressed into a discussion about God at the moment.

"Can we talk to you?" the taller of the two said while the shorter one reached into a purse and pulled something out. She held it up in the sunlight, the contents hard to see behind the plastic. But I could tell even from a few steps away that it was some sort of badge. Some sort of official government emblem. I stepped closer. Squinting. Department of Children and Family Services.

"We'd like to speak with you about this child," the taller one said, walking closer, her face a blotchy shade of tea, as if she'd bleached it accidentally. A beige overcoat buttoned up to her neck.

"This is my neighbor's daughter," I said, hoping I sounded

clipped and intimidating instead of scared and alone. Why had they come?

"She's the neighbor," Lydia confirmed from the doorway, the glass door still pushed open, Winnie pressing herself into Lydia's waist as if fearful or just aware that a drama was about to take place. How many dramas had she already witnessed?

Meanwhile, Lydia's face betrayed nothing, a faint mustache of sweat above her lip but her look and demeanor still confident. As if she'd been expecting the women. Or wasn't worried about their arrival. Shouldn't she tell them to go away until the Edwardses returned? Shouldn't I? My impulse to protect the Edwardses kicking in before I remembered that I didn't fully trust them! My ears hot, my breath short.

"All right, then," said the one with the tea-colored skin. I looked from her to the shorter one, taking in her yellow parka. Her bored, solemn face. What was she bored with already?

"I think I should leave," I said, willing my voice to sound calm. Steady. Willing my wave to appear jaunty. Unafraid. And then I ran. Actually turned and ran down the front yard to the street, my clogs slapping the pavement, my toes clinging tight to the front of them as I loudly made my way up my porch steps and to my front door, resting only when I'd reached my kitchen, standing next to my granite island, breathing deeply, my toes aching, terrified to tell Lorraine or Drew or Jay that Family Services had come. Terrified that this meant something truly awful had happened. Or was happening. That we had failed to detect it.

I drank some water. Thought about having something stronger. A shot. White wine straight from the bottle. But I knew it would only make me queasy. Already I felt queasy. Instead, I went outside to wait for the boys' carpool. Sitting on my porch steps despite the cold against my butt, eager to feel the weak sunshine on my face and legs and shoulders, to hear the hum of the distant cars on the streets just beyond mine. The little blue Chevy visible to my right if I peeked around the side of our house, strained to catch it in my sight. I stood once, saw it there, then returned to my spot on the porch steps, fixing my gaze instead on the shiny leaves of my holly bush. Touching the leaves to see if they were as sharp as I remembered them to be. Pricking my fingers over and over again.

* * *

As soon as dinner was served—mac 'n' cheese with frozen peas, apple juice—as soon as the plastic bowls had been stacked in the dishwasher and the kids were bathed and parked in front of the TV set, I waited near the kitchen door for Jay to get home, believing his presence could save me, could make me understand this thing that had happened. Jay listening intently, then rubbing his greasy face with the palm of his hand, a five o'clock shadow already creeping around his chin, up his cheeks.

"Well, fuck her," Jay said when he'd finished rubbing his skin, finished thinking.

"Do you think I should say something? Call her?"

"Definitely not," he practically shouted, walking abruptly past me and pouring himself a scotch from our tiny bar in the corner.

"Should I pretend I don't know about the visit, then, if I see her?" I asked, aware that this was the last thing I should be thinking about, but trained my whole life to behave this way. To act normal. To pretend that nothing was wrong. Even when it was.

Deep sighing from Jay, who lifted his glass and took a long swig of his drink.

"Well?" I pressed, hoping for some advice, some insight, something that would make this situation all right, understandable. Already I was hoping there was a benign reason for Family Services to be there. That it didn't have to be dire.

"This is what has to happen, unfortunately."

"What do you mean?"

"Honey," Jay said, putting down his glass and staring at me seriously.

"What?"

"Paige is in way over her head. You cannot stop this. You cannot undo things. And you cannot make Winnie's life perfect. A lot happened to her before she even got to Fair Lawn."

I put my head in my hands and started to cry. Angry with him for being so harsh. Angry with him for being right.

* * *

Morning came, and the school buses rumbled through. Pale sunshine, the snow crumbling in halfhearted banks near the corners of our driveways. The grass naked, yellowed and stiff. Drew already crossing the lawns when I went out to retrieve the morning paper, heading toward my front walk in what looked like pajamas. Lorraine in her Range Rover across the street, creeping toward my house as if this had been choreographed.

"Do you know?" Drew asked when he'd climbed the steps to my porch.

My heart racing, my eyes darting around the corner as if at any moment Paige would appear.

"Inside," I said to him, motioning the same to Lorraine, who was parking the car, getting out. I wished her car weren't so conspicuous. Right there, practically on my front walk! Paige would know we were talking about her if she walked past. But what could I do? Tell them to go away?

We sat in the pale gloom of my living room, the sun not quite reaching all the way in, the windows covered with sheers that my decorator had convinced me were appropriate for this sort of thing. What sort of thing? Not letting people see into your house? Not being able to ever properly look out? I hated the living room in the daytime, the feeling of being trapped. I preferred the kitchen, with its sunny views of the trees.

After a moment Drew said suddenly, "You know, obviously?"

"I was there," I admitted, my heart racing at the memory of it.

Lorraine said, "Paige called me last night."

"She knew the authorities were coming," explained Drew, nodding his head self-righteously like he and Nela could have predicted this. Which was ridiculous and also insulting. Which was hard to take seriously from a man wearing plaid flannel pajamas!

"She said she didn't care if Family Services was coming because she had nothing to hide!" Lorraine said, the hint of a snort in her voice. "She phoned me! And I was dumb enough to answer because I had no idea what was coming," said Lorraine, suddenly standing and leaning over me. Implying that I had wronged her. Which I could see from her point of view that I had. I hadn't warned her! Which I truly didn't care about, for once! How Lorraine would have handled the situation. My feelings more important, for once.

"Paige said she tried to call you, but you didn't answer," Lorraine added, beginning to pace my room in her dark gray pantsuit, wagging her chin back and forth in disbelief as if I were no longer present.

It was true. The phone had rung and rung. I had ignored it. I didn't care who it was. Or rather, I feared it was Drew or Lorraine or worse, Paige.

"Didn't you hear the phone?" Drew asked, clearly taking Lorraine's side.

I ignored the implication. That I had done something wrong by ignoring the phone, by ignoring all of them! I breathed in my fiercest, loudest breath. The kind of breath that said I was an independent, educated woman, not to mention a feminist with a formerly big job. In short, I was a person not to be messed with. Then I let the breath out and said, "Go on."

Lorraine stopped pacing.

"Finally she reached me. Me! The last person on earth interested in talking to her!"

I doubted this. Lorraine couldn't resist a good story. And to get it firsthand no doubt pleased her.

"Apparently Yazmin called Family Services! She said she wasn't comfortable with the atmosphere in the house, or with the 'rituals.'"

"Rituals!" Drew said. "It sounds like Satanic worship."

I glared at Drew. Aware he was trying to be funny but not amused by his sense of humor.

"Paige told me she'd fired Yazmin for stealing. That's why Yazmin called the authorities. Payback," Lorraine explained.

I opened my mouth, too shocked to speak, then closed it. What would I say anyway? That I doubted Yazmin was stealing? That she had more to lose than Paige did by calling the authorities. Especially if Paige now filed a police report.

"Yazmin told the investigators that Winnie told her she wished she had a different family!" Lorraine added.

"Jesus Christ!" Drew said softly, shaking his head.

"Why would she say that?" I asked, my hands suddenly cold, shoving them under my thighs to warm them.

"It's not that uncommon!" Lorraine continued. "Paige told me it's part of Winnie's syndrome. Part of spending her early years in an orphanage!"

We moaned. We shook our heads. We wondered if this was true and if Paige was still an unfit mother. At least to Winnie. Both facts suddenly possible in the gloom of my living room.

"Why'd Lydia let them in if Paige wasn't home?" I asked, moving toward the edge of my couch. Which made a terrible crackling sound. My faux down cushions cheaper than I realized when I'd bought them. Which I regretted.

"Paige knew they were coming and didn't want it to seem like they were hiding something," Lorraine said. "That's what Paige told me, anyway."

"And?" I pressed. Aware there was definitely an "and" but not sure Lorraine would acknowledge it.

"And they probably also wanted to buy time until Gene could get there," Lorraine said, tucking her hands into her slacks pockets as if making a presentation to a client. "Gene knows Paige has a temper. She could make things worse. Screaming at the authorities. Shooting herself in the foot. So he came home from work and did the interview with her at night. But he also knows now that things have got to change. That Paige can't continue like this. Angry at Winnie all the time. Sending her to her room for every minor infraction. I think if she knows there's something at stake, she'll be able to change. She's probably seeing a shrink right now!"

I looked toward Drew on the couch, who merely shrugged. Not willing to offer an opinion. Or maybe he'd just stopped having them, cowed by Nela into seeing things as black and white.

"So you think things will get better now?" I asked, turning back toward Lorraine.

"Yes, I do," Lorraine said, shaking her head with satisfaction. "Everything will be better now."

I thought Lorraine was probably a very good recruiter, or at least very good at convincing her clients that she was. Because she made you believe the things she was saying, even if deep down you knew that you shouldn't. And so I said nothing to contradict her. Her conviction not an illusion unless we laid it bare for discussion.

THE WOUND ALWAYS STINKS

A DAY PASSED. THEN two. The sun continued to rise pale and yellow in the January sky, and the school buses continued their slow rumble through the neighborhood. The Edwardses going about their normal work and school routine, Lydia visible in the yard with Winnie, playing quietly, coming and going occasionally in her tan-colored station wagon. All of this reported to me by Lorraine, who made a point of stopping by the Edwardses' house and introducing herself to Lydia. Offering to help if she needed anything. Refraining from mentioning the authorities' visit, but hoping, I knew, that Lydia would confide more details to her.

Instead, all Lorraine got was a "Good morning, Miss Lorraine." Followed by instructions from Lydia that Winnie should do the same. Lydia helping Winnie form the words. Lydia perfectly calm and neutral, as if nothing had happened.

Lorraine wanted me to go over and ask questions. To press my advantage. I had been there, hadn't I? I had a right to ask questions. I ignored her. I pretended she was joking. I told her she was naive to think that Lydia would trust me. Plus, I didn't want to get more involved. Afraid Paige would find out and somehow blame me for something.

And then on the fourth day, Lydia appeared on my front porch with Winnie.

"Winnie wanted to say hello," Lydia said, smiling widely, her short orange hair covered by a black fisherman's cap. Winnie in a purple quilted jacket that looked new, which pleased me.

I stepped outside. I hugged Winnie. I looked up carefully at Lydia, wondering what face would greet me. I was expecting blank eyes, a bland face. The look of a woman who was merely employed and wanted to remain that way. Instead, she looked right at me, the whites of her eyes slightly red, as if she hadn't slept well.

"I didn't tell Paige that you were there the other day," Lydia said calmly. Not in a hurry. With a certain kind of confidence that she was in charge and would remain that way. Which surprised me, given the state of her eyes.

"I think that was a good idea," I agreed. My mouth going dry and my torso suddenly weak. I leaned against my glass door to steady myself while Lydia turned and said over her shoulder to Winnie, "Do you want to walk just to the end of the circle and back? I think we left your chalk on the driveway." Her voice warm and pleasant. I didn't think I'd ever heard Paige speak to Winnie so calmly, with no implied hint that she was about to be disappointed.

Winnie stood on her tiptoes and nodded happily, her chin bobbing up and down with excitement.

"Just stay on the sidewalk and come right back," Lydia continued firmly, bending down to place a tiny foil-wrapped candy in the corner of Winnie's palm.

Winnie smiled, the corners of her mouth making her cheeks bunch up and her eyes sparkle. "I love it!" she said, rolling on the balls of her feet twice before unwrapping the chocolate and popping it in her mouth. Her cheeks puffed up and silly-looking as she skipped down my porch steps toward the sidewalk, out of earshot. We were alone.

"How's Winnie?" I asked, hoping I sounded worried. Hoping Lydia could tell I put Winnie's welfare above that of her mother.

"Paige called me at home all night after the ladies came."

I squinted. I cocked my head to the side. My fingers starting to tingle with cold despite the bright sun above my lawn.

"Why?" I demanded, hoping to show her how angry I felt. How good I was at heart despite supposedly being friendly with Paige.

"She wanted to know what Winnie said to them before she got there," Lydia continued.

"Why all night?"

"Because she didn't believe me."

"What *did* Winnie say?" I asked, curious about exactly what had been reported and whether a six-year-old could even be a reliable witness.

"I don't know. I wasn't in the room," Lydia said calmly, gravely.

"Why not?"

"Because they asked to talk to her privately, and I said okay, as long as the door is open," Lydia replied. "Paige told me to let them in," she explained. Which suddenly made me not trust Lydia. She knew all along that the authorities were coming and she stayed there? What person in her right mind would work for a parent who had been reported to Family Services?

"I told everything to my employment agency, of course," Lydia added, as if reading my mind. "But I can't just leave. I have my own grandkids to think of. They live with me. Along with their mother."

"So why did Paige want to know what Winnie said if she knew

people from the agency were coming and wasn't afraid of them?" I asked, wanting to return to the bare facts and circumstances, away from the conjecture about Lydia's judgment and loyalty. I was still friends with the Edwardses, and I didn't even need their money!

Lydia shrugged.

"How is Paige now?" I asked, afraid of the answer, knowing I needed to hear it.

"All she can do is yell at Winnie; Winnie this and Winnie that! Sometimes Winnie gets wild and starts thrashing around the room. I think she scratches herself by accident."

Hand to my mouth, my head throbbing.

"Finally, I told Paige, 'She's just six. You need to have patience. This isn't good for her.' But Paige doesn't listen to me. She says I don't understand about adopted children."

"Oh my God."

"I pray to God. That's what I do."

"For what?"

"For Paige to calm down."

"But how does she seem besides the screaming?" I pressed, determined to get to the bottom of things.

"How does she seem to you? You're her friend," Lydia said, raising her eyes to look at me.

"I'm not really her friend," I said, lowering my eyes to my porch floor.

"They lock her in at night," Lydia said. "Which I told Gene not to do."

"What do you mean?" I asked, lifting my gaze back toward Lydia, my eyes starting to tear.

"Gene goes up after I tuck her in," Lydia continued, unaware of my confusion and growing discomfort. Or maybe well aware of it. Willing me to face it.

"He gives her cough medicine to help her sleep before he locks the bedroom door," Lydia said, nodding her head, looking right at me. "They have a monitor if she needs something."

I raised my hand to my mouth again. Eyes on my porch floor. The locked door was all part and parcel of the original story Paige had told us about Winnie having sleep issues and refusing to stay in her room. Which meant what, exactly? That the locked door and cough syrup were necessary?

When I looked back at Lydia, she was still standing there calmly, waiting, no doubt, for me to say something.

"Did you tell Family Services about these things?" I asked, anxious to have a third party evaluate these decisions.

"They didn't ask me any follow-up questions," Lydia said, opening her cracked and empty palms as if to reveal something. The nature of nothing.

"But you could call them. Couldn't you?" I pressed.

"You know what they said to me?" Lydia asked. Still calmly.

"What?" I asked.

"One of the agency ladies said to me, 'Look at this house. Look at this pool. These cars.' She waved her arms around the whole property and said, 'I doubt something bad could happen in a neighborhood like this.'"

"They didn't mean that!" I said. Confident it couldn't be true. People had been going on talk shows for years, spilling the gory details of their childhood misery. White families. Thin families. Fat families. Rich families. Families from every corner of the universe. Surely by now people, especially the authorities, knew how to look beneath the surface. They wouldn't be blasé simply because Paige and Gene lived in a marvelous brick Tudor. I prayed this was true even as I worried that it wasn't.

I must have looked forlorn. And disappointed. At my inability to do anything. At my knowledge that doing something wouldn't fix this.

"Don't worry," Lydia said, smiling gently at me, no doubt sensing my despair. "I once knew a Kenyan nanny who used to say, 'The wound always stinks.'"

I looked at her quizzically. Confused by the proverb.

"The Edwardses can try to cover up what's happening, but if they're wrong, they'll be found out. Eventually the stink of the wound will reveal itself."

I smiled like I knew she wanted me to. I tried to pretend I could put my faith in the universe as the proverb was implying I should. But I doubted it was true. Just like I doubted Lydia truly believed it. Otherwise, why had she told me the things that she had? Wasn't she hoping I'd intervene? Wasn't she hoping I'd reveal the wound myself?

* * *

Inside, I went straight to my office and looked up Children and Family Services, willing myself to jot down the number even as I lingered over the stories that poured forth on my search page. One father tying his daughter to a bathtub drainpipe whenever she asked for seconds at dinner. Another child spun around by her hair, her face smashed into walls. There were burned children. Beaten children. Foster parents who were worse than the biological ones. The

Edwardses were nothing like the families described on the Internet. And yet. There it was. I sensed it when I closed my eyes. The black trickle of something dangerous. It didn't have to be obvious, draped with a sign that said trouble. Even though I'd been waiting for that all my life. A sign that what I felt was true. I turned back to my desk and shut the computer screen, not eager to be drawn back into the misery that greeted me there. Picking up my cell phone before I could change my mind. Dialing the hotline as I paced my office, my fingers numb, my mouth dry.

"Would you like to begin with your name?" the woman asked when I'd finally established what I was calling about. Which took forever. Which took much longer than I thought it should. How many people had been turned away by the hold time and the confusion at an agency that was supposed to protect children?

"I don't want to be identified," I said, my voice steady, even if my insides were shaking.

"So this is an anonymous call?"

"Yes."

"If it's anonymous, you can never call back and add more information. You can't update us."

"That's okay."

"If it's anonymous, we can never call you and ask questions. Get clarification."

"So you're saying you want my name?" I asked, suddenly on the verge of crying. Which was so embarrassing. How powerless I felt in the face of this nameless authority.

"We can identify you in some other way if you want," the voice responded. Dispassionately. Unaware of my vulnerability or simply not caring.

"Will the Edwardses be able to identify me?" I asked, trying to breathe deeply and regain my composure.

"We do our best to protect the identity of those who call us, but we can't guarantee anything."

I wanted a guarantee. I wanted safety and protection. I couldn't imagine what Paige might do to me if she thought I'd betrayed her.

A long pause ensued.

"Are you still there?" the voice asked.

"I'm thinking."

"Would you like to identify yourself?" she continued.

"How about 'a neighbor'? Can you say 'neighbor' as an identity?"

"Yes."

"Okay, then let's begin," I said. My voice shaking.

I told her how long I'd known the Edwardses. I told her I thought Paige was unkind to her adopted daughter and not to her biological son. Cringing as I said this. Aware that being mean wasn't necessarily abuse, even if it was just as insidious and painful to tolerate.

The woman on the other end was silent. Was she typing? I kept talking.

"The nanny told me that they lock the girl in her room at night. They give her cough medicine to help her sleep at night."

"How long have you known this nanny?"

I sighed. Embarrassed. "I just met her, but I have no reason to believe that she's lying."

"Are you concerned for the girl's safety?" the voice asked. Clearly bored. Worse than bored. In deep disbelief that I was worth listening to.

I breathed deeply. Was I worried that Winnie was in life-threatening danger? No, not life-threatening. But I did think Paige might continue to scream at her. Possibly lock her in her room. Maybe even lose control if Paige was angry enough about Family Services being called in. Which I didn't want to believe but I had to contemplate. Paige harming Winnie. Wasn't that why I'd called the hotline to begin with?

"Yes, I'm afraid," I said finally, feeling like a fraud when I said it. Someone who exaggerated circumstances. "The new nanny told me that the mother screams at the little girl so much that she hurts herself and throws fits."

"So you're saying the girl throws tantrums?"

I wanted to scream. I wanted to hang up. How could I possibly convince this woman to take my claims seriously?

"The mother, Paige Edwards, admits that they've never had a birthday party for their adopted daughter!" I said stupidly. Aware this was insipid, not worth repeating.

"Okay," the woman said. Obviously bored.

"Listen, they limit what the adopted daughter eats. And in what order she eats it. And she's super skinny," I insisted.

"So are you saying they starve her?"

"No!"

"What, then?"

"Maybe start with the girl's teacher. See if there's any basis for my concern."

"Anything else?"

I clenched my fists. My fingers were cold, numb. What else could I add? That Paige was my friend and therefore I suspected things about her I couldn't explain or even articulate, but that this made them more worrisome, not less?

"Are you there?" asked the bored voice on the other end of the line.

"I think that's everything," I said. Knowing that nothing else I said was going to convince her to open a case if the agency hadn't already.

"Thank you for your call. Would you like your case number?"

"Yes, please," I said, dutifully scribbling it down on scrap paper.

"Are you going to interview the girl's teacher?" I asked.

"We can't discuss the details of the case."

"But I'm the one calling you."

"We have a process," the woman repeated.

"Does that mean you'll open a case?"

"I just gave you the case number."

"So you're going to investigate my claims?"

"I will pass on your concerns."

I hung up the phone and was immediately shocked by how messy my desk appeared. Invitations and bills scattered in half-formed piles, rocks and picture frames propped awkwardly as paperweights. Deciding immediately to buy a fancy bulletin board, the kind with quilting and ribbons that didn't require pushpins. Something that would make my office look beautiful and naturally effortless. Getting up and heading for Target before I could change my mind. Aware that no matter what bulletin board I bought, the chaos would continue to spread.

GARBAGE

A DAY PASSED. THEN three. I tried to forget about the call. I tried to pretend I hadn't really made the call. Slowly resigning myself to the fact that no faded blue Chevy would pull up to the Edwardses' driveway. Slowly resigning myself to the fact that people might judge me for inserting myself into the case to begin with. Wasn't Gene getting help for Paige? Wasn't Paige herself seeing an expert who had told her about the oppositional defiant disorder? What could the government do for Winnie that Gene and Paige couldn't? And yet I was glad I had voiced my fears. Glad I had tried to do something to help Winnie.

It was early the next week, the sun barely up, when Paige snuck up on me. My head buried in a garbage can, my mind on how to shove the remaining bags into the bin, worried that I was revealing my underwear in my too-short nightgown.

"Nicole, I wanted to catch you," Paige said, her voice suddenly right beside me in the driveway, causing me to jerk free, drop my bag.

"You startled me!" I said, reaching down to pick up the dropped garbage, swiping at something gooey that was starting to drain out of a hole in the bottom of the bag. It was disgusting. Viscous and slightly smelly. And I had nowhere to wipe it but on myself. Which

I refused to do! Paige didn't notice. Or she noticed but didn't care, her own distress clearly so much larger than mine. Her whole countenance so nervous, she appeared to be subtly shaking.

"This will only take a minute," Paige said, crossing her arms in front of her Burberry trench coat, crossing her ankles, revealing her brown suede boots. It clogged my brain. That she looked so stylish despite her ragged countenance. Why was she so dressed up at this hour of the morning?

"I know you were there when Family Services came. Lydia told me," Paige began.

So she'd gotten it out of her. What could I say? I nodded like I knew she wanted me to, trapped already in some sort of alarming web she'd created.

"Well, I just wanted you to know we're all right. Everything's fine. I've told Lorraine about it, just so we're all on the same page," she continued.

"I'm so glad," I said, my own voice shaking, unsure what stance to take, friendly or accusatory, doubting or reassuring.

"So, they came back again last night. Did you know they were coming back?" she demanded.

I was so stunned, I couldn't answer her. Instead, I breathed in and out, which seemed good enough for Paige.

"We had all our paperwork in order documenting Winnie's problems," Paige continued. "I have copies of the doctors' reports, if you want them," she said, looking at me squarely in the face now, forcing me to look at her.

"It's not my business, Paige," I said. Willing myself to sound helpful and supportive instead of judgmental and disgusted. Not sure I'd gotten the tone right.

"Someone else called Family Services. Not just Yazmin. A

neighbor," Paige said, taking a step closer. I willed myself not to move. Not to be afraid. My mouth dry. My face as blank as I could muster.

"I know you wouldn't betray me," she said, walking still closer. Our faces only inches from each other. I could smell her minty toothpaste. See the sleep still crusted in the corner of her right eye. I wanted to brush it away. To hit her. But I stood perfectly still. My throat closing. Afraid to speak.

"How could someone do this to us?" Paige asked angrily, her face narrow and sunken, as if she hadn't slept all night. As if she had lain awake pondering this betrayal. Determined to root it out. Determined to confront each of us. Or maybe only me. I couldn't be sure. I couldn't think straight. Sweat had begun to drip down my leg and onto my ankle, despite the freezing cold. I wanted to reach down and wipe myself dry, but I couldn't move. Afraid to break the tension. The silence ballooning and growing heavy. I had to take command or she would accuse me. Possibly harm me. I set my face, prepared my voice before I asked coolly, "What did the people from Family Services say?" Looking Paige in the face, daring her to doubt my loyalty.

"They said that a neighbor had called and said we never had a birthday party for Winnie. You were the only one who knew about the birthday parties!" she hissed.

"I would never do anything to hurt you," I said, clenching my stomach muscles tight beneath the nightgown. Willing my face to appear kind. My eyes warm. Aware that I was lying to her. Aware that I'd been lying my whole life. My betrayal the first true thing I'd done for as long as I could remember. A fact I clung to desperately as I watched Paige watching me. Paige turning on her heel. Paige walking away from me without another word. Which relieved me. That she wasn't going to stand in my driveway and threaten me. Even though I was terrified of what she might do to me now.

MISSING

A SENSE OF UNREST followed me to bed and into my dreams. Waking in a cold sweat at five the next morning, remembering the sequence of terrifying events I'd vividly imagined. A summer house with no working phones and yet a message that kept ominously following me. "You have an emergency." Panicked because I couldn't figure out who was having the emergency or how to get in touch with them. Walking through the summer house looking desperately for a telephone, finding myself without warning in a car, trying to steer from the backseat, my arms stretched uncomfortably around the headrest; the car gaining speed of its own accord. Unable to reach the brake to avoid veering off into oblivion.

My body clammy and cold beneath the duvet cover, my mind racing with fear and anxiety about what the dream meant and what I should do about it. Telling myself it was merely about my dislike of driving, particularly carpools, and the knowledge that I wasn't as watchful as I should be when driving them. Aware that something else was wrong and unable to face it. Aware that it was coming toward me like a slow-moving freight train. That my unconscious mind had perceived the rumble of something black that was bearing its way toward me. The dream a preparation. The dream a reminder to be watchful and careful. I promised myself that I would be, then lay awake till morning trying to think of ways to prepare myself.

Penny called in the afternoon as I was contemplating my messy kitchen. Annoyed that it was still in disarray from breakfast. Annoyed that I'd let my daily housekeeper go. Even though I'd grown to dislike her presence. Eager to have my own space. To make my house more fully my own. My sister crying before I'd finished saying hello, telling me our mother had been in a car accident.

"What happened?" I asked, immediately recalling the dream, convinced that this was what it had been portending.

"She fell asleep at the wheel," Penny wailed.

"Jesus Christ," I said, my hand to my heart, my breath tight and constricted in my chest.

"The other woman wasn't even hurt. Mom had six stitches in her neck where she hit the steering wheel. They found traces of diet pills in her bloodstream. Illegal ones, I think." I felt queasy. Certain this was my fault. Even though it wasn't at all what I'd told my mother to do.

"She's, like, jittery all day, is totally erratic, and then gets in the fucking car. Who does that?"

I wanted to say that Penny did. Or had. I wanted to say that everybody made mistakes and that my mother had made her fair share. But all I really wanted to know was whether anyone was dead.

"Dead?" Penny said. "No, not dead. Why would you even ask that?"

"Is anyone pressing charges? Will she be sued?"

"Why are you all about money and not how someone is feeling?"

I wanted to reach through the phone and strangle her. I wanted to tell her I was sick of being the responsible one! Instead, I asked, "How long has Mom been on the diet pills?" hoping it was long before I had suggested she go on a diet. Long before I confronted her about her health and the fact that she was killing herself.

"You can ask her yourself. I'm walking into Mom's hospital room now."

I felt my mouth open in shock, then closed it as I heard my mother say hello. Her voice groggy and gentle.

"Mom," I said, choking up with tears. "Are you okay?"

"Never a dull moment," my mother joked. Even though she didn't sound like herself. Her words weak. Her spirit diminished.

"Where were you coming from?" I asked, unable to ask her what I really wanted to know. Was she medicated? Unstable? Not taking care of herself in the way I had begged her to?

"If you really want to know, Al-Anon," she answered. Which shocked me more than the possibility of diet pills.

"Okay," I said, curious how Penny felt about this change in our mother. Realizing suddenly that she hadn't called her Phyllis the whole time she spoke with me.

"I've had a lot of nice visitors. People I barely know who were there when it happened."

"I wish I could be there," I said, sorry I couldn't comfort her in person. Wondering if I should get on a plane in the morning.

"Don't come now," she said. Her breath labored. "I'm going to rehab in a few days."

"Why rehab?" I asked, worried she was more injured than I'd realized.

"Because I live alone. They don't want me to be in the apartment without an aide and insurance won't cover someone decent."

I closed my eyes and pictured my mother shuffling from room to room with her stitches. I wondered if I should offer to pay for someone, but knew this wasn't really what she wanted.

"Maybe I'll bring everyone for spring break," I offered. Quickly. Before I could change my mind. Aware that once it was out there, it would be hard to take it back. Aware that once I committed, there would be no end to the fighting. Between Jay and me over why I wanted to go. Between the boys, who hated long car trips. And of course, between Penny and my mother and me. Over all of the usual stuff, and things I hadn't even dreamed up yet. But still. I wanted to go. To ensure the boys had some sense of their family. To ensure that I didn't lose them completely. Swallowing and trying to quiet my breathing when I glanced at my watch. Shocked when I realized what time it was. Panicked that I'd missed school pickup by a full fifteen minutes.

* * *

I drove fast out of our cul-de-sac, aware of the older children who were already dotting the sidewalks heading toward home. When I arrived at the pickup spot, nobody was waiting for me. I cursed myself. Prayed the boys weren't already in the school office calling me. Or worse, calling my emergency contact, which was Jay, of course. Jay having no tolerance for lateness. Jay worrying obsessively that something could happen to the boys if they walked anywhere alone for even a minute. I got out of the car and sprinted toward the school. Telling myself not to worry. Not to make too much of this. It was impossible for something to happen to them on the two-hundred-yard walk from the schoolyard to my car and back again. Not with so many parents walking by. Not with the crossing guard and the two of them together.

I ran, calling, "Josh?" and "Lucas!" Hoping that they would magically appear from behind a hedge or a tree. Hoping they were merely playing a trick on me. I promised myself I wouldn't yell at them if this was the case. Wouldn't raise my voice and tell them how stupid it was to frighten me. If they appeared right then, I would hug them. I would save the lectures for another time, maybe never. I would apologize for my own lateness and inconsideration!

When I reached the office I quickly glanced inside, scanning the two small chairs, the secretary desk crowded with folders and papers.

"I can't find my boys," I said, hysteria creeping into my voice as I spoke to the school secretary, a stern strawberry-blonde who didn't like parents. I doubted she liked children.

"Who are your boys, exactly?" Miss Mallory asked, her glasses pushed toward the tip of her nose. Her hair framing her freckled face in a frizzy halo.

"Lucas and Josh Westerhof," I said. Trying to smile. To win her over. She needed to help me.

"What do you mean, exactly, you can't find them?" she asked with irritation.

"They usually walk to my car together, and they didn't show up today," I said, my voice shaking, tears rushing in. "I was late," I admitted. Embarrassed in front of Miss Mallory.

"What grades are they in?" she asked, the glasses still hanging on the tip of her nose. Eyeing me from beneath them.

"Second and fourth," I answered.

Miss Mallory shuffling some papers, looking up numbers, finally saying absentmindedly to me, "I'm calling their classrooms."

I could have told her the teachers' names. She didn't need to waste precious time looking them up! Turning from her to look around the office again, hopeful I had merely overlooked the boys, that they were in fact sitting somewhere. Which, of course, was impossible. The office was too small.

"Should I go back outside and look for them?" I asked, even though Miss Mallory was just hanging up the phone.

"The teachers said the boys left together, but they're coming down to talk to you."

Waiting. Pacing the office. My armpits sweating profusely in the hot, stale air of the school. The teachers looking worried when they saw me. Mrs. Meade assuring me that Josh had left with Lucas. All of us agreeing to go back out into the schoolyard. Mrs. Meade canvassing the back of the school while Lucas's teacher, Mrs. Likely, took the front. I walked from the school to my car again, calling their names wildly into the wind. Knowing I looked out of control, that other mothers who saw me would surely gossip about me in the morning. Arriving at my Subaru and seeing nobody waiting there. Running back the way I came and finding Mrs. Likely and Mrs. Meade deep in conference in the schoolyard. Neither Josh nor Lucas anywhere near them.

"Should we call the police?" I asked. Panicked. Knowing what the answer was. All of us returning to the office, calling Jay from my cell phone on the way there. My voice shaking. Jay saying, "Think! Are you sure they didn't have a playdate this afternoon?"

Not able to answer him clearly. The tears running down my face. My voice clotted with them. But no, no, they didn't have a playdate.

"What about the neighbors?" Jay asked. "Would they have gone home with one of the neighbors if you were late?" The word *late* seeming to drip with accusation. An image of Paige's silvery head popping into my mind, pushing it out, knowing she drove nowhere near the school. Winnie receiving bus service from her special needs kindergarten. Cameron at his private school. Terrified all the same that Paige had something to do with this. Hanging up the phone and calling Lorraine's babysitter, then Drew, and finally Lorraine herself. Nobody having seen the boys. Calling Paige's house. Paige's phone ringing and ringing. Telling the office that I was going up to canvass my neighborhood and that they should send the police to my house after they were through with them. Running to my car, rushing home, driving too fast, screeching to a halt in front of Paige's house, and ringing the bell. Laughter in the backyard. Walking behind the house and letting myself in through her pool gate. Josh and Lucas standing in the far corner playing badminton. Winnie and the Guzman-Veniero boys all standing with them. The scene confusing to me with its contradictions and subtle surprises. That the Guzman-Venieros were there. That Winnie was wearing our Burberry scarf. I'd never seen her wear it before. Which I didn't want to be thinking about! Running to hug Josh and Lucas, who seemed confused about my worrying.

"Why are you here?" I kept repeating, whirling around to accuse Lydia of something, unable to find her. Watching, astounded, as Paige calmly let herself out of the French doors of her great room, walking toward me in her suede boots and Burberry raincoat as she called, "Thank God you're here," with false concern. "The kids were really scared, Nicole. Did something happen? Is everything all right?"

I was speechless. What was she implying? That I was a bad mother? Of course, I wasn't a bad mother. I was late! But that didn't stop me from feeling like the worst kind of mother: lazy and self-centered. Someone who didn't put her kids first.

Paige didn't care that I didn't answer her question. Or she did care and was thrilled to see me so tangled up and angry. Cocking her head and saying, "I mean, they were standing on the sidewalk looking all around and confused, and you know what? That's when pedophiles grab kids. They lurk around schools and wait to prey on the kids who are alone, walking home."

I felt my fingers start to go numb with cold despite the relative warmth of the day. The nerve of her! Even though I knew it was true. That pedophiles did do this kind of thing!

"They were together!" I said, my voice starting to shake.

"No, Nicole. They weren't. Josh was pretty far down Forest, almost a full block, and Lucas was nowhere to be seen. You definitely have to talk to him about being a good older brother," she said, nodding her head in his direction. Then whispering, "He didn't even apologize when he got in the car."

"I'm sure there were other mothers around," I hissed. Ignoring her swipe about Lucas, which I knew was on point. Lucas wouldn't apologize for ditching his brother. Or say hello when Paige greeted him. He would have demanded a soda and a snack when he got here and not thanked her for that, either.

"Nobody was around, Nicole, I swear," Paige said, crossing her hands over her heart in a way that was completely disingenuous. I hated her! But I was still afraid of her.

"I'm not comfortable with you picking up my kids," I forced myself to say.

"Nicole!" she answered, clearly shocked by my sudden honesty. This wasn't how we talked to each other. She had, no doubt, thought our little sideswipes and innuendos would go on forever. Not just this afternoon but long into the future, as we pretended to be friends and eventually were again. Wasn't that how it had worked until now? Wasn't I part of the lies and collusion?

"Please don't ever pick up my kids from school again," I repeated more forcefully. For a second Paige looked hurt, her cheeks seeming to sink in on themselves, her eyes watery. But in another second she recovered, angry, aware that in my cutting her off, I was no doubt accusing her of something.

"Nicole!" she said, more loudly now, the children looking up from their badminton game, sensing some disturbance in the air, some crack in the natural order of things.

"I thought we were like family!" Paige called out. Clearly desperate to cling to this false idea we'd all created back when we thought we knew everything there was to know about one another. Even though our presented selves were always just that—presented. The subtle undercurrents of our true selves always rippling just beneath the surface.

"I'm just not comfortable with it," I said coldly, turning my back on her and calling for Josh and Lucas to wrap it up. Josh and Lucas eyeing me warily as I walked toward them, whispering low in their ears, "Right now!" Tugging at them to come with me. Walking quickly to the side of the yard, through the gate in the fence where I'd long ago heard Winnie crying.

* * *

At home, I sat Josh and Lucas down together at the granite island.

"I'm sorry," I said. "I shouldn't have been late."

The boys waited, looking at me. Aware there was something more I'd planned to say.

"Also, if it ever happens again, which I don't think it will, go back to the school. Lucas, you stay with your brother and walk back to Miss Mallory in the office, okay?"

Silent, solemn nodding from Josh.

Lucas thinking it over, then arguing, "But it was Paige." Staring at me boldly. Not acknowledging his misdeed in abandoning Josh.

"I don't want you to play at the Edwardses' anymore," I said.

"Can we go in a car with them?" Lucas pressed.

"No."

"What about Lorraine and Drew?"

"No one. Let's just say you only get in a car with Mommy and Daddy from now on."

"Are we still friends with everyone?" Lucas asked. Josh silent. Not comprehending. Or else comprehending but uncertain how to unravel things.

"Yes," I lied.

"But why'd you say we can't play at Paige's house?" Lucas pressed. Always aware when I was lying or hiding something. Which I'd never fully contemplated before. How intuitive he was. How much like me.

"It's just for now. While we work things out with them," I offered, willing to hint at a fight but not the reasons for it. Hoping to reassure him with the fact that it was temporary. Not wanting to scare him.

"Is it about Winnie? Because she lies all the time?" Lucas asked.

"What are you talking about?" I asked.

"Cameron told us that Winnie makes up stories and is ruining their family."

I tried to keep my face composed for Lucas, but already I felt the tears coming. Wiping at my eyes and saying, "Honey, I'm sure Cameron is confused. She is their family." Standing up from my stool at the island and leaning over to hug Josh and Lucas in quick succession, whispering, "I love you." Hoping they knew how much I meant it. Hoping they knew I would always protect them, even though I'd failed miserably at pickup today.

Lucas and Josh silent as they thought about this. Lucas asking, "Can we go to Target since you forgot to get us?"

I was shocked at how manipulative he was, how shrewd and single-minded. Even as I was aware of how well suited it made him for the business of living.

"Yes, definitely. To make up for my being late!" I said, hoping he wasn't thinking of the long-ago slapping incident, as I was. Target forever reminding me of my poor judgment. Lucas all smiles. Excited. Not remembering the past, or at least not burdened by it.

Josh turning toward me and asking, "Me too?" as if there were any doubt.

"Of course, you too," I said, gathering them both up and squeezing them tight.

* * *

"We should adopt her," I told Jay later that evening, unable to sit on the couch for even a moment and watch what he was watching, some terrible auction show in which people bought unwanted junk out of storage lockers. Why did he care? Why did they? It was cheap and depressing and not even entertaining! All the accumulated waste of a lifetime, things people had once loved or never loved or suddenly needed to exchange for something they would have no use for down the road.

Jay got a hard look on his face. Not mean, but serious. He

lowered the TV volume and turned to look at me. "Don't do this to me," he said.

"I told you what Lucas said that Cameron said."

"That doesn't mean anything."

"But what if they want to give her up? What if we could somehow be the ones she was given to?"

In front of me, Jay shook his head some more and motioned for me to sit next to him, reaching out his arm to bring me close, the musky smell of his body making me breathe deeply, relax. Making me realize how upset I was.

"Poodle, you're not thinking straight," he said, reaching out to rub the top of my hair.

"Why?" I said, burying my head in his shirt, my voice muffled by his body.

"Because Winnie's not a pet. She's not even up for adoption."

"We don't know that. We could at least make some inquiries. There must be some lawyer somewhere who can advise you on this sort of thing," I said, still not looking at Jay, still burrowed into his side.

"Please don't make me the bad guy," Jay said, sighing deeply.

"Why won't you think about it?" I begged, sitting up straighter, preparing to plead.

"One, there's nothing to think about. And two, even if I lived in fairyland, where a child could be miraculously transported from one family to another, we wouldn't be that family. It's not the right situation for us," Jay said, looking at me seriously.

I breathed in and out. I considered all the ways I could force Jay to at least consider the possibility of adopting Winnie. To go through the same torturous calculation that I knew I would go through. Weighing the pros and the cons. The good and the bad. Feeling guilty. Hopeful. Sad. Redeemed. Knowing deep down, even as I stared at Jay and tried not to stare at the TV set, that I didn't have the patience. That I wasn't willing to risk it all. My own safety and security so narrowly won. That I wasn't willing to take on the problems of another vulnerable and imperfect being.

"Okay," I said finally, tears welling up behind my eyes, blocking my throat, making it difficult to speak.

Jay kept his arm around me but returned his attention to the television program, my gaze floating to meet his. In front of us, a giant bald man was trying to sell a metal coffin to an even larger tattooed man. The coffin had been converted into a meat smoker. Who the hell wanted a coffin meat smoker? Jay turned up the volume so that their interaction filled the room, surrounding us.

GLASS

THE WEEKEND CAME, AND with it, a clear sky. The snow and the salt cleaned from the asphalt and the sidewalks. Jay showing the boys how to scooter fast down the slope of our street, away from the cul-de-sac. I was watching from the driveway when I heard it. The sound of glass breaking. Spinning around to see the Edwardses' storm door in pieces, Winnie screaming and running away from the house. In another moment, Gene streaked through the opening and began to race after Winnie, catching her near the street and kneeling down to hug her close to him. My mind racing, my limbs trembling, uncertain what to do. Finally turning and sprinting in the other direction, hoping to catch Jay, breathless when I reached him and whispered about what I had seen. Bribing the boys with Nutella pancakes if they'd head home now. The boys reluctantly following me, ditching their scooters and plodding into the house. Nobody on the Edwardses' lawn when we returned.

Inside, Lucas got out the stool and climbed up the counters to pull down the flour and the baking soda while I clumsily reached for the egg carton. My arm shaking. The container nearly falling as I watched the flashing red bubble of an ambulance stream by our kitchen window. Trying to steady my breathing as Jay and I made silent eye contact. And then my cell phone trilling. Lorraine's name flashing. I motioned Jay to take over and made my way toward the library.

"I have to tell you something," Lorraine said, before I'd even reached the paneled room.

"I know about the door. I saw Winnie screaming," I said, my arms shaking wildly, as if I were shivering. Even though I knew it wasn't the temperature in the house that was making me cold.

"Winnie was playing chase with Cameron. She thought the storm door was open and ran right through it!"

Hand to my mouth, imagining the impact as I took a detour to search for the shawl that I kept in the downstairs closet, desperate to get warm.

"Paige said Winnie's going to be okay. The cuts are mainly superficial. They called the ambulance just to be careful."

I swallowed, trying to digest this, wrapping the shawl tightly around me before asking, "Do you think Winnie was really playing chase?" My voice low, the words nearly stuck in my throat.

Sighing from Lorraine. Not willing to enter into my darkest imaginings. Not willing to conjure up the shadow that was crawling along the edge of my consciousness.

"I'm worried that she was running away from Paige," I said, tears climbing into my voice. "You'd have to be pretty frantic to run through a glass storm door."

"I don't think so," Lorraine insisted. "I mean, Gene's a wimp, but he loves Winnie. He wouldn't let Paige threaten her and then lie about it to the authorities."

I closed my eyes and tried to picture Gene in one of his brightly colored golf shirts. The brightness of the color doing nothing to energize the image that came back to me. Of Gene with his loose collar and rubbery face. Of Gene with his long vacant stares and glib, unconvincing answers. Wishing with all my being that Lorraine was right. That Gene was stable, rational, a foil to Paige's temper and nastiness. Even though I feared it wasn't true.

"Well?" Lorraine asked. Softer now. Aware that my silence was its own kind of answer, a response she didn't want and was hoping I might temper. When I refused to say anything more reassuring, we said our good-byes, the silence too miserable to contemplate.

*   *   *

At two, Lorraine came over with Gabe and Jesse. She needed to talk to me. Privately. The boys herded outside to scooter while we stood at my dining room window, vaguely supervising.

"He was on the verge of crying," Lorraine said without preamble.

"Who was?" I asked, already confused.

"Gene!" Lorraine said, her eyes swollen. Had she been crying? "Jeffrey and I went to confront him. We saw Paige leave."

"Do you want something to drink?" I asked, suddenly desperate for a scotch or even a beer. Desperate not to hear how she confronted Gene. What he said. How awkward it was with Jeffrey there!

Lorraine waved me off, obviously eager to get on with her story. Obviously not bothered by the direct nature of her confrontation. Wasn't that Lorraine's hallmark? Blunt force and direct questioning. Even if she never went deep enough.

"I told him, 'Gene, you know we love you and Paige and the kids, but we're worried. What happened with Winnie?'"

I swallowed. She'd really said that?

"Gene sits there blinking, like he has a nervous tic. His skin is this sickly shade of gray."

I could picture it. The pallor. Even though I'd never seen him blink like that.

"Finally he says, 'Look, if we don't move forward in the right way, Paige could wind up killing herself or Winnie.'"

"Jesus!" I said, the image of Paige driving into a tree suddenly rising up in front of me, she and Winnie dead in their seats.

Lorraine swallowing, staring into space, no longer speaking. I wondered if we could take a break for one quick drink. But Lorraine seemed not to notice me any longer, looking somewhere into the deep recesses of her own mind. Both of us standing in the weak winter sunshine, the children racing back and forth unattended on the other side of the glass.

Finally Lorraine began to speak again, staring straight ahead.

"So I ask Gene again, 'What happened with Winnie? Why did she run through the glass?' I thought he was struggling not to cry. I sensed he was going to break. We were going to hear the truth. And then Jeffrey says, 'Gene, we're really sorry. I hope you don't think Lorraine's being a nosy neighbor.'"

I closed my eyes. Held my breath. Aware that I would have done the same thing. Covered up the ugliness. Made an excuse not to hear it. Even though we desperately needed to know it.

"Jeffrey ruined everything!" Lorraine wailed, turning toward me fully for the first time. Her face sagging. A jowl appearing where I'd never noticed one before.

"It was like the old Gene roared back to life inside the blinking man," Lorraine continued. "He turned from gray to red in an instant, stood up, and knocked over the coffee table. He says, 'Why would you doubt us? Paige told me you were all snakes!'"

I was shocked. That Paige had said that about us. That Gene had repeated it! Instantly upset that Paige thought so poorly of us now. Which was ridiculous. I thought poorly of her. Worse than poorly. I thought she was terrible!

"Now what?" I asked. Not that I really expected something more, but hopeful that this situation could still be salvaged. That we could help Winnie somehow.

"Gene told Paige about our conversation, and now Paige isn't speaking to me. I just saw her on the way over here and she literally snubbed me. She's probably not going to talk to you, either. To any of us!"

"Good!" I said, pretending to be relieved. Even though I was disturbed. That Paige hated me for all the wrong reasons. That without a connection to her, I'd no longer have access to Winnie.

THE WINDOW

By February, people had started to disappear. Not eager to be on their lawns, to greet each other and to pretend that everything was fine. Lorraine suddenly busy with a trainer she met at some fundraising dinner. The trainer meeting her three nights a week at her country club and teaching her the art of paddle tennis, a game I assumed Lorraine already knew, but that she claimed her trainer was teaching her better. As if paddle tennis needed such attention! Drew busy trying to expand his baseball card business, adding framed jerseys, signed game balls, cheap tin signs that kids could hang above their beds. Drew insisting that he couldn't keep up with business. Which seemed promising, if also unlikely. I'd never seen anyone in the store, personally. Nela telling me bluntly, "I can't solve the world's problems." Hinting that her parents were being taken advantage of by a home health aide. That it was causing her to lose sleep, to gain weight.

I knew what she meant. I hated what she meant. That you had to take care of yourself first. Had to be sane and stable and able to weather the storms that got hurled at you frequently. Josh suddenly fighting with one particular boy in his second grade class. Josh appearing with a black eye, which he claimed he got from falling off the jungle gym. Teachers were called. Statements taken. The whole thing roiling me to the point that I couldn't bear to think about Winnie.

Except that I did. Alone at night I tried to picture her. Her pale face. Her Disney smile. Desperate to believe she was still in school. Still safe and watched over. Even though none of us had seen her since the glass door incident. Winnie never seen getting on or off a school bus. Never once witnessed in the yard with Cameron. The curtains in Paige's house always closed. The shades drawn upstairs and down.

* * *

And then, six weeks after Winnie's disturbing collision, six weeks after we'd stopped talking or seeing or confiding in each other, Lorraine stopped by after work to tell me that Gene was going on a buying trip to Italy.

"Can you believe this? He says his family's in danger and he's going on a buying trip to Italy!"

I was on my front porch pulling up old plants from my stone planters, my hands covered in mud since I'd forgotten to wear gloves.

"If you even believe him," I said, looking up at her and raising my eyebrows before returning to my pulling.

"Well, why would you say such a thing and not mean it?" Lorraine asked, dumbfounded.

"Some people are really manipulative," I suggested.

"I don't think Gene would lie about something like that!" Lorraine said. Clearly angry. Clearly doubting me.

"Some people don't even remember half the stuff they say after they say it!" I said. Mad at her, for doubting me. For not sensing how much more insightful I was than her!

"Gene's a really nice guy," Lorraine insisted.

I stopped pulling plants and stared at her, incredulous.

Lorraine swallowed. "I know. He's not acting right. But I like Gene. He's a lot of fun. Or he was before. Now he looks like an old man."

I murmured something that could have been support or total disagreement, taking my pile of plant carcasses and dumping them in a Hefty bag.

"I don't think he's a bad guy, but I do think he's a little reckless. I mean, if he's that worried about their home life, why's he going away?"

"Man's gotta do what a man's gotta do," I said, not interested in analyzing Gene's motivations. Just glad that he was going. Aware that there was now one less person to worry about when I wanted to try to sneak into their house. My plan not really a plan, just a desire that I hoped I could execute when the opportunity presented itself. And here it was. Gene going away. Paige more likely to go out if she was alone in the house at night.

I finished pulling the dead plants out of the second planter, threw the remains in my Hefty bag, and then rubbed my hands vigorously over the opening, hoping to rid myself of the dirt that still stuck to me.

"So now what?" I asked when my hands were as clean as I could make them.

"Gene tells me he always buys Paige this special hand soap in Sicily and asks me if I want some. Like we were friends again! Like none of the other stuff happened."

I sighed deeply, tied up the Hefty bag, and motioned for Lorraine to follow me to the garbage cans. When I was through fiddling with the lids, I turned to Lorraine and said, "Please do me a favor."

"Anything. You know that," she said, her eyes bright, her smile eager. Lorraine never so alive as when she thought she was going to help a friend in need, especially if the "help" consisted of something trivial but thoughtful, like driving a carpool or recommending a cleaning lady.

I stopped and drew my breath in sharply. "Please don't ever come here again and tell me what a good guy Gene is. You're better than that."

Lorraine started to open her mouth in protest, but no words came out. For once, I didn't care if I had hurt her feelings. For once, I didn't care if she liked me. I wanted her to hear the hard truth, to hear it plainly and without adornment. To make her go to the uncomfortable place where she had, for a lifetime, refused to travel. Where I myself was an infrequent visitor.

We both stood for a moment in the dying twilight of the day, staring at each other, waiting for something to happen. When after a moment neither of us spoke, I turned and walked away from her.

* * *

At eight p.m., the dinner cleared and the children in front of the television set, I told Jay I was going out for a walk. The evening cold and not suited for walking, but Jay was oblivious to anything that wasn't on his computer screen. Not thinking to question me.

I walked quickly toward the end of the circle, stopped next to the Edwardses' driveway, and peered around the house to see if a car was parked there. Paige's white Lexus visible when I craned my neck. I continued walking around the cul-de-sac, searching the cloudy sky for a pattern of stars, disturbed when I couldn't find even the Big Dipper hidden somewhere in the firmament.

The next night, I excused myself again and again I found Paige's car exactly where I'd last seen it, the bad angle making me think she hadn't moved it all day. The bad angle making me think she was a shut-in. Nobody could park that badly twice in a row. And so I left, trying to feel the beauty of the late winter evening as I walked slowly down our street.

On the third and fourth nights, I arrived at the Edwardses' driveway and found exactly what I expected. Paige's car where she had left it. The house silent and in some sort of perpetual lockdown.

On the fifth night, I considered abandoning my plan altogether. The weather had turned sharp. The wind blowing my hair up as I poked my head outside my kitchen storm door. But how lazy to give up. How selfish and also unhelpful. I grabbed a hat and warmer gloves, then set out toward the Edwardses'. Surprised and pleased when I discovered the Lexus was gone. Which was exactly what I was looking for.

I crossed Paige's front lawn, broken branches cracking beneath my boots, and rang the doorbell, rehearsing my story. If Lydia answered, I'd tell her the truth and hope for the best. Even though I doubted it would be Lydia. I hadn't seen her since before the glass door incident. If it were another sitter, a college kid or someone gullible, I'd say I had a present for the kids and could I give it to them? I'd been carrying light-up tops in my pocket for days, ready for just such an occasion.

I rang the bell and heard the gonging somewhere inside. No footsteps. I rang again. Knocked with the knocker. Waited some more. I was about to give up dejectedly when I saw Nela come out her front door and stare at me accusingly. Or at least I felt accused. For being on the Edwardses' property. For the appearance that I was still friends with them. Not that I could see anything but the dimmest outline of Nela's body in the darkness. Her front light just barely illuminating her silhouette. I walked to the edge of the Edwardses' vast lawn, said, "Hey," then quietly crossed the grass to Nela's stoop.

"What are you doing?" she asked when I reached her, more curious than accusatory.

"The truth or the story?" I asked, still holding the plastic tops in my coat pocket.

Nela laughed a little. "I guess I'll take the truth for two hundred dollars," she joked, motioning for me to sit beside her on the step. But I didn't want to sit. I didn't want to linger. I wanted to move forward with my plan before I lost my courage.

"I'm trying to find Winnie," I said, even though it didn't make sense. That I'd be looking for Winnie in an empty house. But Nela didn't seem to question my faulty logic. She merely nodded and waited for me to go on.

"I know Paige is out. Gene's in Italy. I thought I could quiz the babysitter. Or pretend I was dropping off a present," I said, holding up the cheap plastic gifts.

"But no one answered," I added, starting to shove the tops back into my coat pocket. Nela licked her lips. I thought I noticed a tremor in her right hand as she spoke.

"I was out here because I noticed the light on in their third floor," she said. "It creeped me out. It's the room where Paige keeps her holiday decorations and all those dresses she never gave Winnie. I'm just stuck staring at the light, thinking, 'What the fuck? And why is it on?' and I came out to sit on the stoop and sort of stare at it like the moon."

I sat beside her then and stared at it, too. The tiny window was indeed golden like the moon, but not promising. Just present, like a panel that illuminated nothingness.

"Maybe they went out to eat," Nela said tentatively, even though we both knew that Paige never took the kids out past six p.m. That she believed in strict early bedtimes, even on weekends. We both sighed, defeated, lost in our thoughts. After a few minutes, Nela said, "I know how to get in there."

I turned and looked at her.

"Wait here a sec," she said, rising and disappearing into her house, leaving me alone in the cold of the February evening. After a minute, Nela returned and showed me a loose key, not even on a chain. Her hand trembling as she gave it to me.

"Gene asked us to hang on to it when they went to Russia. 'Just in case.' We forgot to give it back," she said. "It's for the French doors."

"What if they come home?" I asked, already feeling the rush of adrenaline from knowing I would use it.

"I'll call your cell," Nela said, holding up her cell phone.

I nodded, starting to stand, starting to walk away from her before I could change my mind.

"Make sure you check out the light," she called from her stoop. "At the very least, turn it off. It's driving me crazy!" No doubt wanting me to break in as much to turn off the light as to find out what was going on with Winnie. She was that single-minded. That focused. Even though I knew that wasn't all of it. That she'd been anxiously staring at the light for the same reason I'd been ringing the doorbell. Because we cared. Because we were helpless not to.

* * *

I let myself in through the pool gate and willed myself to walk slowly across the patio and up the steps to the terrace and French doors. I fitted the key into the narrow lock and jiggled it back and forth until I felt it catch, then turned the handle to let myself in.

Waiting to make sure I didn't hear an alarm go off, even though I knew Paige never set hers.

Inside, I felt my body begin to shake, my mouth suddenly dry. What if Paige were upstairs sleeping? I walked to the front hall and listened. The house quiet, settling. The house seemingly empty even though a piece of me doubted it. Even though a piece of me feared that Winnie was locked up somewhere inside of it.

"Winnie?" I called up the stairs and into the stillness. I half expected to hear banging or pleading, but nothing answered me. I walked up the carpeted stairway, the green-and-white design plush and springy beneath my feet. I remembered when Paige had gotten the new runner, how much we'd all admired it. All of us wanting to replace our old runners with new ones now that she'd done it. Not that we liked her taste in particular.

On the second floor, all the bedroom doors were shut, which was strange, and meant someone could be inside one of them. Who closed the bedroom doors when they went out for the evening?

I knocked on Paige and Gene's room first, turned the knob and swung the door open, worried I'd find Paige resting on her bed, afraid she might spring up and pounce on me. But I was merely greeted by a muslin headboard, white pillows propped up at attention, a discarded handbag and a pair of pumps turned over next to the closet. She'd switched outfits. Which made sense if she was going out and wanted to look stylish. Gene's things put away. Or at least not visible. A feminine room.

I closed the bedroom door softly and felt less afraid, Paige's specter hidden behind the door. I tried to remember whose door was whose and moved quickly toward Cameron's room, turning the doorknob and peering in at the deep blue and red walls, the monogrammed throw pillows tossed on the floor. A flat-screen

TV built into a footboard that rose above his messy, unmade bed. He was so spoiled! I suddenly hated Cameron, backing out of the room, eager to get away from his presence. Turning left toward the final door, which had to be Winnie's. I pushed at the door and was surprised when it opened, the latch not in its place, as if someone had recently been there.

Inside, Winnie's single bed was stripped of its sheets. A pillow lay without its case on the mattress and stuffed animals remained upright, abandoned against the wall. I opened the closet and saw row after row of empty wire hangers, then tugged at the dresser drawers, disturbed by how empty they were. Which meant what, exactly? That Winnie was gone with her clothing? Or maybe Paige had done something worse to her. Something from which she needed to escape? The thought making me dizzy and light-headed as I stepped out of Winnie's room, terrified about what to do next. I squeezed my eyes shut, then opened them, my breath turning ragged as I walked toward the third-floor staircase.

"Winnie?" I called at the bottom, desperate to believe she was in the house with me. Possibly abused, locked up, but still breathing.

Silence. Or did I hear a rattling?

"Winnie?" I called again, louder.

I felt it rather than heard it. A presence. Someone or something was definitely in the house with me.

I pulled out my cell phone and clutched it in my palm as I carefully climbed the wooden stairs, no runner to cushion the sound of my steps, the creaking like something out of a bad horror movie.

When I neared the third-floor landing, the presence was stronger, another being upstairs, aware of me, waiting. I prayed it wouldn't be too terrible. To see Winnie emaciated. Maybe even tied up. My hands slick with sweat as I opened the door to the bonus room and stepped inside.

After that I remember very little. The light blinding me, or maybe the stench merely felled me. The brown extension cord. Gene's bloated face. The hand-me-down dresses like a gauntlet on either side of his body. And then, blankness. A certain confusion. My head and neck still tender from where I must have fallen. Or from the board the paramedics used when they carried me out of the house. My memory filled with clanging sounds and strange, disorienting perspectives. Gene's body on a second board alongside mine. Or did I merely imagine that part? The heart and mind forever in battle. Against the things we mustn't know. Against the things we desperately wish to anyway.

* * *

Gene's mother came. His brother from Wellesley and a sister from northern Michigan. Their teenage kids. All of Gene's colleagues from his company. Plus their wives. Paige's large and contentious family. Her father standing in the far right corner of the funeral home, not far from Gene's casket, talking to no one. Paige's mother too fragile and shaken to stand; Lorraine sitting next to her for a while before the crush of visitors made it necessary for her to move on. All of this reported to me by Lorraine, who came over immediately following the funeral to tell me about it.

"Paige's mother told me that all Paige ever wanted was a large family," Lorraine said, her voice catching. Both of us on my front porch, the door open, cold air blowing into my living room.

I sighed. I'd heard that before. From Paige. It was one of the reasons why she wanted to adopt so badly in the first place. Because she felt like a failure with just one child.

"I don't think there's anything we could have done differently," Lorraine said, her face wobbly, her skin loose along her neckline. She'd aged suddenly. I imagined she'd say the same about me if she thought about it. Thick, silvery hairs shining at my root line. I rubbed the bridge of my nose, guilty and full of remorse about calling Family Services. Trying to focus on the facts, the specifics. Asking Lorraine if she'd gotten any more details.

"Winnie was homeschooled for a few weeks. That's why nobody saw her."

I nodded. I knew this. The police had told me this when I'd been investigated about my break-in.

"Winnie's with a new family now," Lorraine added. Very softly. Because she knew, no doubt, how I would take it.

I swallowed. Tears streaming down my face before I realized they were coming.

"That's where Paige was when you broke in. They did a private rehoming. It's not the standard process, apparently, but they didn't want her in the foster system."

"What does that mean?"

"It means they worked some back channels to find a good home for her. Paige's mother said the family had been adoptive parents before and were familiar with special-needs children. They're willing to go through the state to make the adoption final. Winnie's with them 'unofficially' at the moment."

I sighed. So many complications. So many rules to protect the innocent. Even if it was impossible. For them, or for anyone, really. Hanging my head. Overwhelmed by the enormity of the situation.

"Did Gene really go to Italy?" I asked.

"He did. He was supposed to meet them afterwards to say good-bye, but I guess he couldn't go through with it."

Both of us silent. Both of us contemplating what this meant. If it was an admission of guilt or just a lack of good coping skills.

"Paige passed out little packets at the funeral. She wanted people to hear about the rehoming from her, and also understand what they'd been going through," Lorraine said, pulling a long white envelope from her purse. The envelope reminding me for all the world of the envelope we'd received when the Edwardses had first adopted Winnie. The promise of being her forever family. The careful way they wanted us to refer to her and think of them.

Lorraine opening the envelope and showing me what Paige had written. I glanced through it, clutching my throat, as I read about how it was common for neighbors to be unsupportive in these situations. Common for adopted parents to feel judged and misunderstood. Had we really been that naive? That unsupportive? Or were Gene and Paige different? Their circumstances unique to them, not the norm? Was there even a norm?

"I think Winnie really had problems," Lorraine said softly, no doubt still smarting from the time I'd chided her for liking Gene.

"But Paige admitted that she was struggling to do better," she added quietly. I opened my mouth to say something but merely swallowed, no words coming out.

"She told me that she used to get down on her hands and knees every night and pray to God that she could be a better mother to Winnie."

"So *did* she threaten Winnie? Is that why she ran through the glass?" I asked, my tears flowing more freely now.

Lorraine shaking her head. Her eyes downcast. "I have no idea. Maybe. Maybe Winnie gets really wild sometimes and that was the first time we saw it. We'll never know."

It was true, we could never know. Which was so exasperating even now, after all that we'd been through. All we'd tried to uncover.

"How do you think Winnie will do with her new family?" I asked, upset that she'd been abandoned again. Upset that now I'd never see her again.

Lorraine swallowed, shifting from foot to foot.

"What?" I asked, aware that she was hiding something from me.

"I asked Paige the same thing."

"And?"

"And she said it's the wrong question. To think of Winnie the way we think of our own children. That Winnie's too damaged."

I closed my eyes and squeezed them tight. Pained that Winnie might never have the life I wanted for her. When I opened them, I saw that Lorraine had begun to cry, leaning her shoulder against my glass door, her body heaving. I knew I should ask her in. Comfort her. Say something half-true and reassuring about Winnie's future, the future of our neighborhood group. But it was too late for that, for me. The desire to quickly move on the same as the desire to cover up. To blur the lines of what you knew and wished you didn't have to. And so we merely stood on my porch in the February cold, neither of us speaking, turning to stare at the end of our cul-de-sac. The Edwardses' Tudor forever outlined against the sky: handsome, stark, and terrifying.

EPILOGUE

What We Knew

WE KNEW WE WOULD never enter Paige and Gene's magnificent home again. Would never welcome the new owners with cupcakes and brownies, never walk under the coffered ceilings or run our fingers down the polished wood banisters. Gene's suicide like an odor that would emanate always from every window and doorway, forever charging the brick facade with menace and horror.

We knew we'd never tell our children the full story about Winnie, why she'd been given away, the exact nature of our misgivings.

We knew we would always wonder what became of Winnie. Whether her new family loved her. Whether she was happy, well adjusted, able to move confidently into the future.

We knew we would always wonder how Winnie would have turned out if she hadn't been adopted by the Edwardses. If she lived with people in Oregon or in Tennessee. Or if she hadn't been adopted at all, but still lived as she had begun, a daughter of parents who decided to keep her. The future as impossible to know for her as it was for our own children. Our own children growing taller and more confusing with each passing year. Our own children shocking us with their strange and mysterious behaviors. Lucas claiming to hate cooking and even building once he discovered the pleasures of football. His frame growing bulkier, his talent as a lineman undeniable. Lorraine's son Gabe beginning to lie about everything. Whether he'd taken a shower. Had done his home-work. Was invited to so-and-so's party. Lorraine and her ex fight-ing constantly. A counselor finally brought in to "fix" Gabe, even though her main focus seemed to be Evan and Lorraine as parents. Sebastian Guzman-Veniero emerging as the surprise genius—not even close to disabled. A hearing test employed to reveal severe hearing loss, most likely as an infant; two hearing aids installed, his test scores and language skills soaring.

We knew we would never be the kind of friends we'd imagined we'd be when we'd first set out to know each other. Unblemished. Without frustrations and petty arguments, fears and suspicions. The tragedy of the Edwardses forging an intimacy among us that made us both more familiar and uglier than we'd ever planned on being with one another. That made us exactly the thing we set out to be when we so naively started. Good neighbors. Like family.

Author's Note

This book is a work of fiction. While I have been blessed to know many friends, family members, neighbors, and acquaintances who have adopted children from all parts of the globe, none of these people are described in this novel—nor has anyone I know been faced with the devastating choices and consequences described in these pages. Rather, I chose to write about the themes of community, parenting, and adoption as a way of discovering my own beliefs about family, the ones we create and the ones we inherit. All of the characters described in these pages are born out of my imagination, as are their struggles, triumphs, and tragedies.

Acknowledgments

This book would not have been possible without the wise and generous support of my family and friends—and of the talented publishing professionals at Aragi and Twelve. I owe a profound debt of gratitude to the following:

Duvall Osteen, my thoughtful and perceptive agent, whose incisive edits made the book stronger and richer.

My editor, Libby Burton, who embraced my vision and then seamlessly made it clearer.

Sean Desmond and Rachel Kambury for their peerless editorial direction; Laura Cherkas, Bailey Donaghue, Yasmin Mathew, Brian McLendon, Lisa Rivlin, Paul Samuelson, Jarrod Taylor, and all the folks at Twelve who championed my work and made sure it was the best it could be.

My wise friends and fellow writers who read the manuscript multiple times without complaint and never failed to offer valuable insight and suggestions: Chris Costanzo, Therese Eiben, Pamela Erens, and Tamar Schreibman.

Liz Carey, who provided geographic background and reference.

Beth Lorge and Mara Posner Metzger for being my tireless sounding boards.

ACKNOWLEDGMENTS

My faithful writer's group, who insisted this short story was a novel and patiently read this book in installments for many years: Philip Moustakis, Lynn Schmeidler, Pamela Erens, and Therese Eiben.

Kate and Arnold Schmeidler, who generously lent their pied-à-terre to the pursuit of writing and art.

My mother and father, who have always believed in me and bragged about me, making it so much easier to believe in myself.

And my husband and children, the loves of my life, who were with me every step of the way. Thank you.

About the Author

JOANNE SERLING's fiction has been nominated for a Pushcart Prize and has appeared in *New Ohio Review* and *North American Review*. She is a graduate of Cornell University and studied and taught fiction at The Writers Studio in New York City. She lives outside of New York with her husband and children and is at work on her second book.

Mission Statement

Twelve strives to publish singular books, by authors who have unique perspectives and compelling authority. Books that explain our culture; that illuminate, inspire, provoke, and entertain. Our mission is to provide a consummate publishing experience for our authors, one truly devoted to thoughtful partnership and cutting-edge promotional sophistication that reaches as many readers as possible. For readers, we aim to spark that rare reading experience—one that opens doors, transports, and possibly changes their outlook on our ever-changing world.